PRAISE FOR DENNIS McFARLAND'S *The Music Room*

"Dialogue you can hear…and detail you can see…McFarland is a brilliant writer."
—*Newsweek*

"Brilliant and graceful, wise and evocative, sometimes funny and always touching… Dennis McFarland's arrival on the literary scene is one thing all of us can be happy about."
—*Mademoiselle*

"Sinewy and seductive, effortless and unaffected—it is a pleasure to read. [McFarland] knows what he wants to say and has the verbal horsepower to say it convincingly."
—*The Philadelphia Inquirer*

"A masterpiece…startling…mesmerizing…pure magic…In pursuit of excellence, just read it."
—*Detroit News*

"A story of dead ends and unfulfilled promises, of suicide and alcoholism, of perpetual adolescence and premature death…without any cheap tricks or false notes…It is superb."
—*Vogue*

"Speaks with such commanding authority, such uncommon grace, it is hard to believe it is a first novel and not the capstone of a distinguished literary career…. Subtle, moving, and heartrending."
—*Newsday*

"Dennis McFarland displays considerable virtuosity…. Handled with ingenuity…strongly registered sensuous detail."
—*The New York Review of Books*

"Strikes all the right notes…powerful and harrowing…Readers have a great fortune in store picking up *The Music Room*."
—*Asheville* (North Carolina) *Citizen-Times*

"Wonderfully well-written, poignant, and tragic…compelling in its truthfulness."
—*Omaha Metro Update*

"McFarland takes the reader on this journey of a shattered life with brilliant insight. His novel is beautifully crafted and a joy to read."
—*Worcester* (Massachusetts) *Sunday Telegram*

"Its themes are simple, as most great themes are: love, death, regret, loss, family. There is humor amid the grief and despair and redemption, too. There is a music to the language and a mesmerizing cadence."
—*San Rafael* (California) *Independent-Journal*

"Extraordinary…McFarland has tapped into some enduring American myths, and he writes like an angel."
—*Kirkus Reviews* (starred review)

The Music Room

A Novel

DENNIS McFARLAND

Picador USA
New York

Picador® is a U.S. registered trademark and is used by St. Martin's Press under license from Pan Books Limited.

For information on Picador USA Reading Group Guides, as well as ordering, please contact the Trade Marketing department at St. Martin's Press.
Phone: 1-800-221-7945 extension 763
Fax: 212-677-7456
E-mail: trademarketing@stmartins.com

ISBN 0-312-27470-X

First published in the United States by Houghton Mifflin Company

First Picador USA Edition: March 2001

10 9 8 7 6 5 4 3 2 1

To Michelle,

WITH ALL MY LOVE

I wish to thank
Larry Cooper, Frances Kiernan, Daniel Menaker,
Det. John F. Gillespie, Mark Simcox, John Traficonte,
Dr. Karen Victor, and Ross for their helpful advice.
The sermon that appears in this novel is adapted from
an actual sermon delivered on December 13, 1987,
at Saint Francis de Sales Church in Boston,
by Mary Helen Washington, to whom I am deeply grateful.
And I thank my wife, Michelle Blake Simons,
who gave as generously and lovingly to this book as she has,
always and in everything, to me.
—D. McF.

The Music Room

In the bicentennial year of our country's independence from Great Britain, a time when I imagined the American masses celebrative and awash with a sense of history and continuity, my wife of only four years decided it would be best for both of us if she moved in with her mother for a while—a trial separation, she said, though we both were so immediately relieved by the *idea* of parting, the real thing was bound to endure. In October of the previous year, she had suffered her second miscarriage—this one quite far along (almost six months); we'd begun to breathe easy, we'd begun decorating a nursery—and afterward, we succumbed to a stubborn disappointment that refused forgiveness, refused sexual and emotional healing. There had never been anything in our marriage quite as coherent as this two-headed tragedy. Madeline left for Santa Rosa in February, a rainy, blossoming-of-spring month in northern California.

By the following August, I had decided to give up our large flat in San Francisco, where I remained, a rambling monk with only random visitation rights to my past. The place, the flat, was a daily encounter with guilt and failure, and though I knew enough not to believe in geographical cures for those conditions, that didn't make me any less eager to escape its sinister Victorian charm. What Madeline didn't have any use for in Santa Rosa I put into storage. I arranged for an absence from my record company, where things had long run better without me anyway. I thought I would travel for a few weeks, perhaps visit my brother in New York. I imagined that on my return I might find better, altogether different living quarters—a houseboat in Sausalito perhaps, a geodesic dome on Mount Tam.

My landlady had told me I should leave the flat "broom clean," a task for which I'd kept a vacuum cleaner behind. In the unused nursery there were cobwebs, and on the walls and ceiling about a hundred self-adhesive stars and moons that glowed in the dark (better than any real starlit sky the night I brought my pregnant wife into the room and switched off the light to show her my handmade heaven). As I vacuumed away the cobwebs, I discovered that the little stars and moons had become dry over the months, and when I passed the vacuum across the surface of the wall, they let go easily. This was just the sort of thing I needed, the sort of thing I'd been needing for weeks. And as I stood there sucking the stars and moons from the nursery walls, and crying like a baby myself, the phone rang in the kitchen: a detective with the New York City police department's homicide unit, informing me that early that morning my brother, Perry, had fallen to his death from the twenty-third floor of a midtown hotel, apparently a suicide.

Stupidly, I asked the man to hold the line for a moment. I returned to the nursery, then moved to the French windows that overlooked the garden. On the south fence, a hummingbird darted in and out of a passionflower vine, and in a distant window, across the length of two gardens, I could see a young nurse in white uniform and cap; I waved to her, but quite sensibly she didn't wave back, and moved away out of sight. When I returned to the kitchen, I saw that the receiver of the cardinal-red telephone lay on the bare floor. I picked it up and spoke into it. I relied on extreme politeness to get through the rest of the conversation. I told the detective how very sorry I was to have kept him waiting and would he be kind enough to tell me his name again, his precinct, and yes, I would be coming to New York on the first flight, thanks very much for letting me know about my brother.

For a minute after hanging up, I wondered why Perry hadn't thought of *me*. Not why hadn't he thought of me as someone to turn to, but why hadn't he chosen a better time to do himself in, a time when I didn't already have troubles enough. And as punishment for this moment of weakness, I then recalled that Perry had left a message on my answering machine a few weeks earlier—nothing special, just hello, like to talk to you—and I'd never got around to returning the call. At that point I had made the decision to give up the flat, which was really a decision to overturn what I currently, loosely called my life, and Perry was not a soothing influence. I loved him, and I couldn't have named some of the deep and thorough ways in which I depended on him, but he was not a soothing influence.

What immediately followed the New York detective's phone call was a lot of practical arrangements—securing a flight and a hotel reservation, disposing of the vacuum cleaner, leaving the key to the flat with the landlady, dispensing with my car, turning off the telephone service, ordering transportation to the airport—and at some point during all this—maybe it was when I saw my two already-packed suitcases standing near the entry hall door—I thought, Sensible people don't allow themselves ever to become this unmoored, they don't allow themselves to reach so frayed a loose end. And why? Because it's very likely that fate will rush in with some great calamity to give new purpose to your life. And for a while, as I sat in the smoky, upholstered cabin of a 747, flying toward the details of my only brother's spattered remains on some grimy patch of pavement in New York City, I actually thought that perhaps I'd developed an interesting life view these last couple of hours. I drank two miniatures of Dewar's Scotch on an empty stomach, and pictured Fate in the style of an editorial drawing—not as the name for what befalls you in life, but as a grisly beast with a thousand eyes, lurking behind a large rock or tree: the landscape is Western, arid (I'm not sure why); you pass by on an ambling horse; Fate, in his hiding place, waits for you to let go, even momentarily, of the reins. It wasn't until we'd begun our descent into Kennedy that I understood what a crock all this thinking was, what a soft, mushy swamp I'd let my mind become lately—that primarily, at least, what had happened today had happened to Perry and not to me.

My flight had left San Francisco at eight-thirty in the evening, which put me into New York at the exotic hour of five in the morning. My cab driver was a black woman in her forties, six feet tall, dressed in a khaki jump suit, her straightened hair dyed orange and trained into a severe flip on one side. In a professional gospel singer's voice, she sang a soulful "Bright

· 4 ·

Lights, Big City" on the way into town, and at first I thought she was putting me on, that the song was meant as counterpoint to the heaviness of her foot on the accelerator and the casual, abandoned way in which she frequently changed lanes. But something in her singing—probably simply how amazingly good it was—told me that she was listening to herself, that I wasn't on her mind in the least.

On the metal frame encasing the Plexiglas protective barrier between us, someone, a former fare perhaps, had scratched into the black enamel, "Boys are my whole life." I assumed this had been written by a teen-aged girl (though surely this was not necessarily the case), and I thought of Perry at fifteen, a precocious fifteen but fifteen all the same, and me, nineteen and home from my sophomore year of college.

It's a moonless summer night on one of the Spring Lake beaches on the Jersey Shore. Somebody whose parents are in Europe for the month of August is having a big house party, one of those parties where the host, whoever he is, has invited his friends and told his friends to invite their friends, and so on. The resulting mixture of booze and partial anonymity has fallen like a gauze over everything at this late hour, and there's something decidedly permissive in the sound of the surf and the wind. I haven't seen Perry for a couple of hours, and Jeanine Clotfelter, my date for the party, has urged me a few times to go find him. I'm older and should be looking out for him. I tell Jeanine that she shouldn't be such a worrier, it's not good for her skin.

As someone throws more driftwood onto a huge bonfire on the beach, twisted screens of sparks fly up, are caught by the wind, and die. Someone plays white, city-kid blues on a guitar. Couples stroll away and are swallowed up by the blackness outside the circle of the fire. Couples return arm in arm. Small groups, mostly of boys, leave—somebody's got dope—and return. Many of the girls and boys are darkly tanned. The sharp smells of the fire and of the sea air dominate, but underneath, there are the sweeter, more tribal odors of coconut oil, cocoa butter, baby oil and iodine.

Shortly after my remark about Jeanine Clotfelter's skin, a younger girl, a Cindy somebody, shows up in the bright glow of the bonfire looking desperate, her cheeks streaked with tears. Jeanine, secretly happy to have arrived at some version of the melodrama she's been imagining ever since Perry's disappearance, finds Cindy's arm and pulls her over to where we are sitting. Lassielike, Cindy manages to convey, not entirely verbally, that something terrible has happened, that we should follow her to the spot.

A half mile or so down the beach there's an old abandoned dirt road with a washed-out bridge; it's about an eight- or ten-foot drop down into a sand gully. Some of the wilder boys have been playing a little game, a daredevil's delight, for which Perry has been kind enough to lend our father's Lincoln. On our way to the abandoned road, Cindy explains—as best she can, for she's still crying—the game. The player sits behind the steering wheel of the Lincoln from a starting place of about a hundred yards from the washed-out bridge; with the headlights on bright, the player drives toward the gully; at about fifty yards—indicated by a boy stationed by the edge of the road—the driver turns off the headlights and, in complete darkness, continues forward as far as he dares. Naturally, the one who gets closest to the gully, without driving *into* the gully, wins.

Cindy, frantic and hysterical, came running to fetch us just when Perry was taking the wheel. But when we arrive on the scene, the game has reached its end—apparently only a moment earlier. With its headlights turned back on, Father's Lincoln squats like a big boat, no wheels visible, in the sand at the bottom of the gully; a great cloud of dust still rises and settles in the swathes of light in front of the car. The circle of boys surrounding the Lincoln is completely silent when we arrive, and they silently clear a path for us as we approach. When I lean down to look inside the window on the driver's side, I see Perry—Perry, with a look of miraculous wonder on his face. What has happened has left him quite speechless. His silence, like the other boys', is almost religious. He looks at me and smiles, shaking his head, his eyes wet with tears of joy. I say, "Jesus, are you in trouble now . . ."

Of course I have failed to understand the moment, the event, and Perry is cosmically disappointed. He continues shaking his head, but his expression has changed to disgust. Then he says, quietly, which was always his way, "At least *I* know what kind of trouble I'm in, Martin."

Now, in the taxi, my recalling Perry's young face, full of wonder, sent a brief but incisive jab of grief to my ribs, and my cab driver, as if she were tracking my thoughts, began to hum, a different song, a melody I didn't recognize, something altogether too melancholy. It occurred to me to tell her that my brother had just jumped out of a hotel window. After all, I hadn't said those words out loud yet, and it probably wouldn't be a bad idea to experiment; I suspected that as a cab driver in New York City she knew something of grief. We were just passing through the toll plaza outside the Midtown Tunnel, the sky had brightened enough to cast an ambiguous glow over everything—not day, not night—and the man who took the money, middle-aged with a droopy mustache and dark pouches beneath his eyes, looked sad and hopeless to me. One too many nights in the neon-lit toll booth.

I closed my eyes: the briefly pleasant, stinging scent of exhaust fumes; the underground roar, like entering the whirling channel inside a giant conch shell. When I opened my eyes maybe a minute later, the interior of the cab had taken on an unsettling domestic look, and in the artificial lights of the tunnel, I noticed that my driver, no longer singing or humming, was glancing at me occasionally in her rearview mirror. After another quick series of curious glances, she said, "If you're cold back there, why don't you roll up the window?"

As I cranked the window handle, which was missing its plastic knob, I realized that I was visibly shaking, which triggered my awareness of a string of neglected physical needs: freezing coldness, hunger, and a by now completely bewildered bladder. The tall black woman nodded approvingly. I thought, judging only from her eyes, that she was also smiling. I cleared my throat and said, "I've had to come here because my brother just died suddenly."

"I beg your pardon?" she said, and I noticed that she had a surprisingly cultured note in her speech, as if she'd been trained in the theater.

"I said my brother just died."

"Oh, that's too bad," she said. "Was he sick?"

"No," I said. "He killed himself."

"What a crying shame," she said. Then she added, quite without astonishment, "I had a brother killed himself, too."

"That's amazing," I said.

Out of the tunnel—only a nod to any transition at best—we were suddenly aimed at the heart of Manhattan. "Wasn't anything amazing about it," my cab driver said, hanging a one-handed right turn that sent me teetering. "I expect just about anybody can blow their own brains out given the right circumstances — and the bottle and the gun."

"I mean, isn't it amazing that here I am all the way from California," I said, "riding in the back seat of your cab, and we both have brothers who killed themselves."

"Oh," she said, as unimpressed as only someone shrugging such wide and bony shoulders could be. "Just goes to show you, I guess."

She'd begun a lively game of dodge and dart up Park Avenue. There was a surprising amount of traffic at this hour and an assortment of drivers — a kind of estuary of the decadent and the ambitious.

Uptown, in the seventies, over to Fifth, down a couple of blocks, and we were stopped in front of my hotel. I had purposely avoided staying in midtown, frightened by the remote possibility of booking a room, by freakish coincidence, in *the* hotel. As I stood outside on the sidewalk, at the rear of the taxi, reaching into my pockets for cash, the cab driver retrieved my bags from the trunk and handed them over to a uniformed doorman. When she told me the amount of the fare, I paid it, along with a tip, and then said, "I thought the fare would be at least — "

"I turned off the meter when you told me about your brother," she said, and as if I weren't already surprised enough, she took both my hands into hers, which were huge and soft and warm.

In a moment, I would have to turn toward the hotel's bright revolving doors at the end of a long arched canopy with brass poles and fittings, and toward an entirely stunned doorman; but just now, I was held firm in the grip of this unlikely navigator's sympathy—her ridiculous orange hair now clearly a wig, she herself now clearly a drag queen. And it must have bolstered me, because after she drove away I was able to ask the waiting doorman, without a trace of embarrassment, to hurry please and show me to the nearest men's room.

After a hot bath in a wonderful, cavernous old tub, I ordered room service. Knowing I should keep it simple, I asked for scrambled eggs and an English muffin, tea instead of coffee, no meat. But when it arrived, caddied by a cheerful young man who clicked his heels after he'd set everything out for my approval, it was not quite simple enough. Though I'm sure the eggs were perfectly fine, they looked like something that might have grown at the bottom of a fish tank. I quickly recovered everything as soon as the porter left the room.

Wearing a robe made of some unseemly shiny material, an anniversary present from Madeline—her favorite old actor was David Niven—I sat on the edge of the bed and stared at the telephone. After a minute or two I went to the windows, which, at the back of the hotel, overlooked a jagged sea of rooftops. I drew the drapes, hoping to shut out the city at least temporarily, and returned to my thinker's attitude on the edge of the bed: if there were a way to erase memory, to escape the resonant sway of the past, then calling my mother and telling her about Perry would be a simpler task. What I wanted was some way to unclutter the thing. I wanted it to be tidy, without echo. Already, as I imagined my mother's voice, I was having to shake the absurd feeling that I was the tattletale, calling long distance to report Perry's having been bad again. And in a vaguer sort of way, I felt some mysterious allegiance to Perry that excluded any grief sharing with our mother. I also needed very badly to sleep—I felt overwrought with fatigue rather than used up.

It was nearly eight o'clock, but I knew Mother to be an early riser these days. I put through the call to Norfolk, and Raymond, the aging houseboy, answered. "It's Martin," I said, and we exchanged a few banalities about how long it had been since my last visit and so on. He told me that Mother was already in the pool. "She's a fanatic about her morning exercise, you know," he said. "Hold on a second, Marty, and I'll just take the phone out to her."

I could hear the sounds of a television, a morning news program, then the yapping of the dogs, a screen door slamming, and Raymond again, calling to Mother. When she came on the line, Mother was using her expansive, outdoor voice. "Marty," she said. "It's so early for you."

"Mother, I'm calling from New York," I said.

"New York?"

"Yes. I'm afraid I've got some bad news."

"Bad news?"

"It's about Perry."

"About Perry?"

"Will you please stop doing that," I said.

"Doing what?"

"Repeating everything back to me. I'm trying to tell you that Perry's had an accident."

"An accident?" she said.

"I don't know any other way to do this," I said, "except to say it, Mother. Perry's dead."

There was a brief silence, then the splash of water, then her voice, away from the phone now: "Raymond, honey, will you please hand me my robe?"

"Mother?" I said.

"Yes, Marty, I'm here. I'm just trying to catch my breath. What happened?"

"I only just got into a hotel," I said. "I don't have any details yet, but the police think Perry killed himself."

Another silence. Then, "I'm all right, Marty, I'm all right. Tell me what to do. I don't know what to do."

"I don't really know anything yet," I said. "I think the thing to do is just sit tight and I'll keep in touch."

"I don't know what to do," she said after a moment. "Tell me what I should do."

"It's very hard to know," I said. "It's a shock."

"A shock?" she said. "Is that what you call it? How did he do it? Jump out of a window or something? Something magnificent, surely . . ."

"Yes," I said.

"What?"

"Yes, he jumped out of a window."

"Oh, God. Oh, Marty, why?"

"I don't know," I said. "I'm going to try to find out."

"Oh, Jesus."

"Mother?"

"I just feel, I don't know . . . why would he do such a thing?"

"I don't know, Mother," I said. "When did you talk to him last?"

"Well, I'm not sure. *I* don't have any idea why he did it, if that's what you're getting at."

"I'm not getting at anything, Mother. I just wondered whether or not you talked to him recently."

"I think Raymond talked to him," she said. "He called once

when I was away, a couple of weeks ago. He talked to Raymond."

"When was that exactly?" I asked.

"Well, let's see," she said. "I was in Palm Beach. That would have been about ten days ago, I guess. Oh, Jesus, why can't I cry?"

"Mother, will you tell Raymond what's happened and have him call me?"

"Of course," she answered. "But you know Raymond's memory isn't what it used to be."

I gave her the number of the hotel and my room number. She said, "Marty . . ."

"Yes, Mother."

After a moment she said, "I don't know what I was going to say."

"I'll call you later," I said.

"I've got people coming for *lunch*," she said. "Raymond's in the kitchen shelling shrimp."

And then, after a pause, she said one word, flat, without inflection: "Perry." After she'd hung up, I sat listening to the clinking chains and wind tunnels over the line, a primitive-sounding music that seemed to darken the already half-dark hotel room.

Perry and I are young boys, maybe nine and five, lying belly-down on the gentle slope of the front lawn to the Norfolk house. Once again nighttime, summer. We can hear music coming from Father's old console radio in the library — Sinatra, something swingy. It's the hour that lies between dinner and bedtime; the help (as we were taught to call them, never servants) are gathered in the kitchen drinking coffee and cleaning up the dinner mess; it is a blissful hour in which,

for once, during a long day of grown-up guesswork and petu-
lance, Perry and I are precisely what we most want to be —
forgotten. It is our chance to observe unobserved, for us to
spin out a commentary unchecked by adult censure. But now
we are mute as we lie on the grass in the dark, watching the
broad, glowing French windows of the library. Inside, our
parents, Father in his dark suit and Mother in a long gown,
are dancing, and though their laughter sails above and below
the music, as they lose and regain their footing again and
again, they look as if they are wrestling: Mother, whirling,
collapses onto a sofa, Father jerks her erect, they both fall
against a desk, sending a lamp crashing to the floor, and their
immense shadows break across the library ceiling. It's a
spectacular thing, and vaguely frightening, and when I turn
to Perry, I see no mixture of emotions on his face. He likes it
very much.

When I was eleven years old, I described to my mother a distinct memory: I recalled a rather heavyset woman with jet-black hair and a deep voice who'd visited our house long ago. The three of us — the woman, my mother, and me — sat on a sofa of red leather with gold upholstery tacks. The two women talked for a while, then the woman with the black hair drove my mother and me to a train station. There was a good deal of train noise and train station noise; we stood on a concrete platform. Soon, a man wearing a white sailor's uniform, the uniform of the United States Navy, walked briskly toward us. It was my father, young and handsome, wearing shiny black shoes whose sharp sound against the platform gave authority to his stride. He embraced us, and for a moment I thought I would be crushed to death.

That was all. The points on the star of this recollection were the red leather of the sofa, its bright gold buttons, the sound of my father's shoes, his approach in uniform, and the brief, biting taste of suffocation. The day I told her of this memory, my mother was astounded, for I had recounted in some detail the night she was driven to the Norfolk train station to meet my father after he was discharged from the Navy. It was August of 1946. She was pregnant at the time—I would not be born for another month and a half.

Apart from that one apparently prenatal memory, it seemed to me, for much of my adult life, that my childhood did not begin until Perry was born. He was born on my own birthday, October 17, the year I turned four, and for me, his arrival was forever linked with early, vivid impressions of autumn: my parents languid on a bright yellow quilt, my father's brilliant red sweater; Perry wrapped in a cotton blanket, asleep, blessedly quiet in the curve of Mother's body; a pile of brown and gold leaves kicked together by my father, their decaying aroma and that of the still-green grass beneath; blizzards of leaves and whirlwinds of leaves in the streets; something more liquid about the light after the stark, straightforward sun of summer; and my parents' heads so frequently bowed, as if in prayer, toward the swaddled thing called my brother. I was an octopus that Halloween, additional appendages fashioned out of old stockings stuffed with cotton by Mrs. Berend, Mother's seamstress, and attached like oblong weights to my shoulders.

My jealousy and the stunts I pulled, driven by it, were standard—almost as if I were merely playing the juvenile role in some ancient and universal myth. The difference, perhaps, was in my motivation, my subtext. I was not reacting to any shift in focus on my parents' part, away from me and onto Perry; I had been farmed out, long ago, to the attentions of my nurse, Marion, a pretty, middle-aged unmarried woman who was dumbstruck on many occasions by her powerful affection for my mother. So while I was spared the trauma of having something that belonged to me taken away and given to someone else, I was driven by the more sophisticated pain of watching this new baby get something I hadn't even known I wanted: it seemed to me that Perry was receiving a kind of study and mindfulness that had never been mine.

But my parents went through most things quickly, and the flurry of their enthusiasm over the baby peaked that year precisely on Christmas Eve: an extravaganza that, though it was held at our house just outside Norfolk, might have been designed and executed by the staff of a lavish hotel. There was an ice sculpture, as I recall, an elaborate life-sized crèche, melting under floodlights on the front lawn. Perry was on display, too, suited up in a Santa's elf costume, carried periodically among the festivities and passed around, even nibbled, like an unwieldy hors d'oeuvre. I remember vividly the little frenetic dance the adults did—the baby coming at them—as they agitated right and left in search of a place to put down a glass of champagne or a cigarette in order to free both hands; and the little cooing, surprised song that accompanied these gestures.

Christmas morning was a terrifying free fall back to earth. Perry, his eyes sunken and gray, was dehydrated, diarrheic, running a high fever, and we were without any help. (Mother, hysterical on the telephone to Marion, to the cook, to the pediatrician: "I don't give a damn if it's the fucking Second Coming, you've got to get over here *now!*") Father booked us a suite in the Fontainebleau downtown, where we could all be looked after properly. A doctor and a nurse were found for Perry, and my parents and I had Christmas dinner in the Egyptian-style, marble-columned restaurant downstairs—

traditional stuffed turkey served in Cleopatra's palace on the Nile.

Perry recovered without any complications from what turned out to be a severe intestinal infection, and the following March, Mother and Father, leaving us in the care of Marion and the other help, departed for an extended stay overseas. That particular party, having begun no more than five months before, was over.

In 1951, my parents were still riding the high gay wave of their alcoholism. After Europe, it carried them to Africa, to India, and back to England. I saved the postcards—with the colorful, exotic stamps—that marked the safaris, the elephant and camel rides, the capitals, ports, and hamlets of that almost year-long binge. And by the time our parents were beached grandly on our doorstep again, two things had happened: having turned five, I had planted a weed of independence that would choke out any garden of love they might have had in mind for me on their gift-laden return; and, bereft of any other suggestions for where my energies should go, I had been turned by Marion into a little nurse's helper—judicious, prudent, attentive to Perry's welfare.

A sunny afternoon in September. My first day of first grade at a private school within walking distance of our house. Happily, I discovered that I could read better than most of the other first graders, though I didn't quite catch on to the fact that I was supposed to follow along in my own primer when other pupils were reading aloud. (I thought that after a turn at reading aloud, I could stare lazily out the window with the primer closed.) But all in all, I liked my first day at school, and walking home—it is a warm, clear afternoon—I like thinking of the seemingly endless string of such days in store for me.

When I arrive at the house, Father is at the grand piano in what we call the music room, a sitting room with Father's piano in it.

The room is decorated in a tropical motif—rattan furniture, bamboo shades, straw mats—and cluttered with many savage-looking knickknacks; on a wall behind the piano hangs a painting of Father as a curly-headed boy, in which he strokes the fur of a huge Saint Bernard. Marion is seated on one of the couches, facing the piano, holding Perry in her lap—clearly against Perry's will, which is considerable now that he is nearly two. In addition to quite a bit of English, Perry has acquired a repertoire of grunts and squeals that sound as if they come straight from a medieval torture chamber. He rehearses a number of these as he writhes and fidgets and strains in Marion's lap.

Father, with a whisky just to the right of the music stand, is giving a piano recital, annihilating a Beethoven sonata, making slush of passage work and banging out chord clusters (instead of the written chords) in the melodramatic manner of a very large-scale loser. When Perry sees me, he wrestles free of Marion and runs toward me, shrieking; as Marion lunges for him, he stumbles, his chin connecting audibly with the hardwood floor. Father's piano stops abruptly, and somehow he manages to upset the tumbler of whisky, which crashes to the floor and explodes in a starburst of glass splinters. Father curses, Marion calls out a warning about the broken glass, Perry screams at a pitch that could open graves—a pitch reserved for serious pain—and from somewhere upstairs Mother's voice cries, "What was that? For God's sake, what's happened?" Though it is not yet three in the afternoon, she has already begun the extensive ritual that will culminate in whatever plans she and Father have for dinner that evening, and when she appears in the doorway of the music room, she is wearing a lavender dressing gown and an abundance of fragrance. Marion has got Perry into an upright position, and then there is this moment—the sound of Father's piano still ringing in our ears, the room reeking of perfume and whisky—this moment in which everyone in our family converges on Perry, and we partake in a small struggle for actual possession of him: a confusion of hands, a repetition of the word "come," I hear my own voice saying, "Let him go!" and Perry is in my arms—I am running with him out of the room, out the front door, and down the lawn toward the line of dark cypress trees that signals the beginning of our neighbor's horse farm and the end of our yard, the end of our parents' property.

Our great-great-grandfather on our father's side was Pietro Lamberti, the popular Venetian tenor, a contemporary of Verdi's, and many tales were handed down through the generations about Lamberti's having spent a good deal of time on Verdi's farm near Busseto. (The implication of these tales, the implication of their persistence, seemed to be that somehow Lamberti would have been a better tenor, or that his life would have been more significant, if he had actually dug potatoes in Verdi's fields, but no historical evidence of any such weekends in the country has ever been found.) One of Lamberti's sons, Fortunino (a middle name of Verdi's), was a minor composer of opera buffa, and another, our great-grandfather, was a violinist. There were musicians in each generation; Peter Lambert, our grandfather, who emigrated to the United States as a child, became a concert pianist, not well known outside his home state of Virginia. But the family's musical fame hit its peak back in the nineteenth century. Some would say that any remnant of a true musical life was lost when my father impulsively wedded my mother, a singer and chorus girl he met at a Las Vegas craps table in May of 1945.

It was a time of celebration, both national (Hitler had just killed himself) and personal (my father's naval squadron was not being sent to Okinawa). My father was spending one night of his leave in Las Vegas, on his way home to Virginia from San Diego, where he was stationed. He took my mother home with him to Norfolk and astonished her with his wealth. They were married during that same leave, Mother was set up, rather surreptitiously, in a room of our grandparents' house, and Father returned to see out the rest of his service in the Navy.

Perry and I never knew our grandparents. All the money came from our grandmother, Elizabeth Stanard, Peter Lambert's second wife, a pretty Virginian debutante whose coal and Bright Leaf tobacco assets alone—this was in 1923, when she was only twenty-one—were valued at something like fifteen million dollars. Peter and Elizabeth Lambert were killed in 1948 when Peter, by then an old man, flew their Piper Cub into the sheer side of a mountain in Colorado. I was only two, and I have no memory of them, though there seemed always to be something vaguely familiar about their aristocratic faces in photographs; Perry, of course, had not been born. And Mother never revealed much about her own family. She had no brothers and sisters, and her parents were always disposed of with one word: dead.

Before Elizabeth Stanard Lambert died, she tried making the best of an awkward situation by teaching Mother everything she could about clothes and food. Though Mother no doubt benefited from this instruction, she never quite lost her own style—you could always detect hints of Las Vegas in anything she did. She wasn't all feather boas and sequins, that's not what I mean, but her jewelry was too big and the colors she chose were noticeably loud; mainly, her style, regardless of the context, was excessive. There was always too much jewelry, too much food, too much chintz, and of course, very soon, much too much booze.

Sometime shortly after Perry and I started school, Mother seemed to retire from society. She was simply drinking too much, and felt too rotten too often, to go anywhere or plan anything. For company, she had a couple of old drinking buddies: an obese woman named Felicia Snow, who had a black-dyed beehive and a voice rather like Popeye's, only deeper, and a friend of Felicia's, a very small homosexual man Father liked to refer to as Little Teddy. The three of them—Mother, Felicia, and Little Teddy—would spend long afternoons together in our house, playing backgammon and cards and getting what they called "house-drunk." When Perry and I would arrive home from school, these three would be our playmates, if only for a few minutes—Perry and I were an interesting distraction to the adults, but a distraction that didn't wear well.

Now that our parents' glory years were over, and Mother had practically withdrawn from public, Father, already in his thirties, made one last attempt to pull his own life together: while Mother and her friends played backgammon and cards and got house-drunk in the library, Father practiced the piano. He was sober during this period, which didn't sit well with Mother. Eventually, he rented a recital hall downtown and hired a publicist to advertise his debut. The performance was well attended, and was reasonably brief. He played a program of classical and romantic music: Schubert's Sonata in A, Beethoven's *Waldstein,* Schumann's *Kreisleriana,* and Sonata in E-flat, no. 49, by Haydn. The recital received a good review in the *Virginian-Pilot/Ledger-Star.* And afterward, over the next eight years, Father, becoming quieter and kinder, gradually drank himself to death.

His beautiful, wealthy mother was only in her forties when she died, and he blamed his own father for the accident, claiming that the old man, in his seventies then, had no business flying a plane at his age. The accident became for Father the single explanation for all his own failures. That small plane smashing into a wall of rock somewhere in Colorado was, in Father's blurred thinking, the basis of his own failed musical career and of his not finding anything else to do with himself. It was the basis of his severe depressions, of his string of DWI arrests, and of the sad, defeated thing that his marriage eventually became.

Perry, Mother, Mother's friends Felicia and Teddy, and I are all in the library, which seems particularly moody this afternoon with rain blowing against the French windows. It's 1957, the year Mother always called us "seven come eleven," our ages. If there is a rare moment of quiet in the library, we can hear distantly, through closed doors, the sound of Father's piano. Perry and I both know by heart all the music Father plays these days—we have heard the same four pieces over and over again.

At this particular moment, I am reclining on a couch in my sock feet, studying spiritlessly a picture in a puzzle book: you are supposed to find a bucket, a shovel, a light bulb, an ink-well, a teapot, and a parrot hidden in the complicated drawing. Perry is tending bar, pouring another Scotch for Felicia—the way he has to hold the bottle steady with two hands somehow makes him look drunk—and Felicia, at the card table with the others, is feigning a slap at the side of Teddy's head, saying, in her barnacled voice, "Oh, you *thing* you!"

"Well, it's true," says Teddy, drawing deeply on a cigarette, executing a French inhale, then looking sidelong at Mother.

Mother, who is dealing cards, says, "Don't look at me. I'm steering clear of this one."

"And wise you are," says Felicia. "It absolutely is not true and you know it."

Perry arrives at Felicia's elbow with the glass of Scotch. She takes it, sips, and sets it down, smiling at Perry, then goes on: "I don't even like the man, the little peacock."

She takes another sip of the Scotch, then notices that Perry hasn't moved, is standing at her side, staring. "Well, what are *you* looking at," she says, not harsh but mildly bemused.

Perry doesn't answer, seems to intensify his gaze.

Mother says, "Perry, I've told you it isn't polite to stare at people."

He looks at Mother and says, "She said peacock."

"Yes, she did say peacock," says Teddy. "I heard her, too. She's a very silly woman."

"Why did you say peacock?" Perry asks Felicia, not even acknowledging Teddy.

Silence for a moment, in which everyone apparently waits for Felicia's answer. She looks at Mother and says, "Do I have to explain this?"

"I really think you should, probably," says Mother, nodding.

"I think you should, too," says Teddy. "It's the least you can do. He fixes your drink and serves it to you like some kind of little lackey . . . then you won't even explain why you said peacock."

Another moment of silence, during which the adults all look into one another's eyes. Mother lights a cigarette and starts to giggle, then they all three erupt into gales of laughter.

Perry saunters over to where I am and leans against the arm of the couch. He looks at the picture in the book and points listlessly to the hidden light bulb. "There," he says.

The rain whips the window glass in such a sharp staccato it makes me think of castanets.

"Don't *show* me," I say to Perry.

Another of those afternoons in the library. Also autumn, also raining. Mother, Felicia, and Teddy are laughing raucously about some other thing. I am trying to show Perry how to make a cat's cradle with a piece of string. Marion, our nurse, shows up at the door to the library beaming at Mother—apparently entranced by the sound of Mother's laughter—and moves to the card table, where she begins clearing a packed ashtray.

"Oh, don't do that, Marion," Mother says, composing herself. "Raymond will take care of it when he brings our snack."

Marion, hurt, abruptly serious, turns to Perry and me. "Well, boys," she says, "what do you say we go out to the kitchen and see what Raymond has cooking for *us*?"

Neither Perry nor I respond. The adults at the table have resumed playing cards, and for a moment it's as if Marion has stumbled into a dream in which she may look, but not touch. "Well, what do you say?" she says finally.

There is a rumble of thunder, after which Perry says, "I want to see Father."

"Good luck," says Mother, not looking up from her cards.

"I want to see him, too," says Teddy with a pout in his voice. "We never get to see him anymore."

"Yeah, me, too," says Felicia. "I'm beginning to think he doesn't like us."

Mother looks up wide-eyed, as if she suddenly has a brilliant idea. "Well, all right," she says, pouring down what's left in the bottom of her glass, then planting the glass noisily on the table. "It *would* be kind of nice to see him, wouldn't it?"

"He's practicing," I say from the couch. I cup my hand to my ear, demonstrating the obvious truth of what I've said.

"Marion," says Mother, "will you please go tell Signore Rudolfo that we would all like to see him?" (Most people know Father as Rudy. Mother sometimes calls him Signore Rudolfo, an allusion to his Italian ancestry, and I can tell, though I wouldn't be able to explain how, that there's something unfriendly in it.)

A dilemma on Marion's face—particularly one involving Mother—completely destroys her looks. "But Marty's right, Helen," she says faintly. "He *is* practicing."

"I know he's practicing," Mother says. "It's daytime, isn't it? What else would he be doing?"

We are all silent for a minute, and it seems that everyone is listening to Father's music, muted by the walls. He happens to be playing Schubert, an especially fiery passage, and Mother finally says, "Well, *I'm* not afraid of him," and rises.

After Mother has left the room, Marion goes to Perry and, gently stroking his hair, says, "I really don't think we should disturb him"—as if this drunken bee in Mother's bonnet is Perry's fault.

"Why not?" Perry asks.

"Because he's *practicing*," I say.

"Oh, don't be such sticks-in-the-mud, you two," Teddy says. "Marion and Martin. Two peas in a pod. You're such an old man, Marty. And you, Marion, you're such an old—"

Marion strides out of the room, past Teddy so briskly that I think I see his hair move. "Well, my, my," he says. "I think I have offended our nurse."

"She's not your nurse," Perry says to Teddy.

"Too bad," Felicia says. "You could use one."

"God knows I could," says Teddy, lighting a fresh cigarette. "I could use an entire intensive care unit, if the truth be told."

Perhaps I am the only one who has noticed that the sound of Father's piano has stopped. Not long afterward, Mother returns to the room and takes her seat at the card table. She sits with an exaggeratedly straight spine and closes her eyes, affecting serenity, then she turns to Perry and says, "Perry darling, why don't *you* go tell Father that we all want desperately to see him in the library. Tell him we miss him."

"Don't do it," I say to Perry, who has already started for the door.

Mother glares at me, and Teddy, cocking his little head in the direction of the door, says, "Atta boy. Thank God one of you boys has some spunk in him."

"Oh, shut up, Teddy," says Felicia, surprising him.

"What's got you?" he says.

"Nothing," she says. "I need a drink."

"That's for sure," says Teddy, rising to go to the bar.

Perry has left by now, on his way to the music room. I start to leave the library as well. But Mother catches my sleeve as I pass the card table. "Stay, Marty," she says. "Don't go. Teddy's sorry. Aren't you, Teddy?"

"For what, pray tell?" Teddy says, placing three full whisky glasses—no ice—on the table.

"Where's Marion?" Mother asks as I throw myself onto a couch.

"Teddy wounded her," Felicia says.

"Oh, I did not wound her," says Teddy.

"Teddy, what did you say?" Mother asks, sighing. "Why must you always insult people?"

"I didn't say anything," says Teddy. "And I didn't insult her." Then he chuckles and says, "She left the room before I had a chance to insult her. And anyway, all I was going to say was—"

Teddy interrupts himself in order to sip his drink, but Mother reaches for his glass, jerks it out of his hand, splashing whisky on the table and shocking Teddy and Felicia both. Holding the glass away from Teddy, she says, "It's really very simple. If you are going to insult Marion, you're not welcome in my home."

Teddy stands as if to go, then sits again, twitters, and lights a cigarette. "Have it your way, Helen," he says. "I didn't know you felt so strongly."

"I do feel strongly," says Mother.

I think I actually see tears in Teddy's eyes. After a moment, he says with some dignity, "May I have my drink back?"

Father is standing in the doorway of the library, holding Perry's hand, and it's clear that he has witnessed at least part of this scene between Mother and Teddy. Mother catches sight of him and quickly returns the drink to Teddy, saying grandly, "Signore Rudolfo!"

Not moving from the doorway, Father says, "Felicia," nodding, "Teddy."

"Rudy," Felicia says, "do come join us. Wouldn't you like a drink?"

"Of course he would," Teddy says, making for the bar.

"What is the meaning of this, Helen?" asks Father, not moving from his spot at the door.

"I told you, Signore Rudolfo," Mother answers, looking intensely into Father's eyes. "We miss you."

Father holds her gaze for no more than a moment, in which he seems to grasp all he needs to know about her, then he says, "Marty, please come with me."

I go to the door, where Father takes my hand. Before we turn to leave the library, he says, "Helen, there's a cigarette smoldering in the rug by your right foot. Do try not to burn the house down. It still has some sentimental value to me."

Perry and I walk with Father down the long dark hallway, back toward the music room, Father holding our hands as if we are in the street.

"Father," Perry says. "Do you like thunder?"

"Oh, I guess I like it all right," Father answers as we enter the music room.

"What are we going to do now?" Perry says.

"I don't know," says Father. "What would you like to do?"

"Nothing," says Perry. He crawls under Father's piano and lies on the floor, staring at the wooden ribs on its underside.

"Don't you want to practice?" I ask Father.

Father sits on the piano bench, and I notice that he has a yellow pencil stuck behind his ear. "Oh, I'm tired of practicing," he says. Then, after a moment's gaze at the music on the stand before him, he says, "Schubert."

Perry, still under the piano, says "Schubert," imitating exactly Father's grim tone.

"Music has here buried a rich treasure but still fairer hopes," Father then says.

"What's that?" I ask.

"It's written on Schubert's tombstone," answers Father.

"But what does it mean?" I ask.

Father closes the fall board, then gets down on his hands

and knees and crawls under the piano; he lies on his back beside Perry. "It means," he says, "that Franz Schubert was a genius and already dead before he was my age. Come and join us, Marty."

I creep under the piano and lie down on the other side of Father—he's between Perry and me.

"It's nice under here, isn't it?" Father says to me.

"Yes," I say, and then there is quite a long silence, during which Father's breathing becomes noticeable, regular. I raise up on one elbow to look at him, and see that Perry is already in a similar position on Father's other side. Father's arms are crossed on his chest; as usual, he appears strikingly handsome, but also uncommonly serene. Perry and I look at each other, Perry suppresses a giggle, then shrugs his shoulders.

Inside a cabinet in Father's bedroom upstairs in the Norfolk house, there was an old reel-to-reel tape recording of his debut (and farewell) recital. The afternoon of his funeral, in 1966, Perry and I hooked it up in the library and listened to it. Father had given a sensitive, flawed performance: there were long, luminous segments—especially in the Schumann and Schubert, and in the slow movement of the Haydn—in which his tone and phrasing were remarkable, enchanting, and there were times when Father didn't seem to have made any decisions about the music he was performing. I recall how Perry at sixteen was a dead ringer for James Dean, and I recall sitting in Father's favorite chair and gazing out the windows of the library, down the sloping lawn and through the trees. It was late November, most of the trees were without leaves, and it wasn't the first time I had sat in that chair, gazing out that same panel of windows, down the hill. It had been a way of charting the passage of time, the year's flight: as more leaves fell, more was revealed—chimneys and rooftops, fences, a pond—and the farther I could see. When the tape was over, I said to Perry that no matter what anybody said, Father had known his playing didn't quite cut it; it was good, but not good enough. But Perry, jerking his narrow tie loose, as if he suddenly needed air, said, "Oh, Marty, you know as well as I do, it was Mother who made him stop. Besides, I think his playing wasn't *bad* enough. I think it scared the living daylights out of him."

Minutes after falling to sleep in my New York hotel room, I awoke with a start from a brutal dream in which I lay in a hospital bed surrounded by medics who observed with horror as my body, one part at a time—a foot, an ankle, a forearm—swelled and exploded. My hands were the size of catcher's mitts on the brink of bursting when finally I howled myself awake.

But I fell back to sleep quickly and slept deeply into the morning. When I awoke a second time, it was from that worst kind of nightmare, a continuation of present reality. In the dream, I am awakened from my nap in the hotel room by the sound of the ringing telephone. It is Mother on the line, and I begin telling her about the ghastly dream I've just had in which my body was swelling and exploding. "That *is* ghastly," she says, and after we hang up, I realize that I didn't learn the purpose of her call. I try phoning her back, but no one answers. I rise from the bed and go into the bathroom, where I scrub my face and teeth. I shave and trim my mustache, just so. I even clip the tiny hairs showing around the rims of my nostrils. I get dressed. I leave the room and walk down the deep-carpeted hallway toward the elevator. The imposing, baroque pattern of the rug, the white-painted wainscoting along the walls, the gleaming chandeliers, all evoke the great palaces of Europe, and as I enter the elevator, I'm aware of a fine feeling of general well-being—almost chosenness— as if the sumptuous decor has worked a kind of voodoo on me. The elevator operator is stooped over with his back to me, tying a shoelace. When the doors close automatically, he stands erect and turns to face me. In a split second I see that the elevator operator is Perry—emaciated, drug-burned— I see that he is wholly demented, he sees that I know he's demented, he laughs like a lunatic and pushes a button on the control panel, sending us falling to a separate but shared death.

It was a cool morning of brilliant, pale sunlight in Manhattan, and as I entered the precinct station, I experienced a moment of blindness. I removed my dark glasses and walked to what appeared to be a reception desk situated near the entry, one of those sad gray metal obstructions with a rubber-coated top scored by countless fingernail gashes. A uniformed officer stood, rather than sat, behind the desk, pinching with the tips of two fingers the butt of a filterless cigarette and talking on the telephone. His face was red and he squinted, as if smoking the cigarette were a painful ordeal. With his eyes he acknowl- edged me, then held up one finger. "So how much do you get for a whole case?" I heard him say into the phone. "Yeah, and you cook 'em and there's nothin' left, right? And that's how many to a box? . . . No, she doesn't like that kind, don't you have any of the ones we got before? . . . So okay already, explain it to me . . ." The officer now pushed a large pad of paper toward me across the desk top. He passed me a pencil and mimed that I should write down my business. Annoyed, I wrote, "My brother just jumped out of a window on the twenty-third floor of a hotel—Detective Karajian please," and spun the pad back to him. "Let me call you back, Andy," the policeman said and hung up quickly. "Sorry," he said, stubbing out the cigarette in a red aluminum ashtray. He handed me a plastic-covered nameplate with "Visitor" stamped on it. "Just clip this to your shirt pocket," he said. "Is the lieutenant expecting you?"

I explained that I didn't have an appointment, but that Karajian knew I would be stopping by sometime today. I was asked to sign a log sheet and note the time (11:45 A.M.).

"That's Lieutenant K.'s office right over there," the policeman said, pointing to one of the last cubicles in a row of glass-fronted enclosures at the back of the large room. "The third from the left. Just give a knock on the door."

Walking from the reception desk to the detective's office, a distance of about thirty feet, proved to be an unexpected challenge. Some combination of fatigue, my early morning nightmares, and perhaps a dash of sorrow (for full-blown sorrow, still brewing somewhere at sea, had yet to find its way into shore) was aggravating what Madeline used to call my "reality problem." The precinct station was surprisingly quiet—its high vaulted ceilings, marble floors, and polished oak trim suggested a monastery or a church—and as I walked toward the detective's office, I was suddenly convinced that I was on some sort of religious mission. It was a fleeting and oddly comforting perception—comforting, I suppose, because it ennobled what had felt, all morning, like mere motions to be gotten through. Three very pretty high school girls sat in a line of oak chairs (not unlike a pew) in the middle of the room, and as I passed, there was something reassuring, too, about their fresh vigorous voices, engaged in some classroom gossip. "All the girls cried, of course," I heard one of them say. "*I* didn't cry," said another. "Well, of course, none of my *friends* cried," answered the first. The scent of their perfume reached me and conjured, for a happy moment, the blind invulnerability of adolescence—I felt firmly awakened by a spirit of adventure, in the grip of indisputable purpose. Then, as I rounded their line of chairs, I saw that the girls were plainly prostitutes—young, admittedly, but already severe, unhealthy. An especially starved-looking girl, the one closest to me as I passed, caught me staring at her and scowled poisonously, pulling up her T-shirt to flash me a hard, businesslike tit. I kept moving. I heard harsh female laughter at my back, loud, then an amplified din of ringing telephones, distressed voices, and rapid-fire typewriters. I would turn thirty in October. I had never been inside a police station. My father's casket, ten years before, had been closed; I had never seen anyone dead. And by the time I rapped my knuckles on the glass of Detective Karajian's office door, I was most assuredly afraid.

I saw him through the glass, a very thin man in his forties, with black hair and thick eyebrows. He was wearing a fashionable, wide-lapeled business suit of dark gray and a very wide tie in a paisley pattern of nearly psychedelic colors, most likely a gift from someone younger. Seated behind an oak desk cluttered with papers, he was just hanging up the telephone, laughing so hard that his eyes were brimming with tears, and as he motioned me to enter the office, he did it broadly, cheerfully, pointing to a chair, trying to compose himself, wiping his eyes. Then, with laughter still in his voice, he said, "Ken Karajian. What can I do for you?"

The office smelled of fresh paint, the floor still covered with a white, bespeckled dropcloth. "I'm Martin Lambert," I said, hoping that fear wasn't obvious in my voice. "You called me yesterday about my brother."

I was immediately consoled by Karajian's poise. He wasn't the least bit disconcerted by the bereaved brother's arriving at this moment of apparent mirth; he smiled as he stood to shake my hand. He asked me to sit, motioning again to a wooden chair that held a red upholstered pillow in the shape of a pair of lips. He inquired about my flight.

"Not bad," I answered, taking a seat. "Long."

"You're from Frisco, right?"

"Yes," I said.

"Great town," he said. "Beautiful."

"Yes," I agreed, though San Francisco's supposed splendor—its bearings and architecture—had always seemed frivolous to me, expendable, as if its builders had been department store window dressers; and lately, of course, all that glory had been nothing but a mocking backdrop to a decaying marriage.

Karajian had already returned to his desk. He picked up a manila folder, opened it, and began reading silently. "Where are you staying?" he asked finally. When I told him the name of my hotel, he said, "Expensive."

"Can you recommend a cheap one?" I asked.

"Not in good conscience," he answered, and for a moment I could have sworn that I smelled whisky. He seemed affable enough, though it now struck me as a salesman's affability—there seemed to be something hidden behind it—and I wanted him to get on with whatever it was. Then I noticed that not only was the desk cluttered, but two wastepaper baskets and a cardboard box rested on the floor, crammed with file folders and loose papers—nervous observation on my part, and it was nerves that made me ask, "Cleaning house?"

He looked up from the file. "Oh," he said, "kind of. This is my swan song, your brother's death. Enough is enough already. Twenty-five years. I'm tired of busting my nut for the taxpayers. I've got a cushy job lined up teaching sociology at Fordham. Law enforcement stuff. Want some coffee?"

When I declined the coffee, Karajian's face turned serious. "Your brother was a music student," he said.

"He would have finished school this year," I said. "He was teaching some classes and finishing up a thesis."

"I'm going to be frank with you, Mr. Lambert. Yesterday, I would have had a bunch of questions for you. Do you know any reason why your brother would have taken his own life? What about your family history? Any mental illness? What about your brother's friends and so on. All that's academic now."

"I don't follow you," I said.

"What I mean is, I would have been asking you to help us determine whether or not your brother committed suicide. But there's no longer any doubt about that."

"You mean you're sure that he did," I said.

Karajian nodded.

"You found a note?" I asked.

"No note," he said. "But we've got forensics and—"

"Forensics?" I said, for "forensics," to me, meant only guns and bullets.

"Fingerprints," he said. "We had to eliminate the possibility that your brother was pushed."

Karajian removed his suit jacket and demonstrated to me

how someone climbing out a window leaves neat, clear hand prints on the sill, whereas a victim who is pushed leaves streaks on the wood that frames the sides of the window.

"But couldn't he have been forced to jump, at gunpoint or something?" I asked.

"Do you have any reason to suspect such a thing?"

"No," I said, feeling entirely ridiculous.

"Which way would you rather go, Mr. Lambert?" Karajian said. "Be shot or jump?"

The question was obviously rhetorical, yet for a moment it seemed to stump me. Karajian did not wait for my answer. "Actually," he said, "we did find some streaks, but they were on the sill, and what I was about to say was that besides the forensics report we got an eyewitness."

It seemed there was a skyscraper under construction on the same block as Perry's hotel, and a welder, on the job early, had noticed a young man climbing out of a window at about five-thirty A.M. He'd tried yelling to him, but he was too far away to be heard, or the young man chose to ignore him. The construction worker watched as Perry, wearing trousers but no shirt, hung there with his hands on the window sill. He hung there for maybe a full minute. Then he pulled himself up and climbed back inside. The worker knew he should alert someone, but before he could raise anybody on his walkie-talkie, he saw Perry climb out the window again. Again Perry hung down, grasping the window sill; this time he was there for maybe two full minutes. And once again he began to climb back inside. But this time he appeared to lose his grip, and fell.

"Jesus," I said quietly. "He didn't even mean to do it."

Karajian looked at me thoughtfully for a long moment. "I think he meant to do it, Mr. Lambert. I think your brother meant to do it."

"Have you checked his apartment?"

"You mean for a note? No luck. We found a student ID that led us to you. We contacted the school and found your name and address on a form—person to contact in case of emergency. But no note. Sorry."

Karajian stood and walked around the desk. He took a seat in the chair next to me. Now I was sure I smelled whisky. He pulled out a pack of cigarettes and offered me one. I watched my hand with an extraordinary detachment as it took a cigarette and lifted it to my mouth. Karajian lit the cigarette for me, I inhaled wrong, and began to cough. I continued to cough, unable to stop, and felt myself receding backward through the large end of a telescope, the world dropping away; I saw, smeared through tears, Karajian's sallow face, its pained expression of concern. I managed to blurt out a "Sorry," but for an eternity I was lost to this humiliating fit of coughing. It felt as if my ears were plugged with wet clay. I heard Karajian's muffled voice: "You don't smoke." I shook my head, still coughing. He took the cigarette away from me and put it out in an ashtray, shaking his head as if I'd been a naughty boy. Finally, I caught my breath.

Karajian said, "You okay?"

I nodded and coughed some more, caught my breath again, apologized again.

"Okay?" Karajian said.

"Yes," I answered. "Sorry."

Karajian went behind his desk, opened a bottom drawer, pulled out two small paper cups, the kind sometimes found near a water cooler, and placed them on the desk top; then a bottle of what looked like Scotch appeared over the rim of the desk. He poured us each a shot, keeping the bottle low. He came back to the chair next to me, holding the cups, one in each hand, down at hip level. He handed me a cup. "Life in a fishbowl, this office," he said, knocking back the whisky in his cup. He wiped his mouth with the back of his hand. "Not that I give a damn. This is off the record, Mr. Lambert, so to speak. I've got all I need for the paperwork. But *do* you have any idea why your brother might have taken his own life?"

"No," I said, clearing my throat. This was all the speech I dared venture for the moment. I drank from the cup, swallowed slowly, and let the whisky burn my throat.

"Were you very close?"

"We were," I said. "But we've lived on opposite coasts for a long time."

"Did you know any of his friends back here?"

"No," I said. "Perry didn't talk about his friends much."

"I thought maybe you might have met someone when you were here on a visit."

"No," I said. "He was private about his private life."

"*Is* there any history of mental illness in your family?"

"Alcoholism, if you consider that a mental illness," I said. "Both my parents are alcoholics. Or were. My father's dead. My mother goes to AA."

"Have you told your mother about this?"

"Yes," I said. "She hadn't talked to Perry for some time."

"When did you last talk to him?"

"He left a message on my answering machine about five or six weeks ago, but I didn't get back to him."

"What was the message?"

"Nothing," I said. "Just hello. Are you getting at something here, Detective Karajian? Do *you* have any idea why Perry killed himself?"

Karajian returned to his desk, wrote something in the

folder. He looked at me in a way that I can only describe as honest. "No," he said, "I don't," and closed the folder. He pointed to the bottom drawer and said, "You want another? It put some color in your face. You needed some, if you don't mind my saying so."

"No, thanks," I said. "Where is Perry now?"

"I'm going to take you over to the medical examiner," he said. "I figured you might have some questions, and I think there's some of your brother's personal effects to claim."

It was probably unavoidable that the particulars of this morning would begin to seem slightly unreal to me—no doubt a mixture of the influence of crime fiction and my mind's effort to distance itself. Without consciously noting the tinge of morbid fascination behind Karajian's off-the-record questions, I'd perhaps been infected by it. Quite coldly, I asked, "And that's where I see the body?"

Karajian looked at me as if he were sizing me up. "Martin," he said, disarming me with the sudden use of my Christian name. "This is a bit delicate. We can request the medical examiner to set up the body for presentation, if you like, but frankly, I don't think he could do it. I'm pretty sure he would refuse. A fall from a height like that. It mangles the limbs, explodes the skull . . . you wouldn't be able to recognize your brother. We had to rely on fingerprints for the identification. And I honestly don't think you want to put yourself through something like that."

There was a knock at the door. A young woman was standing on the other side, and Karajian motioned her to come in. She entered the room wearing glasses and a tan trench coat, cinched tight at the waist with a wide belt. Her face appeared pale, and her dark hair was pulled severely back—the sort of girl from an old movie who wears glasses and a matronly braid at the back of her head, the bookstore clerk or librarian whose natural beauty you're not supposed to notice until the male lead, to swells of harp music, removes her glasses and asks her to take down her hair. She was serious and intelligent looking, and though all I heard her say was "Detective Karajian?" I immediately liked her voice. She closed the door, turned, and looked straight at me. All the blood left her face, quite visibly, and I was already on my feet when I heard Karajian's chair hit the floor.

"Oh, boy," he said, and we both fumbled at catching her. We managed to break her fall, and after we'd laid her out flat, Karajian opened the door and called to someone. "Oliver, we got a fainter over here! Get Weiner!"

Karajian began loosening the scarf from around the young woman's neck and undoing the top buttons of her trench coat. He placed his fingertips on her neck, feeling for a pulse. "Do you always have this effect on women?" he said.

A blond policewoman entered the office carrying what must have been a medical kit and knelt quickly to the floor.

"Here, come with me, Martin," Karajian said. "Let's give her some room."

We sidestepped several onlooking cops just outside Karajian's office door. I followed him to the reception desk.

"Who the hell is that, Oliver?" Karajian asked the officer stationed there.

The officer lifted the clipboard with the log sheet and read off a name: "Jane . . ." The officer squinted at the clipboard, drawing it closer to his face. "Owlcaster?" he said. "Jane Owlcaster?"

"Oh," said Karajian, nodding.

"Know her, Lieutenant?" the officer asked, but Karajian turned to me as he answered.

"Your brother's girlfriend," he said.

Even when we were boys, the physical resemblance between Perry and me was thought uncanny. As we grew older, and the apparent difference in our ages diminished, we really could almost pass each for the other. Perry had skipped the second grade of elementary school, moving us one year closer, and eventually we attended Harvard together. (Father had insisted that we get a conventional liberal arts education before entering any conservatory; specifically, he insisted on Harvard, so that's what we did.) During the year at Harvard in which I was a senior and Perry was a freshman, we inadvertently confused a number of teachers and classmates. The theory instructor—Perry and I both majored in music—would enter the classroom, find me already at my desk, and stare at me, stupefied: the instructor was certain that he had just said hello to me in the hall only the moment before. Perry eventually grew his hair much longer than mine—shoulder length, in fact—but even then, as I crossed the Yard or sat on the Widener Library steps, a girl completely unknown to me might see me from afar and call out cheerfully as she rushed to class, "See you at eight!" However, we had never before, to my knowledge, caused anyone to faint.

After Jane Owlcaster came to, Karajian went in and spoke with her in his office. I waited, seated in one of the oak chairs where the young hookers had sat earlier, and every now and then, I saw Jane Owlcaster turn and look at me through the glass. Karajian kept her for only five minutes before he summoned me back to his office. When he introduced us, she stood and shook my hand—rather bravely, I thought, since in her eyes I was a ghost. Karajian snapped his fingers in recollection of some detail. "There's something else that has to be taken care of," he said. "Wait here. I'll be right back."

Jane Owlcaster sat, and I took the chair next to her. She adjusted her glasses—the large, round, horn-rimmed kind that had recently become fashionable—and lightly touched the braid at the nape of her neck. She stared at her hands in her lap. Then, without looking up she said, "Let's see. You're four years older, play the cello, or used to. You're married, wife's name Madeline, but separated. You like German *lieder,* especially Schumann—and you've soloed with Philadelphia and Cleveland."

"He told you all that?" I said.

"And lots more," she said.

"Did you know him long?"

"Two years," she answered. "I work at the school."

"Well, there's something you should know," I said. "I never soloed with any orchestra, much less Philadelphia or Cleveland."

She looked at me. "But why would he tell me?"

"Maybe he wanted to impress you."

She shook her head, closing her eyes for a moment. "I've slept about one minute in the last twenty-four hours."

"Me too," I said.

"All night I lay in bed and tried to figure out how I feel about this."

"You didn't have any idea?" I asked. "I mean, that anything was wrong?"

"Are you sure you didn't solo with Philadelphia?"

I shook my head. "Not Cleveland either."

She stood and walked toward the door, looked out through

the glass. "Because . . . something like that," she said, "it makes me question everything."

"I would think you'd be questioning everything anyway," I said.

She nodded, then said, "No note. Boy, is that ever like him. You know, I think I'll write the story of your brother's life and call it 'No Note.' "

I said nothing.

She turned and looked at me apologetically. "In the middle of the night last night I searched my apartment. To see what I had of his. And you know what? There wasn't anything. I had some pictures of him, but even those weren't pictures he'd given me."

"Can you tell me anything at all?" I asked.

"Not much," she said. "He wasn't particularly depressed. He wasn't on drugs or anything like that. He'd recently done some of his best work. He was the man who had everything going for him. And yet—this is the weird thing—I don't feel all that surprised. I can't figure out why I'm not more surprised."

"That's okay, I'm surprised enough for both of us," I said, and I thought of my father for a second time that morning. Again I recalled the closed lid of his casket, and then I thought of Father during the period shortly before his death, when he would gather himself into a dark, impenetrable isolation and seem to be listening intently to the urgings of his own self-destruction. With Father, we thought the liquor, the drug, was speaking, stripping him of hope, securing and preserving its tyranny over him. But Perry hadn't been given to that sort of contemplation—I didn't think—and he wasn't under the sway of any substance. Perry didn't drink. Or do drugs. Ever.

"Listen," Jane said. "If there's anything I can do to help. I mean, I'd like to help, but right now I've got to get out of here. I've never fainted before in my life. I'm not the fainting type, believe me. But I'm afraid this paint smell is going to make me pass out again . . ." She turned and looked directly at me. I was still sitting in the chair, and I suddenly saw myself as she must be seeing me: a dejected effigy of someone she must have loved, of someone she had now lost, slumped in a chair in a police station. And seeing myself this way—person to contact in case of emergency—filled me again with self-pity. Jane said, "I wonder if you know how he felt about you. It was completely unsentimental. You were like . . . I don't know . . . like this great unquestioned thing in his life."

Just then Karajian opened the door to the office and a young black Labrador retriever on a red leash with tiny gold hearts rushed in ahead of him. Karajian reached down and released the metal clasp on the dog's collar. "We found him in your brother's apartment," said Karajian.

"Oh, Molly," Jane cried, holding out her hand, but Perry's dog went straight for me, planting her enormous paws in my lap and going for my face, licking to beat the band.

I heard myself making sounds of some sort, not words, as I embraced the dog, and just before I buried my face in the scruff of her neck, I saw Karajian quietly back out of the office and close the door, heading off a young officer's approach, giving him a look that fully imparted what sort of thing was going on inside.

Karajian was to have lunch with an administrator from Fordham, someone he referred to as his future boss, and he suggested that I try the Greek place around the corner from the precinct station, or the Blarney Stone on Broadway. He told me that I could leave Molly with Sergeant Weiner, the policewoman who had revived Jane, and he and I agreed to meet back at the station house at three o'clock to go over to the medical examiner's.

Jane had slipped quietly out of Karajian's office a few minutes before me, and at the time I had been glad to see her go; her anger and confusion were no help to me. But I wasn't sorry when I found her waiting for me on the precinct station steps. Jane had heard Karajian's luncheon suggestions, which had conveyed vivid, aromatic images of goat cheese and greasy lamb, steaming cabbage and watery mashed potatoes, and the first thing she said to me outside the door was, "Don't worry, I know a great deli nearby."

The day was no longer sunny, but overcast, and as we walked west, toward the river, I found myself pushing away thoughts of Perry's contorted body, his exploded skull, of his hands slipping from a window ledge. I listened to Jane as carefully as I could. She told me that a clarinet piece of Perry's was being recorded by a famous clarinetist in Washington, D.C. "Some friend of Max Dolotov's," she said. "Do you know Dolotov, the composer?"

"I used to," I said. "He was a friend of my father's. We didn't like him much. Especially Perry."

"No," Jane said. "He used to say that Max Dolotov was only an illusion. He's really Harold Greenberg from Queens, and you had to always keep that in mind."

"Is that true?" I asked. "I never knew that."

"Oh, yes," she said. "Perry came across it in some obscure who's-who listing. He used to call Dolotov 'Harold' sometimes, just to watch him turn bright purple. It drove Dolotov crazy that Perry didn't bow and scrape like everybody else. He was very possessive of Perry. Perry was supposed to be his protégé."

I hadn't seen Max Dolotov in ten years, not since my father's funeral. He was a hanger-on, an older, white-haired man, a bit of a snob who used to come around and drink with Father. He had known our grandfather, and had drunk with our grandfather as well. But aside from the drinking, there never seemed to be much purpose in Dolotov's presence; he was just *there,* because he had always been there.

After a moment Jane said, "There are a few things I need to check out with you, if you don't mind. All you have to say is true or false."

"Okay," I said. "What?"

"You like to read."

"True."

"You tend to be moody."

"False."

"You worry a lot about money."

"True."

"Unnecessarily."

"False, I think."

"You own a record company in San Francisco."

"True."

"The Sage label? Minority composers and women?"

"That's the one," I said.

"You like fast cars."

I laughed. "I drive a Volkswagen," I said.

"You always try to do what's right. You're a bit of a per-fectionist."

"Maybe."

"Maybe you drink too much."

"Not always," I said.

"You once went to Greece with Perry and lived on a beach."

"True."

She paused. Then, "Your father died in a car crash."

"False. Cirrhosis."

"In Yugoslavia?"

"Yugoslavia? How about in a hospital in Norfolk, Virginia."

She paused. Then, "I don't get it. I mean, what was the point? It's all so trivial. Why would he lie about stuff like that?"

I told her I didn't know. I told her that my brother had always been quirky, but that I thought he was basically a truthful person. Sometimes, in fact, he had been astonishingly truthful and had told the truth when a lie might have been a better idea. But I also told her it wouldn't be unlike him to ad lib a bit out of boredom. I immediately regretted having said this, because it came out wrong: it sounded as if I were suggesting that Perry had been bored with her.

"Oh," she said, stopping for a moment on the sidewalk. "Well, it wasn't a very nice thing to do."

Somewhere out on the Hudson a boat sounded its horn, and I noticed that the sky had grown dark with rain clouds. I said, "No, it wasn't," and we looked at each other in a certain way, for these last words seemed to refer not to the pointless lies, but to the suicide.

At the deli, Jane produced some kind of coupon she'd saved entitling her to a free sandwich and soda. She said she'd brought the coupon along because she knew she was going to be in the neighborhood and thought she might end up at the deli for lunch; she seemed very proud of herself as she explained all this to me at the deli's display case. The young man behind the counter who took our order said brightly, "Is this to go or to take out?" and I said quite seriously, "No, we were hoping to eat it here," before I caught the joke. The young man laughed and pointed at me, saying, "Gotcha," and it so reminded me of Perry that I felt the muscles in my face do something weird—everything seemed to tighten. As I counted out the money to pay for our sandwiches, using Jane's coupon, I noticed that my hands were shaking.

There were only a half-dozen small round tables in the back of the place, but most customers were buying sandwiches to take out. As I sat down, I wondered if part of Perry's legacy to us would be that we should see him everywhere. When I looked across the table at Jane, she said, "This is hard, sitting here with you."

"Sorry," I said.

"It's not your fault. You can't help looking like him."

I told her that the young man behind the deli counter had reminded me of Perry and that I hadn't much liked the way it made me feel.

"Oh," she said. "I know. That 'gotcha' business. I hated that."

After a minute of silence I noticed that both of us were taking small, unenthusiastic bites at our sandwiches, pushing potato chips around with our fingers, staring down at our plates. Seeing Perry's dog back at the police station had released something in me, punctured my self-confidence, and leaky little unobtrusive tears had begun lingering modestly at the rims of my eyes until I brushed them away. It was more physical than emotional; I could even joke about it, but I couldn't quite turn it off.

"Why don't we get out of here?" Jane said. "My apartment's a five-minute cab ride."

I stood and headed for the door, leaving all the food on the table. A light rain had begun, and when Jane caught up to me just outside the door, she was carrying our sandwiches swaddled in paper napkins, and a black umbrella. She asked me to hold the sandwiches while she opened the umbrella.

"Where did you get that?" I asked her.

She popped it open and said, "Be prepared. That's my motto," then walked into the street and expertly hailed a cab.

I thought this a surprising philosophy from someone who had so recently fainted. And considering the circumstances that had brought us together, the idea of preparedness seemed almost comical.

She told the cab driver her address, West 73rd Street, and we were on our way up Eleventh Avenue. We didn't speak all the way uptown, our silence more reverent than awkward. When we arrived I paid the driver, and as Jane opened the door to the apartment building, a smallish one near West End Avenue, she said, "There's something I should tell you."

"What?" I said, prepared for another shock.

But she didn't speak again until she had pushed the elevator button. "I live with my mother," she said.

"You do?"

"Weird, huh?"

The elevator doors opened and we stepped inside. (Happily, there was no operator with his back turned to us, bent over, tying a shoelace.) Jane explained that her parents were divorced; that the apartment was huge; that her job at the school was only part time — she was also taking some graduate courses at Columbia — and she couldn't afford a decent place of her own; that she and her mother got along most of the time, mostly.

"Is your mother home now?" I asked. I didn't feel like meeting anyone new.

"Oh, no," Jane said. "I wouldn't do that to you. She's at work."

When we were inside the apartment—it *was* huge; one of those West Side apartments from a bygone era, complete with maid's room—Jane told me that she had a rehearsal in an hour, but that I could stay and rest if I liked. Her mother wouldn't be home until dinnertime. Then she said, "What I really feel like is some ice cream. Want some?"

I told her that what I wanted was a drink, and she motioned me to follow her out to the kitchen. She showed me the cabinet where the liquor was kept, and when I opened the door I saw an extraordinarily organized cupboard that resembled shelves in a supermarket—everything in surprising quantity: dozens of cans of tuna, seven or eight boxes of the same yellow cake mix, a half-dozen boxes of linguine . . .

I found a bottle of Scotch, one of three arranged in a neat row alongside the other liquors, on the top shelf. "You certainly are well stocked," I said.

"It drives my mother crazy," Jane said, taking a container of ice cream from the freezer, "but don't you hate running out of things?"

"I don't think I ever thought about it," I said.

"Everybody makes fun of me," she said. "But in a blizzard or a blackout, who do you think everybody comes running to for this and that?" She tapped her finger to her breastbone. Then, for a surprising moment, before she remembered who she was with and why, she burst into laughter.

Back in the living room, I sat on a couch and sipped a whisky over ice. Jane did not remove her trench coat or even loosen the belt; I wondered if she wanted to be prepared in case it might rain indoors. She took a wing-back chair opposite me, drew her legs up under her, and began eating the three perfectly scooped, perfectly round globes of chocolate ice cream she'd placed in a clear dish. I was vaguely aware of a clock ticking somewhere in the room, but to let my eyes explore the mantel, the walls, and the bookshelves that were in my peripheral vision felt ridiculously daring. It occurred to me that perhaps the way I was feeling was what people meant by being in shock. I recalled having witnessed an accident once in which a young man, swerving to miss a cyclist in a crosswalk, rammed into a steel lamppost, driving the post deep into the front end of his car. The hood popped open, the horn blasted continuously, steam spurted from the radiator. When I reached the car and looked in at the driver, he appeared to be unhurt; he sat turning the key in the ignition, trying to restart the car. When I finally convinced him that the car was not going to start, he reached into the back seat, lifted shirts and socks and underwear from a laundry basket, and began neatly folding them on his lap. Now it seemed to me that the driver had been desperate to find a focus, something, no matter how trivial or absurd, that would narrow his vision, something to contain him. And now I found myself studying the ice inside my glass: getting to Jane Owlcaster's apartment, out of public view, a means to some end, had quickly become an end in itself. What next? I looked at her.

She shrugged her shoulders, nodding toward my whisky glass, and said, "I guess you're not like him."

"No," I said. "Not much."

She asked me if I was sure I didn't want something to eat. "If you don't want the sandwich from the deli, I could make you some eggs. What about eggs? Scrambled eggs and toast?"

"No thanks," I said.

"Do you want to take a nap, then?" she said. "There are lots of beds here."

"No, really, I'm fine."

"Cheese and crackers?"

"No. Thank you. This is all I want."

For the first time that day, Jane looked honestly sad to me, sitting there with her legs folded under her and eating ice cream. The large glasses, the braided hair, and the trench coat were meant to lend an air of sophistication, but all that had faded now and what I saw opposite me was a lovely young woman who seemed surprisingly wronged and unprotected. I wished I could have said to her, as she had to me, that she was a great unquestioned thing in my brother's life. As it was, I couldn't even tell her that Perry had loved her—I'd never heard of her before that morning—but maybe she didn't need any outsider for that. I hoped that she didn't. What I did say finally was, "Well, *most* of what he told you was true."

She forced a smile.

I knocked back the Scotch and poured another from the bottle I'd brought out to the living room with me. It was the only thing I could think to do. I didn't know exactly why I had come to Jane's apartment—because she had asked me, I supposed. After a minute she said, "He didn't smoke dope either, you know. My mother called him Mr. Clean."

"The funny thing was," I said, "he never criticized Mother and Father for their drinking, even when they were blotto from sunup to sundown. But let me so much as order a beer with dinner—"

"He was afraid for you," she said.

"He was?"

"What was it he used to say? That the statistics weren't in your favor."

"Oh," I said. "He said that to me, too."

"Do you want to see the pictures?"

"Of Perry?"

"There, in that envelope on the table."

In a long white envelope were perhaps a dozen snapshots, all of Perry, all apparently taken on the same sunny day, somewhere outdoors. Jane came over and sat next to me on the sofa, looking at the pictures with me. "We had a fight that day," she said, pausing over a photograph of Perry high up in a tree. "I was furious because he climbed so high and wouldn't come down. He was deliberately trying to scare me."

"Daredevil," I said.

"Fool," she said, and looked at me quickly to see how I'd taken it. When I shrugged, she stood and asked me again if there wasn't something she could get for me. I declined everything again, but she went into the kitchen and returned with a bowl of apples, placing it on the table and saying, "Just in case." Then she told me she should be getting ready for her rehearsal.

"What kind of rehearsal?" I asked.

"Chorus," she said. "That's what I do at the school. I assist the choral conductor. Classes haven't actually started yet, but the chorus has an early concert this fall and I'm doing all the drudge work. I rehearse them until they've learned all the music, then the real conductor steps in to put on the finishing touches and do the concert. We have a medieval system at the school. I'm somewhere between a serf and a vassal. It's all very bad for your self-esteem, but I think it's supposed to make you a great artist."

"You have a legitimate excuse for skipping it," I said. "If you want to."

She shook her head. "No . . . I'm glad I have it," she said. "It feels like a . . . what are those things on ships? You know, those things they throw you if you fall overboard?"

"You mean a lifesaver?" I said.

"That's what I was going to say, but I thought that was just candy."

"Life ring is the official name, I think. What they call them on ships."

"Sounds like something in a science fiction movie," she said. " 'We all have to be sure to wear our magic life ring.' "

She asked me to make myself at home, and went to her room to change.

Left to my own devices, I roamed the apartment. Vaguely, I was looking for distraction; I didn't like being alone with my thoughts. I knew it was crazy, and it made me *feel* crazy, but I kept having these queer little sensations of falling, the kind you have when you're dropping off to sleep. And everything kept going back to the image of Perry's fingers on that window ledge (if only he'd been wearing his magic life ring). The apartment was decorated with very traditional-looking furniture, pretty but not expensive. Everything looked more handed down than bought: there were worn oriental rugs on the floor, a wine-colored corduroy slipcover on the sofa—nothing like the overly decorated childhood homes Perry and I grew up in. I wondered about this woman with whom he had finally, apparently, established a connection. There was something about her that was like him: an obvious vulnerability, yet also a reserve, a strong sense that you weren't getting the whole picture, a hint of something carefully withheld. Just as I was thinking this she suddenly reappeared to retrieve her purse on the coffee table. I was standing at the window behind the sofa, and when I turned she looked at me inquisitively. "I often wondered what kind of woman Perry would end up with," I said, as if I needed to confess my thoughts.

She smiled. "I was perfect for him," she said. "I'm a musician, but not a genius, not a threat. Even though I took care of him twenty-four hours a day, I'm just unhappy enough to make him think that *he* was rescuing *me* from my troubled life. And I squealed when he did scary things." As she started back toward the hall, she added, "But he didn't exactly end up with me, did he?"

After a couple of minutes, I wandered down the hallway, Scotch in hand, toward the rooms in the back of the apartment. Jane abruptly entered the hall from one of the white doors, wearing only a half-slip and a bra. No glasses, her hair was down, and I noted with surprise lots of dark curls. "Oh, what are you doing?" she said quickly, scurried into the bathroom at the end of the hall, and closed the door.

"Sorry," I called out. "I shouldn't be nosing around."

"It's all right," she said, but she didn't sound particularly convincing.

When I returned to the living room couch, I decided that I would wait for her to dress, then we would leave the apartment together. Perhaps I would take a walk before meeting Karajian back at the precinct station. But the whisky was making me very sleepy, or perhaps it was relaxing me so that I could feel how tired I really was. I lay back on the couch, closed my eyes, and almost immediately Dolotov, the composer Perry had studied with, loomed before me, his round face reddened and angry, shaking his finger at me, scolding me, though I couldn't understand his words. We are in some dark place full of huge, severe shadows, some enormous room that doesn't seem to have a roof. Tall black curtains, billowing like sails, hang from the sky, ropes and thick electrical wires dangling. And Dolotov comes at me, his face darkening. I can see a bright red Exit sign behind him as he closes in on me, his pointed finger changing at the last moment to a fist . . .

. . . music, something very early, choral, the thin, woody voices of boys. Jane Owlcaster returns to the living room, naked beneath her tan trench coat, which, unbelted and unbuttoned, opens and closes with the motion of her legs as she approaches: an interval of white thigh, the ephemeral triangle of darkness just above, bisected once, twice, three times by the rise and fall of the coat. She shrugs the coat off her shoulders, and I feel a surge of orgasm, like a drug rush, an inverted centrifugal force that stops precisely at the tip of my erection, and she is swimming toward me, toward *it,* her dark unbraided hair spreading across the surface of the water like fire. Her face now close to my own, she cups my balls in her hand and loops her thumb over the base of my penis, whispering, "He won't mind," pulling down on me, not too gently, so that my knees bend, then up, pulling me into her and quickly back out again. Then back in . . .

These were the bookends of my sleep—my brother's teacher, my brother's lover—Perry in there claiming my slumber for his own use, leaving behind a jumbled wake of fear and grief and confusion and shame. Jane's living room had grown dark. Alone, I lay on the sofa, a woollen afghan draped over me, a pillow under my head, my shoes off. There was a note next to the bottle of whisky on the coffee table:

Dear Martin,

I didn't have the heart to wake you—you were sleeping so soundly. I even took the liberty of phoning Karajian. He

said you could go to the medical examiner's later, and that
you should call him (Karajian). You need to pick up Molly,
though, before six. Molly could stay here for a while if you
like (my mother's crazy about her). And so can you, for
that matter. Your jacket and shoes are in the hall closet.
Your sandwich from the deli is on the kitchen counter in a
brown bag. I've left a note outside on the door for my
mother, warning her that there's a man inside the apartment, that she shouldn't be afraid, that he looks a lot like
Perry, that she shouldn't faint. Please take it down if you
leave before she gets home. And please call me if there's
anything you need.

J.

Miraculously, Perry and I have managed to avoid the local police—the abandoned road outside Spring Lake is that isolated—and we've managed to find a towing company with a truck big enough to get the Lincoln out of the sand gully. The repairs needed are minor: all the shocks have to be replaced. Perry telephones Mother in Newport early in the morning, saying we need to remain in Spring Lake an extra day or two, that we'll be staying at our host's another night. "But why?" Mother says. "It's deadly here without you." Perry recounts, in precise detail, the exact truth—the hellcat game he and the other boys played the night before—and by the time he reaches the part where I showed up at the car window and said, "Jesus, are you in trouble now," he has Mother laughing. Then when she asks him the name of our host in Spring Lake and Perry says, "I forget," she's practically in hysterics.

Of course it would never, ever have occurred to me to tell the truth. Which is just as well, because I don't have Perry's talent for telling it. He is especially good with Mother. He has an impeccable sense of timing and a knack for stunning her with the truth when she least expects it. At fifteen, almost sixteen, he plays her like a harp. He often knows what she wants better than she herself knows, and, as on this morning in Spring Lake, he can surprise her with that knowledge and surprise her into laughter; she has an especially ferocious hangover this summer morning and desperately needs a laugh. Perry knows that a laugh partially at Father's expense — after all, it is Father's car that was risked — has a good chance of hitting the mark. He also knows that she'll see Father in my seriousness at the scene of the accident, and see herself in Perry's not remembering the name of his host.

Back in Newport, we are spending a portion of the summer in the secluded "cottage," a twelve-room stone house with a slate mansard roof and a view of Narragansett Bay that has been in Father's family since he was a child. For the past ten or eleven years the house has sat empty, but last winter, on a whim, Mother decided to have it done over and then spend July and August here. It is a negligible departure from her usual reclusiveness, since we are as isolated here, by our circumstances and personalities, as we are at home in Virginia, or anywhere else. The house, on the other hand, seems full to me: Felicia Snow has descended for a stay of indefinite length (without Little Teddy for a change); Father has as his guest the semifamous composer with whom Perry will later study, Max Dolotov, up from New York, also an alcoholic, and attracted to wealth as pitifully as Father is to any sort of musical success; and we have the extraordinary Raymond, who, with local temporary help, oversees everything—cooking, shopping, cleaning, laundering, gardening.

Mother has done the interior of the house in such bright colors that when you enter a room, your first impulse is to recoil. There's a good deal of trompe l'oeil around as well, so the overall effect is hostile: first your eye is assaulted, then tricked. Felicia is quite fond of all this. When she enters the garden room (spring green and fuchsia), where Mother, Perry, and I are having our morning coffee, Felicia stands near the threshold for a moment and takes a deep breath, oscillating her head and smiling, not at us but at the room. Perry leans over to me and whispers, "She's trying to figure out how to *drink* it," and I nearly choke on the gulp of coffee I've just taken.

We can see Father and Max Dolotov strolling out on the lawn in the distance. Dolotov, in his sixties, a contemporary and friend of Father's father, has grown more and more comical looking out here in the sun as his hair has turned whiter and his face redder. Father is increasingly soft-spoken and gentle these days, as if he has been beaten into submission by some consummate authority. Lately there are times when it appears that he is quietly listening to the uncharitable voice of that authority. He goes still as a statue, his face twitches, his eyes tear in response to whatever verdicts he's hearing. Worse, he has developed a number of phobias—fear of tunnels, of bridges, of close rooms—all of which have the same effect: he loses his breath, his heart flutters, and during an especially bad attack, he will begin tearing at his clothes. His interim doctor here in Newport has told him that he suffers from severe gastritis and must abstain from liquor, so Father drinks Scotch and milk. Out on the lawn with Dolotov now, he gestures broadly with his arms, tracing arcs—he must be describing to Dolotov the extent of the Newport property, what it is nowadays as compared to what it once was in his own father's day. I have noticed during this visit to Newport that Father, though he is only in his forties, rambles recurrently about the past.

"Come on," Perry says to me, wiping his chin with a linen napkin, then tapping me on the arm.

"Where are you boys off to?" Mother asks, putting down her newspaper and scissors. (For years she has clipped articles from newspapers, stored them in shopping bags for no purpose that she will reveal. She calls this idiosyncrasy, this pastime, "Everything Interesting.") Perry is already out of the room when Mother looks up to ask her question, and I, trailing behind, am suddenly face to face with Felicia, who is giving me a bawdy look, even though all she says—no, *sings*—is, "Good morning, Jesus." It's as if each day is newly intriguing for Felicia, as if she awakens wondering what mischief she can stir up. She calls me Jesus this summer because I've grown my hair down over my ears and have a scraggly beard. Felicia herself still has the beehive, still dyes it jet black, and now that she is extremely tan, she's taken to wearing lots of gold hardware, heavy chains and enormous hammered things stolen from the Mayas. Perry, who claims to be writing a book about Felicia, has said that in this way she carries music with her everywhere she goes.

"Marty," Mother calls as I'm about to leave the garden room. "I asked you where you boys were off to this morning."

I haven't the slightest idea where we're off to, and I see that this is a way of life this summer: Perry has the agenda; I follow. In truth, I don't much care what I do. I've returned from my sophomore year of college with my mortal soul in peril. I lost my virginity to my best friend's girl, and I'm trying to pretend that I'm beyond the reach of this recent past. I'm happy to have Perry chart the course of the present—*someone* has to. We spend most of our days at the beach club, we have lunch there, swim in the ocean, swim in the pool, and snub most everyone we see. We're quite above all the idle cabaña talk—the state of one's tennis game, one's plans for Europe this winter, and the like. We boldly declined two party invitations the first week we were here—news that spread quickly—and now we are no longer invited anywhere. Perry writes in his spiral notebooks, about Felicia, about all of us, I suppose. I'm reading *A Separate Peace*. We sleep. From my viewpoint, the days in Newport are dull, without substance, but this perception may have something to do with whatever success I've had at distancing myself from the world. I'm long inured to the chaos going on around me, fueled by the flow of liquor in the house and at the beach club; that's an old habit. But recently, I've occasionally wondered where my feelings are. I've heard myself over and over again, for example, saying to Jeanine Clotfelter, on the beach in Spring Lake, "Don't be such a worrier, it's not good for your skin," and I am further numbed by the perplexing impression of not knowing the speaker of these words. On the beach here in Newport, I've caught myself once or twice in such a torpor, in such a state of numbness, that I've wondered if I might not levitate. The one constant in all of this, the miracle, is that every day at four, no matter what else happens, Perry and I are in the house, in separate rooms, practicing our music. Often Father visits us, listens to my cello, to Perry's piano, and sometimes comments. After Perry and I are done, one of us always asks the other, "Did he say anything?"—as if Father were already a ghost, an apparition haunting the corners of our rehearsal rooms, and we were eager to know whether or not it spoke this time.

I take a stab at answering Mother's question: "We're going to the club, I guess."

"Well, it seems to me that you might ask someone if they might like to go to the club, too," she says.

In stark contrast to Father's failing health this summer, Mother is experiencing a reborn gaiety, which seems to have taken Perry as its focus, and what Mother means now is that she is feeling abandoned by him. Apparently, I am giving her a curious look, because she says, "Well, you *might* . . ."

"I'll tell Perry," I say, and leave the room.

Perry is playing backgammon with Mother at a low wicker table in the shade of our cabaña at the beach club. Father and Dolotov sit in chaise longues nearby, talking, drinking. I'm close by too, but I've pulled my chair into the sun near the edge of the short concrete wall that drops to the beach. Felicia has not yet returned from lunch; she tends to linger with martinis in shady spots, and she has become one of the sights here this summer (as we all have in varying degrees, I think). Felicia strolls the boardwalk, from cabaña to bar and back again, in a silk muumuu of a different electric color each day. Whether sitting, standing, or walking, she is never seen without the cumbersome leather purse she wears soldier style on a long strap crossing her breast. I have it from Perry that she has a secret identity as a cleaning lady, and that she carries her change of costume in the bag; she enters the homes of the very rich for one-day stints, steals whatever she can find of value, then changes back into the apparently well-to-do Felicia Snow. (I think this is the basis of Perry's book about Felicia.)

The rattle of dice, muffled by felt and cork, and the slap of the markers that punctuate Perry and Mother's games begin to have a meaning of their own, a new language, a code of stresses and rapid reports and innuendo. Or so it occurs to me, in an entirely sun-drenched sort of way. Occasionally, I hear Perry say, "You die," and later, often much later, Mother say, "Oh, *do* I?" Just as you can sometimes discern the woman who is a golfer though she is far away from any course, you can tell, if you know what to look for, that Mother attaches a lot of importance to her backgammon game. Some of her game-table mannerisms have crossed over into everyday life. For example, she has a way of sitting forward, half-bent from the base of her spine, with the palm of one hand planted, fingers inward, on one knee. Mother is wearing a bikini and still looks good in it. She's very dark, her hair long and sun-bleached, pulled back and held at the nape of her neck with a gold barrette. She is addicted to her appearance, and so far the old habits of grooming haven't been wasted by her other addiction; she is sure to spend enough time flat on her back in the sun so that no white lines mark the creases of her stomach.

Oddly, I am just thinking about how she likes to play backgammon for money and how she can't keep her hands off the doubling cube when I hear Dolotov, moving his drink glass in small circles, churning the ice, say loudly to Father, "Well, you must like a lot of doublings in the strings if you're fond of his chamber music."

I've already overheard them talking of Brahms, and this remark sounds to me like an attack on Father's taste—I know for a fact that he is practically reverent about the piano quintet and the clarinet quintet—but now he would rather reminisce than defend himself, and simply squints out toward the ocean and smiles. "When I was a child we had a copy of that famous drawing of Brahms," he says, and I notice Mother stare at his profile for a moment, then roll her eyes: he's *off* again. "The one with the potbelly and the long beard," Father continues. "Each Christmas, my mother would paste a felt Santa Claus hat on the picture's glass, just over Brahms's head . . ."

Dolotov scrutinizes Father for a long time after this, then follows Father's gaze toward the greenish water and the sky, as if to find some clearer intelligence on the horizon. Eventually, Dolotov brushes the thick mat of white hair on his chest — an insect has flown into the snowy forest — and quietly sips his drink.

Mother offers Perry the doubling cube, this time placing it delicately with two fingers, like a laboratory specimen, in Perry's quadrant. "Give me a break," Perry says, plucks the cube from the board, and throws it far out into the sand. Mother is instantly up and around the table, delighted, ready to roughhouse, and begins slapping at Perry's head, saying, "You get out there this minute, you little chickenshit, and find that cube!"

Perry covers his head with his hands, pulling his legs up into his chair, laughing. "All right, all right," he says until she stops. Mother stands with her hands on her hips, the task-master waiting for orders to be carried out. "How *dare* you?" she says as Perry rises and walks toward the steps that lead down to the sand. When he reaches the first step, however, he quickly turns and sprints toward the pool behind the line of cabañas. Mother shouts after him, "You are no gentleman, you chickenshit!" and then saunters, still with hands on hips, after Perry. Father buries his face in his hands, appalled. Dolotov clears his throat and looks right and left, very embarrassed, very much the gentleman himself, and I notice that one white-bearded testicle hangs out below the hem of his trunks.

After a minute Perry returns, breathing hard. Father's index finger is up, beckoning him silently. Then Perry does something he does very well. He goes to Father, lays a thin brown arm across his chest, affectionately, and wearing an expression of genuine concern, puts his face quite near Father's. "Pop?" he says.

"Where is Helen?" Father asks.

"Getting a drink."

"Mr. Dolotov has never seen anyone conduct in three-four and four-four at the same time," Father says.

"You mean like this?" Perry says, and he gets the triangle going with his right hand, then adds the inverted T with the left, three against four, easy as you please.

Dolotov laughs and turns to me, his head at an odd angle, his mouth slack so that I can see an abundance of gold fillings. "Can you do it?" he asks cheerfully.

I suddenly think of my best friend's girl, Camilla Parker, as thin and frail as a pipette in the school science lab, about our fumbling and finally successful night on her family room couch, as we lay in pitch dark listening to the enraptured groans and barks of her psychiatrist father making it with his college-student girlfriend in the bedroom down the hall—it's the blossoming of the sixties—and I push all these images away with an effort of will greater than any I've had to muster so far today. "No," I say to Dolotov and stare determinedly down at the heat-blurred words on the pages of my novel.

"Any good?" Perry asks, squatting in the sand, looking over my shoulder at the book.

I've pulled my chair out onto the sand. "The print is nice and big," I say. "Boarding school types during World War Two. Everybody's going a little crazy."

"At least it's not one of those where some woman has to go out in the rain for some reason and then dies because of it. I hate those."

"Not so far," I say.

"Want to take a walk before practice?"

"Sure," I say. "You don't think Mother will be jealous?"

"What do you mean?"

"Don't tell me you haven't noticed."

We both look back at the cabaña: Felicia sits in a chair, rattling on about something, gesturing with her hands, her gold bracelets ringing; she's situated just behind Mother's chaise, so she can't see that Mother is sound asleep. Perry laughs. "She's just lonely this year," he says.

We start walking toward the water and I think, What a peculiar pair we are, off for a promenade before retiring to our practice rooms, to our cello and piano. Aren't most boys our ages playing softball, tennis, chasing girls, carousing, sneaking beer and (nowadays) marijuana? We would never have survived a public school, sheltered as we are by the roomy sanctuary of extreme privilege. It occurs to me that we have saved the world the trouble of casting us out. One of the differences between Perry and me is that I'm aware of this division between us and the rest of the world, and he is not. Or at least it's not something he *experiences*. (Once when Perry was twelve, a neighbor kid named Clarence Ward called him a sissy. We were in our yard, and Perry, having quit whatever game they were playing, was about to return to the house to practice. Perry, a small boy for his age, looked considerably younger than he actually was, and there was something comical and endearing about his voice having already changed, earlier than most boys': what you got was this kid who looked eight or nine but with the voice of a bassoon. Perry walked back over to Clarence and took his hand. As he bent Clarence's middle finger back, bringing him to his knees, Perry said in his deep, resonant voice, "You're probably right, Clarence.") I am cursed with a consciousness of options in a way that Perry has never been. Though I auditioned for orchestra at college, for example, and won first chair my sophomore year, I still think sometimes that I'll put down the cello, take up sculling on the Charles, be normal. This is a curse that comes with having a smaller gift: it's possibly expendable. But it would never occur to Perry to do anything of the sort. Not using his gift would be like not using one of his senses.

"Dolotov's a clown," Perry says as we walk toward the fence that divides the sparsely populated private beach from the very crowded public one.

"Why do you say that?" I ask.

"Because he is," Perry says. "And he's not very nice to Father. He's so superior. And he's a drunk."

"He wouldn't be here if he weren't a drunk," I say.

"No," says Perry, "I guess not. He's a sponge to boot."

"That's not what I mean," I say. "I mean, he wouldn't put up with us if he weren't a drunk."

Perry is quiet for a moment. Then he says, "Why are you so angry, Marty?"

"I'm not," I say.

"You are," he says. "All summer. Mother thinks so too."

"Mother doesn't think," I say. "She *distills*."

"Well, she distills that you're angry," Perry says. "And I agree."

"Sorry," I say. "Summer's almost over."

"I'm worried about Father," he says. "Mother's bored with

him this summer. Dolotov's a clown. And you're angry. What's he got to cheer him up?"

"You," I say. "That's your area."

"Marty," says Perry, "I haven't done anything to you."

"I didn't say you had. I just mean that you're the one who cares. You're the one who's always making everything all right, so you're the one who ought to do something."

"You're angry," he says.

"Perry," I say. "Do me a favor. Don't play shrink with me, okay? You're always cutting to the goddamn heart of the matter and if you want to know the truth it's pretty tiresome."

"I don't know what you're talking about."

"You do too," I say. "That's another thing. You walk around day and night being Mr. Incisive and then when somebody tries to talk to you—I mean really talk to you, about *you*—you go stupid on him."

"Well, what *about* me?" he says.

"I don't like the way you manipulate them all the time, that's all," I say, floundering a bit.

"Who?"

"There you go again. Heckle and Jeckle, jerk-off. Who the hell do you think I mean?"

"All this just because I said I'm worried about Pop?"

"You're not worried about him," I say. "You just have this need. You can't leave anybody alone. I guess you were worried about him when you were driving his car off that bridge in Spring Lake. You could have wrecked it, you know. Or you could've been thrown in jail. That would have cheered him up."

"Oh, you've been sulking ever since I conducted three against four for that clown Dolotov," Perry said. "I don't see why you hold something like that against me. I could teach you if you like. It's not that hard. A lot of people can do it."

"Oh, would you, please?"

"Look," Perry says. "I've got an idea. Why don't we start over? Why don't I say, 'Why are you so angry?' and then you answer the question?"

"Go fuck yourself."

"Oh, I'm sorry, I've made a terrible mistake," he says. "I thought you were angry when obviously you're not." He turns and begins walking back the other way.

I stand watching him retreat for a moment, then he stops dead, shading his eyes with his hand, looking out at the water. "Marty," he calls with alarm in his voice, "what's that?"

I jog to where he stands, and follow the line of his pointing finger but I don't see anything. "What?" I say.

"There," I hear him say, and when my attention is thoroughly trained on the horizon, he gives me a sharp jab to the stomach. "Go fuck *your*self," he says, tearing through the surf and diving into the breakers.

He disappears under the water, and as I search the swells for him I am surprised by an odd feeling of something like panic — the realest thing I've felt for some time. Then I see him, surfacing about fifty feet away. He stands in waist-deep water, looking at me. When our eyes connect, he points at me, lets out a horselaugh. I begin walking through the water toward him. The beach noise grows louder, I can hear the high-pitched squeals of teen-aged girls and young children, the chomping percussion of the breakers, and more distantly, the frantic prattle of an AM-radio announcer. Perry's eyes and nose are red. I hold out my hand to him, saying "Truce," but he stares warily at it, shaking his head.

"No way," he says, but I don't move my hand, and after another moment he takes it and says, "Truce, you angry son of a bitch."

Almost midnight, a cool breeze blows in from the bay, whispering in the cedars. I lie swaying in the enormous hammock that is suspended from the ceiling in the garden room. I've turned off all the lamps, bringing on a meditative darkness: I'm in the dark, looking out at dark. Occasionally, a pinpoint of light appears—a boat in the bay—and travels across the black scrim of the water like a slow meandering comet millions of miles away. Dinner was the usual circus. Felicia reached new heights of self-degradation. What had been, on previous evenings, flirtation aimed at Dolotov evolved tonight into genuine raunch. Mother lost her patience, pulled Felicia out of the dining room into the pantry, and then proceeded to scold her loudly enough for all of us still at the table to hear every word.

Now Perry enters the garden room, closing the door behind him, walks quietly over to the hammock, and climbs in. We lie in silence for a moment, then I hear his voice, even more hushed than usual. "Guess what I just saw," he says.

"What?"

"Dolotov," he says. "Upstairs. Coming out of Felicia's room wearing nothing but his underwear and flip-flops."

I feel the hammock shaking before Perry's laughter becomes audible. Then we're both laughing, and I suddenly recall something Father used to say years ago: that the sound of laughter can brighten a room so that you can see things once hidden in darkness.

"I guess she wore down his resistance," I say, still laughing.

"I guess," says Perry.

"Or maybe the chemistry was right," I say. "The proper strength of alcohol in the bloodstream."

"Old Felicia probably just finally started speaking Dolotov's language," Perry says.

Suddenly I hear the door open, and the overhead light goes on, causing both of us to squint. And then Mother's voice: "What on earth are you boys doing out here in the pitch dark?"

"Mother, turn off the light," I say.

"I'm *sorry,*" she says. "All right, all right." She turns it off, then, after a moment, I feel her hand on the top of my head, stroking my hair. "What's so funny, you two?" she says.

"Nothing," I say, and she removes her hand abruptly.

She goes to Perry's end of the hammock and begins stroking *his* hair. "What's so funny, Perry?" she asks.

"We were just thinking about Felicia, tonight at dinner," Perry answers.

"Oh, God," Mother says. "Don't remind me. When Felicia's determined to make a fool of herself, there's absolutely nothing that will stop her. I love her dearly, but when she's determined, there's nothing to do. Why are you boys sitting out here in the dark?"

"Helen, are you out there?" It's Raymond's voice now. He has turned on a light in the hall, and his slim shadow stretches across the floor almost the full length of the room.

"Yes, Raymond, I'm coming," says Mother.

Raymond is accustomed to seeing both Mother and Father to their rooms at night, as if they were children who needed to be reminded to go to bed. As the door closes and the garden room returns to darkness, I hear Mother saying something in a bewildered tone to Raymond about those two crazy boys sitting in the dark. When they're gone, Perry says, "I wish you would go inside to the study and look at Father."

"Why?" I ask.

"Just go look," he says.

The house is entirely quiet except for the soft pop of the window screens pushed and tugged by the wind. When I reach the study door, I see Father sitting at his desk, the single desk lamp with its green glass shade the only light in the room. He's holding a stack of photographs about an inch thick under the cone of the lamplight. He looks up at me, unstartled, as if he had been expecting me to appear at that instant. He smiles and says, "Marty. Did I ever show you my old Navy pictures?"

"No, Father," I say. "I don't think you ever did."

"Come over here and sit down." He points to a nearby straight chair. "I took some of that goddamn stomach medicine that quack is giving me and I . . . well Marty, frankly, I'm having some trouble telling which way these pictures are supposed to go. I can't tell what's right side up."

I bring the chair over to the desk and sit next to him. There's something sweet smelling about Father, mixing with the bleachy smell of the white pajamas he's wearing. He holds an old yellowed photograph with scalloped edges under the light. "What in the hell is that?" he says.

"No," I say, turning the picture between his fingers. "This way."

"I still don't know what it is," he says.

"It's just some palm trees, Father," I say. "There's a building and some palm trees."

Perry comes in and gives me a collusive look. He pulls up another chair on the other side of Father.

"Perry," Father says, "I bet *you* can tell us what this is."

"Marty's right, Pop," says Perry. "It's just some trees and a building. Probably something you thought was pretty. It looks like San Diego."

"Oh, Perry, I know that," Father says. "All of these are San Diego. The question is not the name of the city."

"Sorry, Pop," Perry says. "It's late. What you say we all go to bed."

Father looks up at Perry, then turns and looks at me, then back at Perry, as if he is noticing for the first time that we are in the room with him. "You boys go," he says. Then he looks down at the photograph and says, "Palm trees. That's helpful."

In the hallway we find Raymond, leaning against a wall, striking a kitchen match on the sole of one shoe, and lighting a cigarette. Dressed in white pants and short-sleeved shirt, and with a stack of white towels under one arm, Raymond looks like an orderly in a hospital. "Marty," he says to me now, "do me a favor. Take these up to the linen closet. Don't make me climb those stairs one more time today."

"Why are you doing laundry this time of the night?" says Perry.

"Insomnia," Raymond says. "Is he still up, too?"

"Yes," I say.

Handing me the stack of towels and turning back toward the study, Raymond says, "I'll see what I can do." There is not the slightest hint of judgment or impatience in his tone. Just before Raymond came to work for us, he had been a chef at the Fontainebleau, in the Egyptian-style restaurant where we had our Christmas dinner the year Perry was born. Father, noticing that night that the food was not quite what it had been, inquired after Raymond and learned that he had suffered multiple relapses of bronchitis and had been replaced at the restaurant because of his frequent illness. The very next day, Father visited Raymond in his room, had him moved to our house and attended by Father's own doctor. When he was fully recovered, Raymond took over as cook for us, and eventually he took over in every other capacity. When Raymond says, "I'll see what I can do," it is a comfort: because he is in Father's debt, Father listens to him as he does to no one else, not even Perry.

Perry and I watch Raymond enter the study. Then, as we climb the stairs, Perry says, behind me, "Now once more, *al dente.*"

It is a reference to a comical thing Father sometimes does when he listens to us practice, a thing he has done since we were young children. At the end of what we're playing, he lowers his head in concentration and very seriously says, "Now once more, *al dente,*" and it invariably makes us laugh.

As we reach the landing at the top of the stairs, Perry adds, "I think he's dying, Marty."

I turn to him. "That's ridiculous," I say. "He's too young."

Nothing I could have chosen by my own lights—not drugs, not liquor, not self-hypnosis or transcendental meditation—could have numbed me as effectively as the paperwork at the morgue. *Perry Christian Lambert, male, died August 30, 1976, white, age 25, born 10/17/50, State of Virginia, never married, student, etc.* not only linked me to the procedures that would get my brother buried but also became a kind of opiate. I thought perhaps the whole prospect of his burial was something that might occur solely on paper, and by the time I was handed the plastic bag containing Perry's things from the hotel room—a prop that belonged to poorly lit crime movies—it felt like a reward for my having been dutiful, for having competently carried out my responsibilities.

Karajian provided the name of a funeral home in Brooklyn, telephoned to arrange an appointment for me that evening, and even offered to drive me there on his way home.

When I asked him why I should go all the way to Brooklyn for a funeral director, he gave me a guilty-sheep grin and told me the place belonged to his sister's husband.

I had met Karajian shortly after my nap at Jane Owl-caster's. It was after six o'clock by the time we left the medical examiner's. The sky had cleared again, and warmer weather was moving into New York, causing, oddly, the temperature to rise as the light died. Karajian drove a brown four-door Bel Air, no frills. He had removed his jacket, loosened his tie, and rolled up his shirt sleeves; he slouched down low in the seat, one elbow resting on the rim of the open window, and steered the car most of the time with one finger. Molly was in the car with us, in the back seat, and distressed by the giant dentist's drill of Karajian's wheels on the grated surface of the Brooklyn Bridge. Big and clunky, she tried to leap over the seat into the front, apparently intent on getting into my lap, but only fell to the floor.

"I hope you don't mind," Karajian said. "They do good work." He was referring to his enlisting me into his brother-in-law's clientele.

"I don't mind," I said, and I really didn't; it felt like help. "You live out this way too?"

"If you call it living," Karajian said. "I got a house, a yard, a wife, a daughter in college. A hibachi. Neighbors who yell at each other at the top of their lungs night and day. A fucking mulberry tree that dumps a shitload of inedible fruit on the ground every year."

"I guess your wife's probably glad about the new job," I said.

"Why do you say that?"

"I just thought she must be happy you'll be doing something safe. It must be tough being a cop's wife."

He laughed. "You've been watching too many movies," he said. "You know, I think you might've put your finger on something, though. Therese has been sulking around ever since this new job first came up. I guess she's upset because she figures I might not get killed now."

"You can't be that cynical," I said, and Karajian gave me that same guilty-sheep grin as before.

"Nah," he said. "She's okay in the long run. She was a good mother. Trouble was, after Sue came along, it seemed like she'd gotten everything she needed out of the marriage. It sounds like a terrible thing to say, I know. Now Sue's off at school, studying to be a psychologist. She's going to come back home and straighten us out."

He took the downtown-Brooklyn exit and headed straight out Court Street. "Therese is wrong, anyway," he said after a minute. "A cop walking into a college classroom these days . . . he could very likely get his head blown off. You married?"

"Separated," I said, glad to have the answer ready—that tidy code word that stood for so much ecumenical pain and complication.

Karajian nodded discreetly, affording me a silence in which I could volunteer anything I wished. I let the silence be. It was like having blood drawn: I had to sit there and be still, but I didn't have to look at it. What he'd said about his wife's having got everything she needed out of the marriage after their daughter was born had struck a chord—it was a quiet little thing with lots of sound, lots of notes in it.

Karajian said, "You ever hear of this guy Skinner?"

"The psychologist?" I asked.

"Yeah. My daughter's all gung-ho on him. She thinks he's the greatest thing since sliced bread. So I looked him up in the encyclopedia, and it turns out he taught pigeons to play Ping-Pong, can you believe it? I said to Therese, just think what *we* could learn to do."

We were entering a section of Carroll Gardens that Karajian described as "mixed," which meant that there were a few Greek and Armenian families in addition to the Italians. The houses, set back from the street with small gardens in front, were mostly three-story brownstones, though there were a few of brick and even a wood-frame or two. Many of the houses had fences in front, confining a dog, an unwieldy rose bush, a shrine to the Holy Mother. Karajian parked in front of a fire hydrant near the middle of the block. He said it would be all right to bring Molly inside, that his sister's kids would love it. His sister, her husband, and two young boys lived above the funeral parlor. Also the husband's mother, who was in the business with them. The house was large, white clapboard with black shutters, a small porch out front, two wooden Doric columns and some black-painted grillwork. There were two doors: one the entrance to the parlor, the other to the apartment above. And two doorbells, lit ivory like little moons. We were let into the parlor by a very short, gray-haired woman wearing glasses—the mother, Maria Spinelli—and Karajian left me alone with her while he took Molly upstairs to visit his sister's family.

"My son is out, Mr. Lambert," Mrs. Spinelli said with a Brooklyn accent so clipped and absent of *r*'s that it sounded like a stagy imitation. "But I'm sure I can help you."

"It's dark in here," I said as we walked slowly down a long hallway.

"I'm sorry," she said and stopped to switch on a light, a crystal sconce that protruded dangerously from the fake mahogany wall at jugular level. She led me into a large room that looked like a banquet room in a family-run restaurant built by a handyman: the same cheap paneling; red carpet with a black pattern that reminded me of the grillwork outside; red flocked wallpaper on two walls; heavy red drapes over the windows. The Spinellis had determined red as the color of death. Folding chairs were stacked in the corners of the room.

Mrs. Spinelli asked me to take a seat before a heavy oak desk at the near end of the room. "My sympathies to you, Mr. Lambert," she said, sitting behind the desk and opening a loose-leaf notebook. "Such a tragedy." Her glasses had thick, squarish lenses that enlarged her eyes—when she looked straight at me, I saw two cloudy, walnut-sized pools in an aged, sagging face, and for a moment it looked like trick photography. But I also saw that she was one of those women whose intelligence and sentiment reside in their eyes, and I saw, magnified, that she was entirely sincere.

I thanked her.

"Have you ever done this before?" she asked.

"No," I said. "In fact, I don't have any idea how to go about any of this. Maybe I should be talking to somebody in Virginia."

What I meant to say was that perhaps I should be making arrangements with a funeral home in Norfolk, since that was where Perry would be buried; but suddenly I realized that I hadn't discussed any of this with Mother. Not until this moment had it occurred to me that there was anything to discuss.

"It can be a little confusing the first time," Mrs. Spinelli said, as if this were something I was just getting started at, but intended to perfect with practice. "First tell me your brother's name," she said, "just so I can refer to him."

"Perry," I said.

"Perry," she said, jotting it down on a blank sheet of paper in the notebook.

"And is Perry to be buried in Virginia? Is that what you meant?"

"I guess," I said.

She looked at me.

"I mean, I assume he is," I added, clarifying nothing. "Do you handle the transportation to Virginia?"

"Oh, yes," she said. "Sure we do. We pick him up at the morgue, and arrange for a flight, and—"

"Do we need to get a company down there as well?"

"Well, you should," she said, nodding. "You should because when Perry gets to the airport down there . . . do you have any connection with a funeral home? Most people do."

I knew somebody must have handled my father's funeral ten years ago, but I certainly didn't know the name.

"Well, *if* you don't," she said, "and you give me . . . where is the cemetery?"

I had to confess that I didn't recall the name of the cemetery where Father was buried in Norfolk. I apologized.

"Yeah, well . . . because . . . he's not going to be cremated, is he?"

I hadn't thought of that either, but the way Mrs. Spinelli had phrased the question made me say, reassuringly, that of course Perry would not be cremated. She explained that there was a network of funeral homes that could be tapped by calling a central office, and that her company would cooperate with a company in Norfolk. What I wanted to hear was that she would take care of everything, and as if she were reading my thoughts, she did eventually use just that phrase: ". . . take care of everything from here," she said, and the weight of my head on my shoulders seemed to lighten. Then she explained, very sympathetically, that because she had never served me before and I didn't have any credit with her, everything would have to be paid for in advance. I assured her that this would not be a problem. She asked whether or not the autopsy had been completed at the medical examiner's and if all the paperwork was in order. The autopsy, which was required for anyone meeting a violent death, was not my favorite subject, and she mentioned it again while explaining that embalming was not mandatory, as most people thought, but that in Perry's case, since an immediate burial would not be possible, and since *he had been opened up already,* embalming would be necessary—deterioration, you see, speeded up once the body had been *opened up.*

There were quite a number of forms to fill out and sign, and we did the best we could despite my ignorance on many questions: I couldn't say how many copies of the death certificate at five dollars each I would like; I didn't know whether we would have a graveside service or a church service. I was shown a lengthy list of expenses: a cement burial box would probably have to be purchased, but that should be done in Norfolk, since it would be too heavy on the airplane; something called a shipping tray also had to be purchased—the airlines wouldn't take a casket plain and simple, the casket had to be in something. The cemetery would have what they called an "opening charge." We shouldn't schedule the burial too soon, because anything could happen (a storm, for example), there might be a delay, and the airlines did not give human cargo priority—produce was given priority. As Mrs. Spinelli filled out one of the forms, she asked me for the place of death. I said New York City.

"But did Perry die in his home?" she said. "He lived here, right?"

I supposed that Karajian had explained that Perry had committed suicide, but hadn't told the method.

"In the street?" was my idiotic answer, which of course caused Mrs. Spinelli to turn her huge eyes on me again. She could tell that I was having some trouble.

"Did he throw himself in front of a car?" she asked weakly.

"Out a window," I said.

She shook her head sadly. After quite a long silence, she said, "Was it love?"

"I don't know," I said. "I don't think so."

"Only twenty-five," she said, nodding. "At that age. Probably it was love."

She asked me if I wanted to look at caskets. I said that probably I should first talk to my mother, to see what kind of thing she might want for Perry.

Already rising from her chair, Mrs. Spinelli said, "Well, you're here, you might as well look." She handed me a price list as she rounded the desk, sorting through keys on a large ring. "It's not complicated to describe a casket," she added.

We went down a flight of stairs into the basement, Mrs. Spinelli flipping light switches along the way. The basement was three large rooms with a concrete floor and glaring fluorescent lighting. "I'll show you the three-hundred-dollar unit," she said, leading me through a maze of bright, gleaming caskets into a small, darker storeroom. (The price range was $300 to $5000.) The $300 unit, which rested on a deep shelf, hip height, was of softwood covered with what looked like the same flocked wallpaper that was on the walls upstairs, only in gray. White crepe interior. Mrs. Spinelli announced, "This is wood," rapping her knuckles on the casket. "If you feel underneath, you'll see it's wood. You see out there"—she pointed to the larger room we'd just passed through—"now there's wood, too. But those are *solid* woods . . . and they spent the time to finish them . . . but this isn't. This is heavy, though. Feel. I want you to see how heavy this is." She wouldn't go on until I had lifted one end of the casket and indicated that it was indeed heavy. "You see," she said. "But they're not going to spend the time to finish it, labor-wise, so you see they cover it. That's three hundred."

She turned and walked into the third room. Passing a casket with bright silver handles and the metallic bronze finish of a customized sports car, she ran her hand along it and said, "Seven-fifty on this."

She showed me several others, lifting the lid panels and encouraging me to feel the interior fabric; all of these caskets were metal, though some a heavier gauge than others. She demonstrated the various closing devices, describing one as being just like "those freezer bags," a remark that prompted me to see that refrigerators were precisely what all these metal boxes reminded me of.

"Are the solid wooden ones the most expensive?" I asked.

"No," she answered, disappointment in her voice, "there are some heavy steel ones and other metals that are more."

"Because I'm not sure," I said, "but I think Mother would want wood." (What I was really thinking was that Perry would prefer wood, but it seemed too odd a thing to say.)

"Well, that's the Protestant background," Mrs. Spinelli said, nodding with resignation. She hesitated for a moment, choosing her words. "Just let me tell you this. It may not matter. We've had clients come in and say, 'We want wood, we don't care if it . . . ah, decays faster than metal.' You see, a wooden casket is porous, and there are elements in the soil, that, you know . . ."

She trailed off, leading me to the solid wood caskets. "Now

these woods here are solid wood," she said. "They're not just sprayed with a veneer."

There were footsteps on the stairs, Karajian's, but Molly—a black streak—came shooting into the room before him, which caused Mrs. Spinelli to let out a whoop and slap her hand to her heart. "Mother of God," she cried.

Karajian pulled me aside and told me that he was leaving now. "My brother-in-law, Carmine upstairs, he'll drive you back to your hotel when you're ready."

I thanked him, and when I turned back to the room, I saw that Mrs. Spinelli—with an entirely bemused expression, her hand still resting over her heart—was watching Molly. Perry's dog was sniffing at the caskets, rather frantically, methodically moving from one to another.

When I insisted that Mrs. Spinelli call a taxi to take me back to Manhattan rather than accepting her offer of a lift from her son, she was both insulted and confused. Considering the cost of a cab all that way—the phrase "an arm and a leg" came readily to her lips—she might have briefly contemplated breaking off relations; how could she be expected to do business with someone so foolish and deranged? Then she must have remembered that I was grief-stricken, that surely I didn't know what I was saying, that probably I should be humored.

Before leaving Brooklyn, I telephoned Jane Owlcaster and arranged to leave Molly at her apartment. No one would be home when I arrived, she told me, but she would have the super let us in. She told me I should've taken my sandwich with me when I left her apartment, and then asked if there was anything else she could do to help.

"Well, yes," I said. "I've got to go over to Perry's apartment in the morning. Maybe you—"

"Of course," Jane said. "You want company. Just tell me what time."

We arranged to meet at ten, and I thanked her. "And thanks for being understanding," I added.

"What's to understand?" she said. "It's spooky going over there. You wouldn't catch me going over there alone."

When my cab driver arrived in Brooklyn, he was a dead ringer for Karajian—same age, same thick, dark eyebrows and gaunt face—and I wondered if Mrs. Spinelli had called another family member for this service. At first, the cabbie didn't want to take Molly, but Mrs. Spinelli's son, Carmine, came out to the curb, put his head inside the car window on the passenger side, and spoke a phrase of Italian, a phrase that had the word *sorella* in it and that made Mrs. Spinelli wince, and soon Molly and I were on our way back to Manhattan. "I got nothing against dogs in general, you know," the cabbie explained, looking at me in the rearview mirror. "It's just that some people, you know, you wouldn't believe what they keep on the end of a leash. Dirty, stinking, shedding . . ."

Molly, as if she sensed her dubious standing, behaved splendidly. Before we had even reached the bridge, she had fallen asleep with her nose in my lap.

After dropping Molly off at Jane's apartment, I returned to the hotel, and the moment I entered the lobby, something about the ornate furniture and carpet, something about the abundance of gold leaf and the blend of muffled voices as if everyone in the large room were whispering, warmed the seed of my "reality problem," causing it to sprout. Nothing too startling, just that the man behind the hotel desk, whom I had never seen before—dark, and sporting the handlebar mustache of a lion tamer in a circus—seemed to know me, and to know my trouble. I watched him cheerfully help a man just ahead of me, then turn decidedly sorrowful as he shifted his gaze in my direction. It was with great sympathy that he handed me the pink slips of paper on which my telephone messages were written, and I couldn't help noticing that the skin on his hand appeared a bit too moist and white, and that the several hairs on the back of it were a bit too coarse and black, individual and rooted, as if magnified.

It happened again upstairs in the long wide hallway. A chambermaid approached from the opposite end of the corridor, pushing a very silent, gleaming metal cart stacked with linens. As we neared each other, I thought her face underwent a metamorphosis of recognition, which reached a peak of completeness just as we met, causing her to cast her eyes down in pity.

The instant I was inside my room, I switched on the light, closed the door, and leaned my back against it, the way people sometimes do in movies or on the stage when they are being chased. I took a deep breath of the stale hotel room air.

One of the messages was from Raymond, who had telephoned from Norfolk that morning not long after I'd left the hotel; and a second one from George Michaels, the man who ran my record company in San Francisco; and a third, already from Mrs. Spinelli.

I called the record company first. George Michaels, an efficient, ambitious man about my own age, disapproved of me in general, and had long pressured me to sell him the business. He had big plans, more commercially successful plans, if only he could get me and my idealism out of his way. Today he telephoned to remind me that one of our artists was performing at Carnegie Recital Hall tonight, in case I got a chance to "drop by." I explained to George what he already knew, that my brother had died yesterday and that I probably would not find a chance to drop by Carnegie Recital Hall. "I didn't think so," he said, suddenly sympathetic. I knew George well enough to guess that he was resisting several urges: to go over a handful of questions and ideas he'd been nursing; to suggest two or three other businesspeople I should look up while visiting New York; and to ask me how soon I planned to be back.

Next I phoned the funeral home—Mrs. Spinelli only wanted to remind me that she would need clothes for Perry—and when I placed the receiver back into its cradle, I felt enormously relieved that I had already made arrangements with Jane Owlcaster to meet at Perry's apartment. I kicked off my shoes and leaned back on the bed. As the light from the bedside lamp flooded my eyes, causing me to cover them with my hand, I recalled the compassionate faces of the man behind the hotel desk and the chambermaid in the hall. In that moment of recollection—as if there were a rational link—I realized that I had left the plastic bag containing Perry's belongings in the back seat of the taxi from Brooklyn. The shock of this—Perry's personal effects set adrift, possibly irretrievably, by my stupidity and neglect—left me to observe with a cold and formal distance two images of myself: first, dumbly making a sandwich in our kitchen in San Francisco as Madeline glares at me from the opposite side of the counter—she's angry, disappointed, perhaps beyond all hope, because I have once again pulled out the heart of a head of lettuce rather than using the outer leaves, which would need washing (near the end, this was the sort of thing that could take on the weight of betrayal); second, a much younger me, carelessly kicking with the point of my boot Perry's pet tortoise, cracking its shell, causing it, astonishingly, to bleed red blood. I was certain that judgment and instruction lurked somewhere inside these two images, and even without analysis, I was getting strong hits of my own malignancy and sloth. I went across the room to the cabinet that housed the booze and a tiny refrigerator-freezer. I found a miniature of Scotch and poured it over ice. I didn't even know the name of the cab company in Brooklyn, which meant that I had to telephone Mrs. Spinelli again, who eventually gave me the number after asking twenty questions. I dialed the number and was told impatiently by some farting, grunting, hairy-chested, cigar-smoking brute in an undershirt that I would have to call back tomorrow. I downed the liquor in my glass and headed—or rather, shuffled slump-shouldered—for the shower.

"She's already in bed, Marty," Raymond told me when I telephoned Norfolk. Raymond was crowding sixty and still chain-smoked Kools, still lit them most often with kitchen matches. Now I could hear the little combustive hiss of a match and the pause and puff of his exhalation. "She usually picks up if she's still awake," he added, "but I'll check if you want me to."

Fresh out of the shower and freezing in the air conditioning, I wore my David Niven robe under the bedcovers. "No, Raymond," I said. "I really wanted to talk to you, anyway. How's she doing?"

"As well as can be expected," Raymond said. "I tried to get her to eat something. It's not good for her to go hungry, you know. I hate seeing her go off to bed like that with nothing to eat. I thought I'd go up in a little while and check on her, maybe take her a cup of hot broth at least. I'm worried about her, Marty, I don't mind telling you. You know how she felt about Perry. I don't know if she's going to be able to take this one in stride. It would help if she'd eat some —"

"What about the luncheon?" I asked. "Did she have the luncheon?"

"Oh, she had it," he answered. "But she didn't come to it. I explained to everybody what had happened and went ahead and served, but nobody felt like eating anything. Except Felicia Snow, of course. She eats when she doesn't even know she's eating. If she'd been on the *Titanic* as it was going down —"

"Raymond," I said, "did you talk to Perry when Mother was away?"

"He called one afternoon while Helen was in Florida, Marty. Said he was about to go out to a baseball game, as I recall. I remember being surprised, because I didn't know Perry was a fan. Was Perry a fan?"

"I don't think so," I said.

"Well, that's what he said. Said he was on his way to Yankee Stadium. I could almost tell you who they were playing if you give me a minute to think."

"It doesn't matter, Raymond. What else did Perry say? Did he leave any kind of message for Mother?"

"I gave him her number in Palm Beach. But I guess he never got around to calling."

"Did he say anything else?"

"Well, this was the conversation in which he told me he had joined the church," said Raymond. "Which is something I've been trying to figure out all day . . . why anyone would join the church just to turn around and kill himself."

"Perry joined a church?" I said.

"You knew Perry had joined the church, didn't you?"

"No," I said. "What church?"

"Jesus, Marty, the Catholic church. You had a Roman Catholic for a brother and you didn't even know it?"

"When did this happen?" I asked.

"I'm not sure. Recently, I think. He said he wanted me to know because he knew I'd be happy. He was very proud of himself. He'd gone to classes and I don't know what all. You can't just walk into a Roman Catholic church and sign up, you know. Not unless you're born Catholic."

"He didn't tell you the name of the church?"

"Maybe he did, Marty, in passing, I don't know. Saint something, I guess. I'm afraid I didn't seem as happy about the whole thing as he expected me to be. I mean, I was glad he joined the church, but he shouldn't have expected me to be happy about him becoming a Catholic."

"Does Mother know about this?"

"Sure," said Raymond. "I can't believe one of them didn't tell you. Of course, the sad thing is . . . of all churches . . . I mean, you know how the Catholics feel about suicide."

"Did he say anything else, Raymond?"

"Well, we had a little chat," said Raymond. "He said it was hot as Hades in New York. He said he was writing some songs. I remember he said I wouldn't like them, and I said he was probably right. I said it was just because I didn't understand serious music, and can you beat that, me living in this house for all these years and never learning to understand serious music? We laughed about that. He was in a good mood, Marty. He didn't seem to be in any trouble. I just can't figure it. Did he leave a note or anything?"

"No," I said. "Not that they've found."

"Well, I guess he would've left it somewhere it could be found," said Raymond. "No sense in hiding it."

"Tell Mother I'll call her in the morning," I said. "Raymond, do you know the name of that cemetery where Father's buried?"

"Oh, sure. Grace. Grace Cemetery. Out on Wilmer Road."

I thanked him and was about to say goodbye when I heard the unexpected, explosive, high-pitched sound of Raymond's sudden crying. "I'm sorry, Marty," he said. "I've never been a crier, you know."

"You don't have to apologize for crying, Raymond," I said.

"It's just that he was the baby, you know. And I can't help but feel that there must've been something we were all missing. I mean, Perry must've been unhappy and none of us knew it."

"I know," I said.

"Well, he could've *told* somebody he was unhappy, you know," said Raymond. "Can you make any sense of it, Marty?"

"No," I said. "I can't. Not so far. But I plan to."

"I hope you can, Marty. I really hope you can."

The phone rang almost the moment I'd hung up: Raymond calling back with something he'd forgotten to say. "Marty," he began, "there was something Perry said that day we talked. It was so nutty and I was so taken with it I wrote it down. Perry told me to look around the room I was sitting in. It was the kitchen—I remember I was sitting at the counter, you know, where the bird has his cage? So I looked around and Perry said, 'Are you looking around?' and I said yes. Then he said, 'Just think, Raymond. Every single thing you see, before it existed in the world, it first existed in somebody's mind.' And I started thinking, well it was true, wasn't it? But then I saw your mother's parakeet and I said wait a minute, Perry, what about the bird? And he said the parakeet first existed in the mind of God, and the cage first existed in the mind of man, and that that was the difference between God and man. He was always coming out with stuff like that—you know, nutty stuff—but it was never about God before. I don't know why I wrote it down, it was just . . ."

I could tell that Raymond was about to cry again and that he wanted to hang up. I thanked him for calling back.

Raymond had told the truth about his not being a crier; in more than twenty years I'd seen him cry only once before. The morning of Father's death, Perry and I found Raymond crying in the butler's pantry, sitting on the floor, his back against a cabinet, his forearms resting on his knees. "I loved him, *too,*" he said to us, and we said we knew he did, though we both were surprised by Raymond's dilemma: we hadn't known that loving Father, and especially confessing it, meant, for him, crossing the barrier of his salary, that it meant over-stepping his "place," that it was a right he had to claim as an insurgent. How could we have known?

I fully intended to order something to eat after talking to Raymond, but I fell into another long whisky nap, and when I awoke about an hour later, I was lying on my back in bright California sunshine—memory, not dream, though with the ardor of dream—Madeline's head resting on my stomach. We are in the secluded garden of my first little cottage on the West Coast, in the Los Altos Hills, Easter Sunday, naked, near the encroaching giant chrysanthemum of shade cast by a walnut tree. I stare at the back of her head as, finished, she says to my stubbornly slow-contracting penis, "You've had a big day, haven't you?" referring to the two earlier times that morning.

This was the first year we were married, our bumper crop year of big days, and now, in the sad luxury of the hotel room, thoroughly doused by a goofy nostalgia for what was irrecoverable—an unthinkable thing were I fully awake—I looked at my travel clock on the nightstand. Almost eight in Santa Rosa.

"I'm really glad you called, Martin," she said when she heard my voice. "I tried calling the flat last night and got a recording saying the line had been disconnected. I spent about an hour resenting that. What if I really needed you?"

I said I was sorry.

"Well, I'm just glad you called tonight," she said. "I did want to talk to you. Can you talk now?"

"I called *you,* Madeline," I said.

"Good point," she said. "Sorry. Listen, I think this is ridiculous, us being separated this way for so long."

"You do?" I said, thoroughly surprised.

"Well, yes," she said. "I want to go ahead and file for divorce as soon as we possibly can."

"Oh," I said. Then after a moment, "What's his name?"

"I really resent that, Martin," she said.

"I'm sorry," I said. "But what's his name?"

Silence. Then, "What difference does it make?"

I hung up and poured another Scotch.

She had been involved with another man when she met me, and she'd told me she had taken up with him to escape yet another sour but tenacious affair. Nothing had happened during our four years of marriage that might have served to break that pattern. I called her back immediately, ready to punish.

"I'm in New York," I said. "Perry killed himself yesterday morning. I had to go to the morgue to claim his things, his clothes and stuff. Then I went to look at caskets. Then on my way back to my hotel, I accidentally left Perry's things in a taxi."

She whispered, "Marty, this had better not be a joke."

I said nothing.

After quite a long silence, she said, "I'm sorry, Marty, but I can't have this conversation with you unless you promise me right now that you won't hang up on me again. That's completely unfair."

"I promise, Madeline," I said and—so much for my readiness to punish—I began to cry for what would be the last time during this whole ordeal, mourning the death of my brother and of my marriage. Finally, I was coming to the end of my crying, and I said again to my estranged wife, "I promise."

I had noticed before that in the permissive, stone and steel theater of New York, thunderstorms seemed the wrath of an avenging God. A series of storms had begun moving through the city, and as I stood under the hotel canopy, waiting for the doorman to whistle up a taxi, I watched throngs of people running as if in terror, covering their heads with folded newspapers, or pulling coats up against the driving rain, or struggling with umbrellas in the wind. There was the usual traffic jam on Fifth Avenue with its din of car horns, but now it all looked like a scene from a disaster movie in which everyone was trying at once to escape the doomed city. A sudden flash of lightning, a prompt crack of thunder, seemed to freeze everything for an instant, then the tableau shuddered briefly and moved on. A few ruined umbrellas—black fluttering omens of defeat—lay in the gutters, torn, inverted, metal ribs exposed.

When my taxi arrived at the stoop of Perry's building on West 46th Street, Jane was waiting in the vestibule, out of the downpour; I could see her through the window of the front door, waving. As I ran up the stoop, she pushed open the heavy wooden door.

"I already got the key from Pascal," she said, and explained that Pascal owned the nightclub tucked into the ground level of the building and owned the building itself. "Pascal says the September rent is due." Then she added, "You look really tired."

"I didn't sleep well," I said. "My dream life is giving me trouble these days."

"Your waking life isn't exactly a party," she said, inserting a key into the lock of the inside door. "Ready?"

I told her that I was as ready as I would ever be.

Perry's apartment was on the top floor, four flights up a noisy staircase, which, as we climbed it, wheezed and rasped like some great dying leviathan. The walls of the hallway were painted the shiny lime green of a previous era; round fluorescent tubes cast a watery sheen over everything. Once inside the apartment, Jane stood in the middle of the large front room, her face set hard: she was testing the air, seeing how it would affect her. Then we stood facing each other, wondering where to begin, *what* to begin, until we were startled by the sudden ringing of a telephone on the counter in the kitchen. "I'll get it," Jane said, and then after a bit I heard her saying, "No, he's not here . . ."

I had been to Perry's once before, but the only thing in the room that seemed familiar was the ebony baby grand that stood in front of the two tall windows facing the street—Perry's piano from Norfolk, an old Baldwin. The piano's music desk was cluttered with miniature scores, yellow pencils, staff paper, an electric metronome, a coffee mug. Otherwise the apartment—one large room with a separate kitchen and bath—was scarcely furnished: a couple of chairs, a mattress and boxspring covered with an Indian bedspread serving as both bed and couch, and a huge roll-top desk, drawers pulled open, papers scattered. (Had Perry left it like that or had the police when they searched the place?) One wall was all shelves: volumes of music, records, a stereo system, a reel-to-reel tape recorder, books. The tall windows, without curtain or shade, were now splattered with rain.

I went to the piano and began looking through the music — six bound scores of the opus 33 Haydn string quartets (the *Russian Quartets,* if my music history served me correctly), Ravel's Piano Concerto in G, Lukas Foss's "Paradigm," and a piano piece by Barbara Kolb — a rather odd assortment, I thought, considering that Perry appeared to have been writing songs. I picked up a song entitled "To the Roaring Wind" and began to study it — very simple, for soprano and piano, only a half page long. The lyric went: "What syllable are you seeking, / Vocalissimus, / In the distances of sleep? / Speak it." The piano accompaniment was written for left hand only, lots of open fifths, sustained, slowly dying chords. "Vocalissimus" was repeated twice, stretched out over long miasmas. "Speak it," aptly, was spoken. Then I had a shock when I turned the page: an unfinished song entitled "Two at Norfolk," beginning with, "Mow the grass in the cemetery . . ."

Jane returned to the room. "A piano student," she said. "Perry missed a lesson. I must've sounded like an idiot. I couldn't seem to find the right words. Finally I just pretended to take down the girl's name and number." She crossed the room, stood next to me, and looked over my shoulder at Perry's songs. "Wallace Stevens," she said after a moment. "I think he has a dozen or so of them. He planned to put together a cycle, all poems by Stevens."

"Have any of these been performed?" I asked.

"The first three," Jane said. "At the composers' concert a year ago. They're really wonderful. Mature, Dolotov called them."

I placed the songs back on the piano and asked Jane if she knew anything about Perry's having joined a church.

"He became a Catholic," she said. "You didn't know?"

"No," I said. "What church?"

"Somewhere in Brooklyn." She shrugged her shoulders. "I don't think I know the name. I always meant to go with him sometime, but somehow I never got up early enough. Technically I'm Jewish, and Catholic churches give me the creeps. I feel like I've got 'Christ killer' written all over me."

"I didn't even know Perry was religious," I said. "He never used to be religious."

"I don't think he was, really," Jane said. "He started going there for the music. He used to joke about it. I mean, he would *only* joke about it. Any time I questioned him about it he'd just say that the Catholics had drafted him."

"Drafted?"

"That's what he said. He started going for the music and then before he knew what hit him they'd drafted him."

"I wish I had the name of the church," I said.

"You could look in the yellow pages," said Jane. "There are probably only a couple thousand Catholic churches in Brooklyn."

"Thanks," I said.

"I'm sorry," she said.

"It's somebody to talk to," I said.

"Talk to?"

"To see if they might shed some light on things."

"Oh," she said. "You mean why he did it."

"Yes."

She sighed, turning her back to me, and went over to the wall of shelves.

"Is there anything wrong with that?" I said.

"No," she said. "I just don't think you're going to find an answer to that question. Not a single answer, anyway."

"Well, he must have done it for *some* reason," I said. "I don't imagine it was a whim."

I detected cruelty in my own voice. I tried to explain that I wanted to find some reason for what had happened, that I was desperate for a reason, and even as I said it, I began searching the apartment for any possible places Perry might have left a note overlooked by the police. I went to the desk and began poking around: utility bills, a ginger jar full of coins, Perry's Nikon, a yellow legal pad on which he'd listed things to do — "book to Garnette, pick up shirts, thank-you to Sam," etc. — nothing that suggested a final ordering of things, not the list of someone planning suicide. I checked the camera to see if there was film in it. There was, so I removed it and dropped it in my pocket.

Jane had sat down on the piano bench. When I turned to look at her, she gazed out the window next to her, away from me. "Perry and I had broken up," she said softly. "We stopped seeing each other about a month ago."

I crossed the room and pulled a chair up nearby.

"I'm the one who called it off," she said. "I thought I was rid of him. I thought it was over. And now this."

"I'm sorry," I said. For the moment, it was the best I could do.

"He did seem happier lately," she said. "After the breakup. I thought he was on some course, some grand path of some kind, and I was just so much baggage weighing him down."

"You don't strike me as baggage," I said.

"I'm not talking poor self-image here," she corrected me. "This wasn't my imagination. He *made* me feel that I was weighing him down. He'd gotten more and more secretive and withdrawn . . . preoccupied. I thought he was bored with me. I even thought for a while that maybe he was seeing someone else. If I asked him what he'd done all day, he'd say 'Nothing.' And then if I asked him where he was, since I'd been trying to reach him all day, he'd say 'Out.' And that was the other thing. He was just out more and more. And even when he was in he was out."

"Do you think he *was* seeing somebody else?"

"I was sure he wasn't," she answered. "I asked him. And I thought he told me the truth. I thought I would've known if he was lying. I don't know anything anymore. But it got to where we were seeing less and less of each other, until I reached a point where I felt I had two choices. I could stay with him and watch him grow more distant day by day, or I could get the pain over with. I tried to talk to him, and at first he seemed surprised—you know, that anything was wrong. Then he was resigned. But immediately. He didn't exactly put up a fight. Of course, I didn't know he was going to kill himself."

For some reason, I found myself becoming increasingly formal in the face of this. "I think it would be a mistake to take this personally," I said.

"Personally?" she said. "How else do *you* take it? It *is* personal."

"I just mean you can't blame yourself," I said.

She gave me an impatient look. "I don't blame myself," she said. "I blame *him*. You want to know why he didn't leave a note? Because even to say goodbye is to acknowledge a person, that's why." She rubbed her eyes and nose with her hand, as if she were trying to scrub away any emotion that might be forming there. "I was good to him," she said. "I was a good friend to him. I wasn't attracted to his goddamned musical gift, I didn't compete with him, and I didn't inspire him. I was just a good friend, and I was faithful to him. I was a good listener, that's for sure." She suddenly, quickly scanned the room and said, "What are we doing here, anyway?"

"I have to get some clothes for him to wear," I said.

"Well, they're right over here," she said, striding across the room to a closet door and yanking it open. A heavy black overcoat came toppling forward off a hook, but exactly like a dead body, onto the floor. Jane gave a shriek, and for a moment I couldn't tell whether she was laughing or crying. It had given me a fright, too. I went to her and quite naturally gathered her into my arms—she wasn't laughing or crying, but some combination of the two—and then the moment turned distinctly ambiguous. We quickly released each other. We did a sort of courtly dance, circling away from and back toward each other, then grabbed hold of each other again. This time I kissed her, removing the ambiguity, and we did the same thing, in miniature, with the kiss: the retreat, followed by the more certain return. We kissed a second time, fully, then she pulled away. "I haven't known you long enough to do that," she said.

"I know," I said.

"I'm sorry."

"What for?"

"For kissing you. It must be confusing."

"I kissed *you*," I said. "And I don't feel like apologizing."

"You don't have to."

"And I don't feel confused."

"I'm glad there's one of us."

"Well, maybe I do feel confused a little, but I'm not sorry I kissed you."

"I don't think this is the right time," she said, "and I know it's not the right place."

"You're one of the things I've been dreaming about," I said, and started to kiss her again.

But she touched her fingers gently to my lips. "It's much too weird," she said. "I feel like I'm *in* one of those dreams of yours. If you want to know the truth, it kind of gives me the creeps."

This made me release her. I put my hands in my pockets, as if at once to control them and to show her that I was serious about controlling them. I thought again of that young man in the wrecked car, folding his laundry, in shock. What on earth was I doing? "My wife's in love with somebody else," I heard myself saying. "She wants a divorce. I'm thinking of moving here."

"You mean permanently?" Jane asked.

"I hate California," I said. "I've always hated it. I don't want to go back. I want to stay here with you."

"That's really nuts," Jane said.

I knew she was right, but in this moment I couldn't tell why. "Why do you say that?" I asked.

"A lot of reasons," she said. "For starters, we met each other less than twenty-four hours ago."

"That's not how it feels to me," I said. "Does it feel that way to you?"

"Okay," she said. "No, it doesn't, not exactly. Weirdly, it doesn't. But I didn't know when I kissed you that you were going to move to New York."

"Oh," I said.

"I didn't mean that the way it sounded."

"You smell like roses," I said.

"I need everything to just stop for a minute," she said. "I'm going to go into the bathroom now. I'm going to take several deep breaths. I'm going to wash my face. And then I'd like to go home."

When she had gone into the bathroom and closed the door, I lifted Perry's coat from the floor. Without giving any special thought to what I was doing, I slid my arm through a sleeve. The moment I slipped it on, I recognized it as an old cashmere coat that had once belonged to me, one I'd given to Perry years ago when I'd quit Harvard and set out for California. The feel of it, its weight and sudden warmth, conjured up that particular time—terrible, nebulous days of disappointment with my life, uncertainty about my future, and the pain of separating from Perry and everything else I'd known and loved. In other words, exactly the way I felt right now, as if all the years between had been nothing but a pointless loop of digression.

In late November of 1966, my father entered a coma of two days' duration and died. This was only months after Perry had said, in Newport, that he thought Father was dying, and I had said, That's ridiculous, he's too young. We were, of course, both correct.

Before we left Newport that summer, Father was arrested twice, only a few days apart, for drunken driving. Much in the tradition of Old West law enforcement, he was told, essentially, to pack up his family and get out of town. As it happened, we left only two weeks earlier than already planned, and our departure, like the arrests themselves, was for Father an entirely passive experience. He endured all discussion on the subject in his best statuesque style — agreeable to most anything, terse when a response was absolutely necessary. He did appear to be listening, but it was always to the voices in his reveries. I finally came to believe that he was in a state of partial anesthesia. Drink, to Father, was like an abusive parent — both source and comforter of pain.

On this, our last day in Newport, Felicia is treating us to lunch at the club. It's midday, very hot even on the club's breezy, shaded terrace. Earlier this morning, Raymond banged on our bedroom doors, rushed us through pastries and coffee, and sent us on our way to the beach. "And stay out" were his last words to us, meaning that he wants to prepare everything for our departure in peace. Dolotov has already returned to New York, but Felicia is loyal to Mother in what she perceives to be Mother's time of trial. Actually, Mother is resilient, even displays some junkie pride: she's been kicked out of chorus lines, barrooms, casinos, and ladies' clubs, but never kicked out of town.

Father is dressed in what has become a uniform these last couple of weeks: white trousers and a long-sleeved white shirt that he buttons at the neck, making him look prim, buttoned-in, as if he were dressed by someone else. He says he's had enough of the sun, and wears this costume even on the beach. For her lunch, Felicia has selected something called the Diet Lover's Special, a beef patty and cottage cheese. The rest of us are having hamburgers, except Father, who ordered a single boiled egg with toast. He wipes egg from the corner of his mouth and says, "George Gershwin's *Rhapsody in Blue* . . ." After quite a long pause, he says, "Ah . . . and Joseph Stalin became dictator of Russia . . ."

Exceptionally talkative today, and more lucid than usual, Father is once again recounting the significant events of 1924 (the year of his birth), 1946 (of mine), and 1950 (Perry's). It was once a familiar chant — we heard it throughout our growing up. Now he struggles and strains for the facts, but cheerfully, as if having to reach for them makes them all the more cherished: long-lost friends, found again.

"*Saint Joan,*" Perry says during the next lull.

"That's right," says Father. "*Saint Joan,* by Bernard Shaw, now please don't tell me any more. Ah, well, Puccini died, not quite having finished *Turandot.* And . . ."

Felicia begins singing, in a mock-operatic voice, the melody to "Un bel dì."

"That's *Madama Butterfly,* Felicia," Father says, entirely serious, pronouncing it *Boot-er-fly,* "but you've got the right composer. Now let's see, there's definitely something else—don't tell me, Perry."

"*Magic Mountain,*" I say.

"Martin," says Father. "Yes, *The Magic Mountain,* by Thomas Mann. And poor Franz Kafka died, author of *The Trial.*"

"I read that," Mother says, her mouth full.

"You most certainly did not," says Father.

"I did," says Mother. "You don't know what I've read and what I haven't. That's the book where the guy splits the old woman's head open with a hatchet and then he can't get anybody—"

"You couldn't be more mistaken, Helen," Father says, "and besides, you're interrupting."

Mother makes a ghastly, priggish face—her eyes wide, her lips pursed—and wags her head in mockery of Father's correctness. This gets a belly laugh from Felicia.

"Now, Martin," Father says, "what two very significant things happened in 1946?"

"You mean you want me to say them out loud?" I ask.

"*If* you can remember," he says.

"Well, the Nuremberg trials were going on," I say, "and the United Nations met for the first time."

"And in the world of music?" he asks.

"I forget," I say.

"And you a cellist," Father says.

"Shostakovich," I say.

"The third string quartet," Perry says. "Now do 1950, Pop."

"Right," I say, rather weakly.

"Nineteen fifty," says Father, gripping the bamboo arms of his chair and squinting into the glare of the beach beyond the terrace. In a fit of fastidiousness he has overclipped his graying mustache—his upper lip, usually in hiding, looks sadly exposed—and the clear light on his face ignites the spidery network of blood vessels beneath the skin of his cheeks. Slowly he says, "Let's see, there was T. S. Eliot's *The Cocktail Party* . . ."

"*I* wrote that," says Felicia.

"And . . ." Father, stumped for a moment, closes his eyes.

"He's gone to sleep," Mother says. "Rudy, wake up."

"Of course, I was just a tiny child in 1950," says Felicia. "But—"

Felicia's face suddenly pales. She is looking in horror at Father, and when we turn toward him, he has dropped his chin to his chest. There is a luxuriant stream of blood flowing down from his nose, over his mouth and chin, drenching the front of his white shirt. Felicia says, "Jesus," repulsed, a gasp escapes Mother's throat as she turns violently away—the sight of blood makes her ill—and she says calmly, quietly, "Boys, do something. Help him."

*

He is stupefied, paralyzed by humiliation. He refuses to be taken to any hospital, says he's had nosebleeds since he was a child (though we haven't seen one before this), and he won't allow Mother or Felicia into the car with us; they stay at the club while Perry and I take him home. I drive the Lincoln, Perry sits with him in the back seat, and by the time we arrive at the house, only a five-minute ride, the bleeding has stopped. Father insists we take him directly to his room without enlisting any help from Raymond.

Inside Father's room, a spacious bedroom upstairs on the corner of the house facing the bay, we get him into a morris chair with brown leather cushions. Father removes the soaked cloth napkin he's been holding beneath his nose, and I carry it into the bathroom. As I drop it into the sink, I hear Perry's voice, shaky: "Marty, it's started again." I return with a white bath towel, and when I give it to Father, he quickly presses a corner of it over his mouth and chin, tilting his head far back, and looks up at me — a meaningful look, which I don't get — and he jerks his head impatiently in Perry's direction. Perry stands a few feet away, rigid, his hands stuffed into the pockets of his shorts, and to my astonishment, tears streak his cheeks. Father jerks his head again. He's telling me to get Perry out of the room, but Perry, seeing this, turns and leaves of his own accord.

The minute Perry's gone, Father takes away the towel and sits up straight. A single drop of blood falls onto his white trousers. There's blood everywhere, his trousers splotched and streaked, his hands and cuffs covered, his mustache and the front of the shirt saturated. But it seems to have stopped again now, and Father begins fumbling with the buttons of his shirt. His fingers are shaking violently, however, and after a moment, he says quietly, "Help me with the goddamned buttons, Marty." He sighs as he slumps back into the chair.

I am aware as I bend toward him, my fingers already coated with his blood, that what's going on here is extreme. But I'm blind to implication, my faculty for drawing simple conclusions numbed and put to bed. A kind of natural selection has occurred: I'm here in this room because Father knows that my heart, especially this summer, is a steady pump—it doesn't skip beats, race, pound, sink, or rise to the throat—it only pumps, and Perry's been urged out because Father doesn't want to watch Perry's heart breaking.

After I've got the shirt unbuttoned, he leans forward so that I can help him out of it, and I see that his chest and upper arms are covered with bruises, dark stains seeping through the skin. He notices the shock on my face and averts his eyes. "How did you get so bruised?" I ask him, but he just begins wiping his stomach with the towel. Soon he hands me the blood-stained towel and smiles, saying, "Thank you, Marty."

"Don't you think we should call the doctor at least?" I ask him.

"Oh, good Lord, no," he says quickly. "That quack is liable to wrap a tourniquet around my neck and choke me to death. Just go down and get me a drink, if you will. And open a window in here, for Christ's sake."

Not moving, I say, "I think you need a doctor."

"Marty, we'll be home tomorrow," Father says patiently. "I'll go see Dr. Gasser."

In the hallway, I can hear Perry's piano through the closed door to his room. He's tearing off a Bach fugue I don't recognize—but loud throughout, no dynamics—then segues into a jazz riff in the same key, an ostinato in the bass, and starts to pound out some diminished chords on top. There's something crazy and spasmodic about it—it's missing the humor of Perry's usual improvisation, for one thing—as if the impulses in it were warring with each other.

When I knock on his door, open it, and put my head inside, he stops playing and props his elbows on the music desk, looking at me blankly through the triangle formed by the piano lid at full stick. "What are you doing?" I say.

"Nothing," he says.

"Are you all right?"

"Yeah. How about him?"

"It's stopped," I say. "He wants a drink."

Perry nods.

"*You* weren't much help in there," I say.

"He wanted me to leave," Perry says.

"Yeah," I say, "because you were falling apart."

Perry smiles ironically, then starts to play again, slumped over the keyboard.

When Perry was about five years old, we used to go, sometimes in summer, to a pumping station, part of the city waterworks on the outskirts of town. It was a popular swimming hole, fed by a huge reservoir and dammed at one end where the water cascaded over a spillway and dropped some fifteen feet to a rocky creek. A small section of the pool was cordoned off in a shallow area for younger kids. One day, Perry, who hadn't yet learned to swim, somehow got into the deep part, where a gentle current moved the water from reservoir to spillway. Unnoticed by anyone, he was in over his head, able to surface and resurface for air but unable to stop his slow drift toward the falls—Perry was small enough that he would have been carried over with the force of the plummeting water. Finally, someone did notice him quite near the spillway, a teen-aged boy who lifted Perry under the arms, guided him to the edge, and deposited him on the grass. Perry coughed and spit up water, assuring the teenager, between fits of coughing, that he was all right. Many years later when he recounted the incident to me, Perry said, "I knew I was going to die. The minute before I felt the guy's hands lifting me up, I had accepted my death."

"But how stupid," I said to him. "All you had to do was call for help. Why didn't you just call out for help?"

"I don't know," Perry answered. "I guess I just felt like I would rather die than do that."

We were to see a great deal more of Father's blood before it was over. The enduring image of his dying is one of cheap, B-grade, Hollywood gore. The nosebleeds became frequent and severe. His gums bled, he bled under the skin, he bled regularly from the rectum. Eventually, he was vomiting up fresh blood. Perry and I, off to separate schools in September, were spared most of this, though by Thanksgiving, when we returned home for the holiday, advanced cirrhosis had caused a buildup of ammonia and bilirubin in Father's bloodstream, which made him into a man we hardly knew—jaundiced and muddled, invaded and thoroughly colonized by fear.

When I arrived in Norfolk the Wednesday night before Thanksgiving, I took a taxi from the airport. It was an unusually warm, overcast night. Besides my cello in its case, I had only one small bag with me, and I decided to get off at the gate to our driveway and walk the hundred yards or so up the sloping lawn. The moonlit blanket of clouds cast a glow over the white clapboard Colonial house, eerie and monumental in the distance. The five great pecan trees, two on one side and three on the other, had lost their leaves and were in silhouette against the sky. As I walked up the lawn, breathing in a nutty smell in the air, I noticed how few lights were on in the house. Then I had a kind of premonition. I saw in my mind an image as explicit as memory, but not memory: the drop leaf of a table set with dishes suddenly collapsing with a great crash. I saw it in slow motion, and I "saw" the silent, shattering sound it made. And then it was gone, leaving me a bit dazed as I mounted our porch. On the landing, beside the front door, a rotting jack-o'-lantern sat, its carved features now black and sagging.

Perry, who had arrived a day earlier, met me at the door, pale, his eyes red and puffy, as if he were long overdue for a good night's sleep. All he said—whispered, actually—was "Welcome to the divine comedy," and made a butler's gesture of entry, bowing and extending one arm in the direction of the library. It was about nine o'clock, and ordinarily at this hour, drinking and conversation would have been proceeding in the library—Mother and Father and anyone they might have had over for dinner; but tonight the house is entirely quiet, and dark, with only a single lamp burning inside the library. What I see from the library door is the back of an easy chair, a table next to it on which the lamp stands, and a hand, presumably Father's, fingers wrapped around a tumbler, also on the table. I turn for a moment to Perry, who is right behind me, and he relieves me of my bag and cello, nods, silently urging me forward.

An old man sits in the chair, quite an old man, with yellow skin and drugged, blank eyes. He wears a silly-looking maroon smoking jacket with cuffs and collar of black velvet, something Mother would have ordered for him from one of her catalogues. He gazes into the few inches of air directly in front of his face, sips his drink, and with his other hand clutches at his genitals through his trousers, like a little boy in need of a toilet. I lean into his light so he can see my face. I think he sees my face, and he says pleasantly, "We don't use coal anymore to heat the house, you know that. It's too goddamned dirty . . ." Then, "Oh, Jesus, Perry, I thought you were Randolph Crane, the old black fellow that used to bring the coal around. Can you imagine that? Caught him eating dog food out of a can one day . . ."

I look at Perry, who stands in the shadows behind Father's chair, but he holds my gaze only for a second, then turns and walks away to the door, where he leans against the jamb.

"Father . . ." I begin, but Father holds up a hand to silence me and says, "All that gold and all that care—caught him eating dog food out of a can. Longer already have I baked my feet and been planted upside down."

I look again in Perry's direction. "Dante," he says quietly. "Mixed with a little memory. He's been at it all evening."

"Where's Mother?" I ask him, but Father answers, "Upstairs, upstairs, trussing the Thanksgiving—"

His eyes suddenly change, no longer boarded up but open, human, and he looks at me with recognition, places the tumbler on the table and gets to his feet, perfect terror in his eyes the instant before he throws his arms around me and whispers my name.

Mother *is* upstairs, in her bedroom, but of course she's not trussing any Thanksgiving turkey. She's at her desk, scissors going madly, making cubist openwork of several back issues of the *Ledger-Star*. When she stands to hug me, her voice is a bit too shrill and she nearly stabs me in the shoulder with the scissors.

"Yikes," I say, holding her away from me and carefully

removing the scissors from her hand. I ease her back into her desk chair.

"I wondered when you were going to show up, Marty," she says cheerfully, but not quite cloaking the accusation.

"I'm here exactly when I said I'd be here, Mother," I say.

"Oh," she says, surprised, lifting her drink glass from the desk. The plastic coaster, a bright turquoise disc with a deep-sea fishing scene painted on it, sticks to the bottom of the glass, then falls noisily to the desk top.

"Everything interesting," I say, passing her the scissors.

"*Every*thing," she says and smiles, warming up a bit. Then adds, "I'm really glad you're here, Marty. Perry's been acting very blue." She resumes her clipping. "I've just been reading the sickest story here, Marty," she says. "About a woman who meant to only kill herself but ended up killing her whole family. You wouldn't believe."

Mother's room is something like a stage set—it's too far from one piece of furniture to the next—and she's still in her floral phase. Everything in sight is covered with a different floral print. The proportions and the jumble of prints make the room seem dead and alive at the same time, also masculine and feminine.

"Mother," I say, "how long has Father been like that?"

"Like what?" she says, turning to look up at me, her eyes overly wide.

"You know," I say. "Like a corpse."

"Oh, that," she says. "Years."

"I'm serious, Mother," I say. "He's down there muttering nonsense, he looks half dead, and—"

"Martin," she interrupts, "your father is intoxicated. You know he's never drunk very well." She puts down the scissors and takes a gulp from the glass, as if to prove how well *she* does it.

"I know he's intoxicated," I say. "You're intoxicated too. I'm not talking about that. I'm talking about the fact that he looks like a seventy-year-old man. Have you looked at him lately?"

"No," she says. "I haven't. Not up close."

"Well, he looks like a seventy-year-old man," I say. "He looks half dead."

"Perry," Mother says broadly as Perry enters the room, "look who's here."

"I know," says Perry.

"Perry's been very blue," Mother says to me.

"What is she, crazy in addition to being drunk?" I say to Perry.

"What's wrong, Mother?" Perry says.

"I'm sure I don't know," says Mother, and she seems drunker suddenly than I had even thought. "Martin seems upset by your father's drinking. After twenty years. *Finalement.*"

"Will you tell her what he looks like?" I say to Perry.

"She knows what he looks like," says Perry.

"Well, I don't understand what's going on here," I say.

"The doctor comes every day, Marty," Perry says. "He says the same thing. Pop's got to stop drinking. But Pop doesn't stop."

"But what's wrong with him?" I say.

"It's his liver," Perry says.

"Why don't you make him stop drinking?" I ask Mother.

"Me?" she says. "*Me* make him stop drinking? That's a laugh."

"But you've got to," I say. "He's your husband."

"Oh, Martin, really," she says. "I'm the *last* person to make Rudy stop drinking."

"But you have to," I say. "We can't make him stop when we're away at school. You're the only one who can do it."

"The only thing I ever made your father stop doing was giving those goddamned concerts," she says.

In the abrupt silence that follows this remark, she quickly reaches for her drink, sensing that she's slipped in some way. "Well, it doesn't matter," she says finally. "No one can make Rudy stop drinking, and that's that." She gives me an exasperated look, puffs out both cheeks, and expels her breath. She moves unsteadily from the desk chair, walks the considerable distance to her dressing table, and finds a hair brush. She turns and looks at me again, this time angry. "What is it exactly you think I should do, Martin? Lock him in his room?"

"What do you mean, you made him stop giving concerts?" Perry says. He says it very slowly, so that it sounds like a threat.

Mother laughs, incredulous. "I don't know what the two of you think you're doing here," she says. "This is not exactly my idea of a good time, you know. Having my children come home for Thanksgiving only to attack me in my own bedroom. Now I feel very tired. I can't imagine why."

She moves back to the desk, where she adds vodka to her glass from a nearby bottle, then drinks. This is as unceremonious as it gets, short of drinking straight from the bottle. Perry turns to leave. Just as he reaches the door, Mother calls to his back, "What do *you* know? You were only a child. It was an embarrassment. A man of thirty-four making his debut! Why, a seventeen-year-old girl outplayed him on that same stage the week before. You didn't have to endure all those sympathetic looks from people. What do *you* know?"

For a brief moment, Perry shows her a face thoroughly absent of expression, an exterminator's face, then quickly leaves the room.

I'm a bit stunned. It's as if some detail has been erased from a complicated drawing, and suddenly the picture makes new sense. I even think that's what Perry's parting look meant: erase Mother from the picture, rub her out, and all at once we can see Father a happy man.

Of course, I am wrong. The picture makes new sense, but it doesn't show a happy man.

"It's been quite a spectacle," Mother says to me, pitiful now, almost slurring—something she never does—as if any surge of emotion she might have felt (regret, loss, fear?) has only pushed her further into drunkenness. ". . . should've been here," she says. "The *two* of you should've been here . . . these last months. Raymond's been spending half his time mopping blood. It's been quite a party. Like something out of a fucking horror movie. Don't you see, Martin? Your father is killing himself. And he wants us all to watch."

"He wants *you* to watch," I say. "I'm just an innocent bystander."

She turns her back to me in order to exchange the hair brush she's been holding for a cigarette. When she speaks next, she's a tough Las Vegas girl, up late and with no time for greenhorns. "You know perfectly well, darling," she says, "that there's no such thing."

But maybe she did wake up feeling something the next day, some resolve pushing through the fuzzy rubber dam of the hangover. Maybe we were all three frightened by what happened that night in Mother's bedroom—maybe we incautiously ventured too near some partial truth, close enough to have caught a glimpse of consequences—and the next day, Thanksgiving, we were all wonderfully gentle, as if we meant to heal one another. And we found that the safest way of doing this, the most comfortably indirect, was to focus on Father: we colluded in a conspiracy of kindness toward Father. I decided that he didn't really look all that bad after all, not nearly as bad as I had thought the night before. He seemed to have his wits about him again, as much as he ever did lately. He wasn't quoting any Dante at breakfast. Midafternoon, when we all gathered in the dining room for the Thanksgiving feast prepared by Raymond, Father was sober and energetic. No wine was served with the meal, a breach of custom that could only have been engineered by Father, and no one mentioned it. Mother fetched her drinks discreetly from the kitchen, and discreetly she drank vodka from a water glass with no ice.

After dinner, in the music room, Perry and I faked our way through part of the Chopin cello sonata. Perry sang the notes he couldn't get to, blah-blah-blahed embellishments, and we laughed through many passages, wagging our heads and making saucer eyes. It was meant only as fun, but Father regarded the performance (as he did the music) reverently. Long after we'd quit, he remained in that elevated place to which romantics are so often carried by Romantic music, that place where they seem to be deeply inhaling some fragrance— eyelids shut, head tilted back (raising the nose slightly), breath phrasal, smile serene. Father must have been extra-vulnerable to suggestion in that state, for when Mother whispered in his ear, he was up and on his feet; his hand at the small of her back, he escorted her to the curve of the piano. He took a seat at the keyboard, and before Perry and I could quite believe our eyes, Mother was warbling sweetly, girlishly: "Most gentlemen don't like love, they just like to kick it around . . ." We were as reverent at this intended fun as Father had been at mine and Perry's a minute earlier. He prompted Mother jovially when she forgot the lyrics, and as they laughed and he played and she sang, the room darkened — a cloud enveloped the sun outside. The silk tiger lilies on the back lid of the piano quaked in their Japanese urn. The old grandfather clock in the foyer chimed one, two, three, four, five. When Father began the introduction to "Embraceable You," Mother faltered a bit; she had a moment of serious doubt. They looked at each other. She seemed to say, "Can we really do this?" and he seemed to say, "I dare you." She started out self-consciously, but before the song was over, she was singing it to him. Perry, either too moved or too astonished, too *something*, left the room but returned in another minute and stood in the doorway, because Father, who was, I suppose, irreligious, had one more idea, one more surprise. At the end of the Gershwin, he began to sing unaccompanied, "In the bleak midwinter . . . ," and Mother at first laughed, saying, "Oh, Rudy, it's not Christmas *yet*," but then quickly abandoned the curve of the piano to stand behind him, her hands on his shoulders, his head fitting nicely between her breasts. "Frosty wind made moan . . . ," he sang. "Earth stood hard as iron, Water like a stone; Snow had fallen, snow on snow . . ." Father didn't have much of a voice, and he didn't finish the carol, because singing it took him too far away to see it through.

Perry escaped the music room again.

When I think of these last days with Father, when I think of this last Thanksgiving, what I recall of Perry is his leaving rooms, or lingering in doorways, about to leave. His standing on thresholds, unable quite to stay, unable quite to go.

We buried Father in Grace Cemetery eight days later. Perry and I had both returned to school on Sunday after the holiday, but we were called back home early Monday, told by Mother that Father was in the hospital, comatose. She called Max Dolotov, too. She felt that Father's closest friend should be present, even though Dolotov was not really a close friend. Father had no close friends. Unless you counted me and Perry, especially Perry. Dolotov arrived on Tuesday and stayed with us at the house. Father died Wednesday morning, around nine-thirty, never having regained consciousness. We got this news by telephone. Father's doctor, Gasser, had urged us all the night before to go on home and get some rest; the chances of anything changing overnight were slim. The news was received quietly—most quietly by Dolotov, who went back to sleep. Mother called us into her bedroom. In her pink dressing gown with the pink ostrich feathers on the sleeves, she hugged us and said she wanted us to know that Father had been a wonderful man, had always taken good care of her, had always taken good care of all of us; he may not ever have made a career for himself, or even held a job for that matter, you couldn't point to him and say, My father, the great scientist or businessman, but he had had character and goodness, and wasn't that important, wasn't that a kind of greatness all its own? Then she took a long bath in preparation for going to the hospital.

I felt very close to Perry that morning. I seemed unable to

let him out of my sight. We went from room to room together, and said things to each other like, "Do you want to sit
in the library for a while?" "Do you want something to eat?"
We found Raymond in the butler's pantry, at the utility basin,
hand washing shit stains out of Dolotov's boxer shorts. He
told us that Dolotov had given him a half-dozen pairs of boxer
shorts — apparently Dolotov had brought his dirty laundry to
Norfolk — and told him to scrub them by hand, with bleach.
Perry collected the wet underwear in a dishpan, I stuffed the
rest into a plastic trash bag, and we carried it out to the garage
and dumped it into a garbage barrel. We returned to the
kitchen, and that was when we found Raymond crying in the
pantry. "*I* loved him, too," he told us, and we attempted to
comfort him, tried to make him sit on a stool in the kitchen
while we made him some tea, but it soon became clear that the
best way we could comfort him was to give him something
comforting to do. So *he* made the tea and we sat on stools. And
it was with Raymond that we began to be able to talk about
Father. We sat around the old wooden refectory table in the
kitchen drinking tea and talking about Father. Raymond
smoked his Kools, striking matches on the sole of his shoe. He
showed us the inscription on the back of his watch, a gold
Rolex that Father had given him one year for Christmas. Two
words: "Long Life." Most of what we said was sentimental
and wouldn't have interested anyone but us. Stories about
Father were quiet, domestic stories, set indoors; they didn't
find him exploring his virility in the high elk country, or con-
templative, in waders, in the middle of wilderness streams;
they found him writing hundred-dollar checks for the mailman so the mailman might have the plaguing warts removed
from his elbow; they found him buying the bad still-life of

a local artist, or wearing the ridiculous string tie given him by a neighbor. The only extraordinary reports about Father weren't stories at all, because they had so little individual shape: they were momentary sketches that began, only in collection, stratified, to form the portrait of a man—an addict—who loved his children.

Astoundingly, crazily, I thought I was falling in love with Jane Owlcaster, falling in love the way men sometimes do in novels, hard and overnight, or with certain music, forever, on a first hearing. Any restraint I might have felt on account of Perry's not yet being buried was dashed by the news that he and Jane had broken up a month before his death. I had begun studying her, learning her—how she sat, crossed her legs, held her head; her occasional irony; her startling kindness; her scent of roses; her voice of midnight blue (my favorite crayon as a boy); her excellent teeth (Perry, on women, as if the subject were horses: "Teeth are important"); her strong hands that ruled whole bass sections of men; the way she had yielded in my arms, in Perry's apartment, allowing herself to be held for a minute; the cherished pearls she wore that had belonged to her grandmother; the champagne-colored slip beneath her dress (I didn't think Madeline even owned a slip); her directness, even her anger and confusion; and, undoubtedly, her love for my brother.

It occurred to me that my being in shock had finally found its focus, its pinpoint of denial — Jane Owlcaster — but even this thought didn't cause so much as a ripple in my determination. Some remote voice whispered intermittently to me of the absurdity of my sudden feelings, but this voice was shouted down by the passionate chorus whose text touched on sexual splendor, domestic bliss, and many children with dark curly hair. Of course, I wasn't entirely free to fall in love — not because of my unresolved marriage, but because of the vague, pervasive claim that Perry's death made on me: any giddiness had first to permeate a cloak of shock and loss. I was pushy, because I felt I had to be, and I embarrassed myself and Jane more than once. I pretended knowledge of things I didn't really have, of academic detail — Ockeghem and Josquin, for example, of Bruno Bettelheim, the Tao — but most recklessly, of romance. I kept thinking that at any moment we would begin enacting one of those epidemic progress-of-the-affair segments from the movies: the couple, to jolly Vivaldi, boat in Central Park, dress in each other's clothing, play peekaboo on the observation deck of the Empire State Building, relish long silences anywhere. The purpose, in movies, was to get past all that is familiar, so the *real* story could proceed, and that, I think, was something like what I had in mind, too. I wanted to avoid the details — the facts of who Jane Owlcaster really was, of who I really was — so the *real* story could proceed. The real story wasn't about our impotence at rescuing each other from marriages gone sour and mutual indictments and alcohol abuse and divorce and suicide, or even about falling in love with your dead brother's lover. It was about the new life that lay on the other side of all that: I'd had my cry, now I wanted to get on with it. Oddly, I thought the real story was about the story's end, an illusion that would prove both stupid and true.

The day after we met at Perry's apartment, I went to Jane's for dinner. Her mother, dressed like a gypsy, in a blouse with embroidered flowers and a long peasanty-looking skirt, greeted me at the apartment door: "Oh, my God . . . I don't believe it . . ."

Jane appeared and introduced us—her mother's name was Dorothy—and we shook hands. "I'm sorry," Dorothy said then. "Jane warned me, but I really was not prepared for this."

"Mother, please," said Jane. "Stop staring."

"She should talk," Dorothy said to me, taking my arm and escorting me into the living room. "At least I don't require smelling salts."

I didn't much care for this remark—it seemed borderline cruel. She had recently turned sixty (Jane had told me), an event for her of such monstrous intimations of mortality that she'd embarked on a dogged rediscovery of her youth, and at the moment she was floundering a bit. She wore dangling earrings that rattled when she moved her head, and I saw her as the kind of woman who competed with her daughter for the attentions of her daughter's male friends. Worse, I saw her as the kind of woman who would affect cheerfulness at wakes, fetching drinks and generally effervescing, believing death a time of jubilation, confident that dancing in the graveyard is carrying out the will of the dead. I immediately looked at Jane for her reaction to her mother's remark, but apparently she'd seen nothing mean-spirited.

Dorothy guided me to the sofa, sat next to me, angling her knees in my direction, took both my hands, and said, "We're all going to miss him very much. I felt very close to old Mr.

Clean, Jane may have told you. If there's anything at all I can do."

Just then, as if on cue, Molly came running into the room and pounced on me, smelling strongly of canned dog food. "You already are," I said, dodging Molly's tongue.

"Molly, get down," said Dorothy, pushing gently at the dog's neck. Molly nuzzled her nose into my lap and lay still, gazing up at Dorothy from the corner of her eye. "What a mess this one is," Dorothy said. "Look at that face. Does that make you think of somebody?"

"What do you mean?" said Jane. Jane was lining up a stack of magazines on a tea table.

"Oh, you know," Dorothy said. "I always thought Perry had this way of appearing more innocent than he really was."

"You mean secretive," Jane said.

Dorothy looked at me, worried, then, cupping her hand to one side of her mouth, said, "She's a little angry, you may have noticed."

"Private is what we used to call him," I said.

After a pause, Dorothy said, "I flattered myself, I'm afraid," and stared for a moment into her lap. "I thought he told me everything. Eventually, I mean. I couldn't be more shocked by all this. Come on, Molly, let's go."

She rose from the sofa, snapped her fingers at Molly, and walked into the long hallway toward the rear of the apartment.

"What are you doing?" Jane called to her, but she gave no answer. Then Jane said to me quietly, "She's a lot more shaken by this than she's letting on."

I felt an urge, as I had when she first entered the room, to take Jane in my arms, to touch her at least. The light in the room was unflattering; it cast a drabness over everything, including Jane. I wondered: did the light in this room always seem to be dying, no matter what the weather or time of day? I recalled my last visit, when I'd had those scary sensations of falling. I'd welcomed the room's privacy then. It had seemed uncluttered, soft-edged—a trick, no doubt, of the light—which I now saw to be a result of long, fabric-covered cornices over the windows. And I noticed an abundance of porcelain figurines scattered here and there around the room: a pair of giraffes with necks entwined, an Indian mama elephant with her calves, a whistling milkmaid with pigtails.

Waiting for dinner, the three of us sat outdoors on a terrace of redwood duckboards built off the kitchen over a lower roof. Petunias in carnival colors and marigolds nodded from wooden planter boxes and barrels. Molly lay in the shade under my chair. Dorothy fussed with the flowers, pinching off wilted blossoms and using a plastic watering can. Jane leaned over to whisper in my ear, and I felt a sudden, unexpected thrill. But all she said was "I don't think he was private. I think he was secretive." I whispered back with my mouth at her ear, "You may be right," and, like a schoolboy, I tried a quick nibble but she pulled away. "Don't," she said sharply under her breath, really annoyed.

I felt foolish, like a scolded child. In the awkward silence that followed, I found myself thinking how fitting that a woman named Dorothy, collector of figurines, would name her daughter Jane—such broadloom names, solid colors, avocado and harvest gold.

Jane whispered, "Sorry, Marty, but your timing's way off."

I tried to look as unsulky as possible.

Later, at the dinner table, Jane and Dorothy collaborated in telling the story of Dorothy's one glamorous night out with Max Dolotov. Perry had introduced Dorothy to him after a concert back in the spring. "Dolotov put the Dracula eyes on her," Jane said.

We were eating cold artichokes, dipping the leaves in homemade mayonnaise and discarding them into a white platter at the center of the table. I had no appetite, and the leavings on my plate amounted to rudeness. I observed that the spindly legs on the dining room chairs looked like Renaissance recorders. I wasn't having a very good time—I wasn't the least bit interested in Max Dolotov—and I drank much too much wine. Two topics could engage me: Jane (where would we find our old covered bridge for shelter from that sudden summer rain?) and, of course, Perry. And yet, through the haze there came this directive, *Keep listening.* Somehow the story had shifted from Dorothy's night out with Dolotov to something that went on between Dolotov and Perry—Jane had the floor now—a public scene between Dolotov and Perry at the school . . . Dolotov's big opera had just bombed . . . a new piece of Perry's had got lots of attention . . . Dolotov's jealousy and drunkenness . . . a quarrel backstage during a student composers' concert . . . Dolotov's calling Perry a prima donna, attempting to pull Perry's piece from the concert . . . Perry's calling Dolotov a drunk . . .

"I followed them backstage," Jane said, "and saw the whole thing. At one point Dolotov said, 'What do you expect, to be spoon-fed?' and he came at Perry, shaking his finger right up at his face. I really thought he was going to hit Perry."

"Wait a minute," I said to Jane, and I closed my eyes, trying to will myself sober, for I could see, a bit vaguely, that the dangling electrical wires were actually fly lines, the black billowing sails the fabric backdrops, the large, dark, seemingly roofless room with the large red Exit sign the backstage area of a theater. I said to Jane, without opening my eyes, "I dreamed this."

"What do you mean?" she said.

That night I stayed in Perry's apartment. I'd checked out of the hotel earlier in the day and dropped off my bags at 46th Street. I'd also paid the September rent to Pascal, the owner of Perry's building and proprietor of the nightclub on the ground floor. When I returned to 46th Street after dinner at Jane's, dreams and dreaming were on my mind. If a scene from my brother's past had found its way into my dreams, perhaps I could also learn something about his reasons for killing himself. Maybe this was how he would speak to me, through dreams. But then, if he'd wanted to speak to me, he could have left a note—that would have been more definite. I knew nothing of the mechanisms of the afterlife, but it struck me that writing a note would've been *easier*. Surely, funneling dreams into a living person's sleep was a complicated business, even for a ghost. And I didn't much like the idea of Perry's being in communication with me now, by dream or otherwise. I didn't really know how he would feel about my falling in love with Jane, and it would be like him to tease me—a gruesome nightmare or two just to alarm me, just to vex me. And if he could author dreams, what else could he do? Maybe he was *making* me fall in love with Jane. After all, didn't I feel as if I were under a spell, smitten by a woman I hardly even knew? Was such a thing among the powers of the newly dead? But why would Perry want me to fall in love with Jane Owlcaster? Was I meant to be some sort of proxy, called up out of Perry's shame over having left her behind? Did I have a will of my own? Was I in control of my life? And why did he kill himself in the first place? As I clambered up Perry's wheezing staircase, I wasn't sure that these questions were the least bit sensible, considering how muddled I was by exhaustion and chablis.

In the kitchen, I noticed a tiny key hanging on a cup hook by the door. I removed it and felt its slight weight in my hand: a mailbox key. Very excited, I scrambled back down the stairs and out into the vestibule. Why hadn't I thought of this before? A letter from a friend, perhaps a clue of some kind. But once I got the little bronze cell open, I quickly saw that there wasn't a single item of personal correspondence. Junk. And a few end-of-the-month bills. I trudged back up the stairs like someone punished. No, I was not in control of my life, I hadn't been for some time—years, if you wanted to know the truth. Racing down those stairs, hungry for revelation; leaving Perry's belongings in that taxi; my inopportune nibble at Jane's ear; overdrinking every day since Perry's death; refusing to eat; alternately heady and petulant—it was only a variation of what had been going on for a long time. The only thing I knew positively was that if you were drinking, disappointment made you drunker, and if you were disappointed, drinking made you hopeless. Back inside the apartment, I threw myself onto the mattress on the floor and lay on my back. I was not a man of prayer—I had not prayed since my wife went to the hospital during her last miscarriage—but now I stared drunkenly at the plaster ceiling, thinking myself a puppet maneuvered by powers beyond my control or understanding, and I shouted, "Pull . . . *pull!*" Nothing happened, of course—it was more a comical, drunken order than an honest petition—and after a minute, I got up and went to the stereo. There was something on the turntable, an old monaural record of Strauss's "Four Last Songs." Appropriate, I thought. Elisabeth Schwarzkopf. Otto Ackermann. The Philharmonia Orchestra. I put it on, this simple masterpiece, exuberant, direct, soaring, this voyage of tension and release with its surprising, astute horns. I got undressed and into bed. Perry's bed. I braced myself for an emotional onslaught, but the music had a neutral, tranquilizing effect, and somewhere during the third song ("*Und die Seele, unbewacht, Will in freien Flügen schweben . . .*") I fell asleep.

Perry used to talk about dreaming music. He said he sometimes dreamed music from heaven, or so it seemed, but he could never retain more than a mood, or perhaps a paltry motif. That night I dreamed not original music but Strauss— another orchestral song I hadn't heard or thought about in years, the one, replete with suspensions, called "Morgen"—a song of amazing lyrical beauty, never more beautiful than in my dream, played by angels, sung by a startling soprano god. And I'd never seen extreme beauty more dreadful, more ambiguous, falling to death as I was, or falling in love. Omniscient, both the dreamer, apart from the dream, and the dreamed, inside it, I was myself, and I was Perry. We watched our common fingers, like clips on a shower curtain popping one by one from a rod, slipping from the granite window ledge . . . our testicles pull in tight inside their wrinkled pouch, I hear our breathing, a mounting, suggestive rhythm, like passion heard through a hotel room wall, Strauss's exquisite organ-swell of harmonic resolution . . . and suddenly we see the sky, pale, pale white-blue and far away, an early morning sky, an autumn sky, a whirlwind of leaves caught up there against it scribbling, and I am a sleepy child, carried down suspiring stairs in our father's arms, pale, pale white-blue, in morning, sleepy . . .

. . . alone, not alone, alone, Perry, not Perry, his presence keeps leaving me and returning as I climb the spiral staircase toward the high room, drawn there by the sometimes sweet, sometimes raspy labor of a bow across a cello's strings. I climb—how long I've climbed—he's here, not here, to the high room, and at the top, the door is open—long, long windows let in the sky—a child, a boy, me, not me, sits in the middle of the plain room on a scarred wooden chair, cello between his legs, music stand a scarecrow before him, his eyes wet with diligence and struggle . . .

The day before Jane Owlcaster and I arrived in Norfolk, I telephoned Mother to say that I would need the guest room for Perry's girlfriend, but Mother was confused by this. She couldn't recall Perry's ever having mentioned any Jane Owlcaster (a name she was sure she would have remembered), and besides, she had already booked Max Dolotov in there. I told her to *un*book him, which annoyed her, and which she refused, at first, to do. When I told her that I wouldn't be staying at the house either, in that case, that I would get rooms for Jane and me downtown, she agreed to move Dolotov to Felicia Snow's place. But she was annoyed. And perhaps she was still annoyed when we arrived the night before Perry's funeral. She wasn't exactly impolite to Jane, but she was distant, almost cold. I was especially sensitive to nuance in this regard, since I had all but coerced Jane into coming with me to

Norfolk. Honestly, it was impossible to judge how much Mother was in control; she seemed very sleepy, strung out.

The next day, she maintained a startled look throughout the reading of Perry's will in the offices of our family lawyer, Welles Barclay. The will itself was not at all startling: Perry had left everything to be divided equally between Mother and me. And her startled look was a bit odd, considering that she was clearly tranqued-up on something that Father's old quack, Gasser, had prescribed for her. She maintained that look, too, that afternoon during the brief service at the graveside. I stood next to her, tightly holding her arm — it occurred to me that she might fall into the grave — and Jane stood next to me, holding *my* arm. Madeline, who'd surprised us all by showing up at the house a few minutes before we were to leave for the cemetery, stood on Mother's other side.

Madeline looked very fit, a woman in love, at the threshold of a new life. She had a Santa Rosa tan, her hair white-blond, and she wore a black jersey dress to the graveyard, some kind of wraparound thing with a scooped neckline that revealed the straps of a black leotard underneath; she could move from funeral to aerobic workout with the tug of a single drawstring. She'd flown in that afternoon and was to get a flight back to California that night, a girl on the go. An hour earlier, when she arrived at the house and we stood embracing in the foyer, she whispered in my ear very intimately, almost tenderly, "I need *money*." I was already in a beastly mood — I'd waked up that way — on the prowl for discord, and I said, "You didn't need to come all the way to Virginia for that, Madeline." I resolved to ignore her the rest of the day, and I pointedly refrained from introducing her to Jane, the mystery woman at my elbow.

There were many people at the service in Grace Cemetery, a shocking number, not friends of Perry's but locals who knew Mother. In her sobriety—or, more precisely, in her abstinence from liquor—Mother had become civic-minded, sat on some committees, held a few receptions for this or that. After we had gathered around the grave, I whispered to her, "Mother, who *are* all these people?"

She seemed surprised to find me next to her, even though I had not let go of her arm since we'd stepped out of the car. She smiled briefly—had I said something pleasant or unpleasant?—then looked piqued. Now that I had her attention, I repeated the question.

"Friends, Marty," she said. "They're friends."

The weather had changed four times that morning, from sunny to cloudy to thunderstorm to sunny to cloudy, and many of us were toting umbrellas (Jane, in her characteristic overpreparedness, brought *two* umbrellas, in case anyone was caught without); but for the service it had become sunny again and unbearably hot. Aside from the heat, the funeral's particulars were smooth and in order, under Mrs. Spinelli's remote control. The service itself was brief, Spartan. The same Unitarian minister who'd presided at Father's funeral ten years before said some kind, general words about "our brother Perry," so that my unique relationship with Perry was robbed from me, made universal, shared by every stranger who so much as knew the family name. Mother had arranged to have everyone back to the house afterward, and when we were dispersing, I asked Raymond and Madeline to escort Mother to the car. I took Jane by the hand and rushed down the dirt road to the parking lot. I'd seen Gasser alone, and I wanted a word with him.

Gasser, elderly, bald, a prolific prescription writer of

dubious medical skills, had grown rich off the rich in this community. I deflected his condolences quickly and said, "What have you got Mother on?"

"She's obviously under great pressure, Marty," he said in his cordial Virginia accent. "She's taking a very small dosage of Librium. It won't hurt her, I assure you."

"She's so goofy I can't tell whether she even knows what's going on," I said. "How is she supposed to know what she's feeling?"

He looked at Jane sympathetically—what was a sophisticated-looking girl like her doing with this hopeless layman?—and said, "I don't expect Helen to have fond memories of today, Marty, regardless of her medication. I wouldn't worry too much about what she's feeling if I were you. I'd just do everything I could to help her get through it."

"I think we have different ideas about what's helpful," I said.

Jane squeezed my arm. My face was sweating profusely. Gasser turned to go, dismissing me with, "I imagine we do, Marty. You're not a doctor."

"Neither are you," I said to his back. "If you were, my father might be alive today."

He turned and began to say, "Your father was a—" But he stopped himself, staring at me, sizing me up, sizing up the situation, and said finally, "That's very unkind, Martin. You're obviously not yourself." Then he walked on, his shoulders slumped, as if I'd really hurt him.

"That wasn't very pretty," Jane said as we proceeded to the car.

"Sorry," I said, and I did feel sorry, not for Gasser but for myself, for that limping stray dog I called my emotions: in lieu of a man grieving, or a man resigned to loss, was a grumbler.

The funeral had seemed perfunctory to me. I thought we should have done more. At least we should have had music; someone could have sung something, if only we'd taken pains. As it was—a bunch of spectators in black, strangers for the most part, sweltering around a hole in the red clay—it felt more like a chore than a ritual. In the flowers I'd seen only the tawdry gladiolus; in the minister I'd seen obsequiousness and a cheap black suit. When we reached the car, we turned for a moment to the slope of an adjacent field—future graves, I supposed—where a trio of very young children, two girls and a boy, were running in their Sunday clothes. The girls, with much high-pitched laughter, chased the boy, who had swiped one of their wide-brimmed white straw hats. When the boy stopped and sailed the hat like a discus, down toward a grove of pines at the bottom of the field, the girls stopped too, dug their elbows into their ribs, and set off two shrill, penetrating screams, a bitonal strain to the long, smooth glide of the white hat through the air. I noticed that Jane was smiling, and if I'd been the least bit yielding, this chance moment might have saved the day, but I trained my eye instead on Mother and her wobbly approach, complacent between Raymond and Madeline, her now ridiculously affable face a perfect mask of a numbed life, and I thought the only real passion my family—any of us—had ever shown was in the extreme distances we'd traveled in pursuit of escape.

I opened the door to the car and got in first, leaving Jane standing outside. With one hand on the open door, she leaned down and put her head inside. "Marty, are you all right?" she asked.

"I'm swell," I said.

*

Back at the house there was an enormous roast turkey, an enormous roast beef, a woodpile of baguettes, a pyramid of ham biscuits, bowls of potato salad, black olives, sweet gherkins, pickled eggs, pickled watermelon rind, spiced crabapples, pecans, banana nut bread, cheese, a bar outside by the pool, a bar in the sunroom, and a staff of six earnest-looking local college students in white dress shirts and bow ties. Jane went upstairs for a few minutes when we first arrived. Mother, Madeline, and I took seats in the library, where Raymond offered us refreshment. Madeline requested white wine. The voice of my better self told me not to drink. Aside from my foul mood, I was tired and had a headache, so I ordered a Coke. This captured Mother's attention; for a moment she stopped staring at the arm of the couch. She said, to no one in particular, "I was thinking about a Coke a few minutes ago."

"Do you want me to get you a Coke, Helen?" Raymond asked with wildly exaggerated sympathy. At any moment he would lapse into baby talk.

"No," Mother said, shaking her head—resigned, possibly, to something like the utter uselessness of desire. "No . . . I was just thinking about one . . ."

Madeline, who had sat very close to me on the couch, whispered, "She's not drinking, is she?"

"Drugged," I whispered back. "Gasser's been writing prescriptions."

People began arriving and the place got instantly noisy. Mother seemed to have acquired many of her friends, the men and the women, for their penchant for shouting indoors. Maybe they felt they had to, if Mother was often in the condition she was in now. A bald man who looked like Fred Mertz on "I Love Lucy" extended his hand toward me, shouting, "You must be Martin!"

Without standing, I gave him a robust handshake and shouted near the top of my lungs, "Yes, I am!"

This startled the poor man and caused an eruption of laughter from Madeline. She recovered the moment by standing, introducing herself, and quickly steering the man toward the food across the hall. When she returned, she had our drinks. She took her seat again and said, "Where'd you get that tie?"

It was an old fifties diamond pattern Madeline had bought for me at a shop on Haight Street called Second Chances.

"You have good taste," I said.

"Marty, I'm sorry about this morning," she said. "I'd just had to go into my change purse to come up with the cab fare, and I was in a panic when I walked into the house. It came out all wrong, and anyway, I didn't mean I needed money in any large sense. I just meant that in my rush to get away, I hadn't brought any with me."

In our phone conversation from my hotel room my first night in New York, Madeline had quickly begun talking about me as older brother to Perry. She spoke in quiet tones, in a way that was calming and helpful, about how Perry had relied on me, and loved me. And I was touched by what she'd done just now with the man who looked like Fred Mertz—a simple kindness; I'd expected her to scold me on her return from across the hall, but she hadn't. When she finished apologizing, I told her I was sorry for what I'd said that morning in the foyer, too. I kissed her on the cheek. She kissed me on the cheek. We hugged awkwardly, the way you have to, sitting on a couch. It was the hug she must have given her sorority sisters in college, punctuated with a pert little squeeze, but I didn't mind. She didn't want to be husband and wife anymore. She didn't want to think about being husband and wife anymore. She wanted to point her face into the cool sea breeze of the future. She meant for things to be okay between us. That's all she meant.

"She seems nice," Madeline said, turning up the volume on a conversation she was already having in her head.

"You mean Jane," I said.

"Helen told me her name was Jane," said Madeline, "but you know, I wasn't sure. Perry's girlfriend?"

I nodded.

After a moment: "You seem . . . close."

"We are," I said.

"I've never heard you mention her."

"I just met her," I said.

"Oh."

I'm not sure what Madeline made of this. I don't imagine she was about to pursue the subject in any case, but just then Jane entered the library. I had struck an agreement with Jane, one I hadn't bothered telling her about: I wouldn't push anything, wouldn't make advances of any kind, until after Norfolk. This agreement had nothing to do with any deference to her own reluctant feelings. I was merely giving myself a deadline, to make myself feel better. It didn't mean I wouldn't be jolted by a vague, pleasant urge to do something whenever she came into a room. It didn't mean my eyes wouldn't track her like twin electronic devices as she crossed toward me. She had changed her dress, from something simple and black to something simple and black with tiny red and white flowers in the fabric. She had changed her hair somehow, too; it was still pulled back, but not quite so severely. Madeline and I both stood when she reached the couch, I introduced Jane, and offered to get her a drink. Giving me a desperate look, as if I'd just saved her life, she said, "Some tonic water would be great. But if they don't have tonic I'll take soda water. If they don't have soda—"

I held up my hands and told her I was sure there would be both. She and Madeline, still standing, began a conversation as I was leaving the library. I heard Madeline say, "You were a close friend of Perry's?"

I immediately regretted having left them alone together. I couldn't have said exactly what I feared, what caused me such discomfort, but by the time I reached the bar in the sunroom, I was miserable. I couldn't recall what drink Jane had requested only seconds ago, and I stood staring at the young bartender for a moment, rubbing my temple like someone who'd suddenly materialized in the room. "A plain tonic," I said at last. It seemed as if a cloud of steam had entered the room, clear enough but distancing, and even the considerable noise of the party seemed to reach my ears through a layer of cotton padding. The bartender's simple question "Lime?" seemed loaded with implication. What would it mean about me if I said yes? I shook my head rather shamefacedly and took the glass. Two extremely tall, thin women, the ancient Mullis sisters, Opal and Ruby, were standing behind me. "Marty," Opal said with great sympathy as I turned. Both unmarried, they lived together a few houses away in the red-brick mansion their parents had left them. For a brief period when Perry was a young boy, Ruby, the older of the two sisters, had given him music lessons. The tall women were very pale, their cheeks deeply stained with rouge. Opal, tilting her head to one side, looked at me sadly. "Marty," she said again.

I must have looked entirely lost, because Ruby said, "Opal and Ruby *Mullis,* Marty."

"I know," I said at last. "How are you?"

"How are *you*?" Opal said, reproaching me for having asked the wrong question.

Before I could answer, Opal said, "You look tired, Martin. Doesn't he look tired, Ruby?"

"He does," Ruby said. "The heat in the cemetery, probably."

Opal said, "Marty, I can't find Helen. I don't think she's here."

"She's here," I gurgled, under water now. "In the library."

"In the library?" Ruby said, as if I'd said that Mother was in Antarctica.

Then my vision cleared, the noise came back like the breaking of an ocean wave, and I blinked my eyes several times. I led Ruby to the sunroom door. We could see across the hall and into the library. I could see the couch where Mother had been sitting, but she was no longer there. Jane and Madeline were seated now, angled toward each other on the opposite couch, absorbed. I needed to get them apart, and yet I had no idea how to go about it. I pointed out Jane to Ruby Mullis and asked her to deliver the tonic. When I thought she looked askance at my asking her to do a lackey's work, I said I would find Raymond and see if he knew where Mother was.

As I turned back toward the sunroom, I saw the long food table—already ravaged—and sunlight, unusually harsh as dusk approached, streamed in through the windows directly onto it. Nausea bucked through me so vehemently I had to reach for the nearest wall, and when I looked up next, three or four strangers who'd been staring at me averted their eyes. I went to the washroom off the foyer and splashed cold water on my face. Mother had a dark-colored pleated chintz on all four walls in the tiny room, and it really was like stepping into a coffin. As I loosened my tie I made the terrible mistake of catching a glimpse of myself in the medicine chest mirror: I had the drawn look of someone recovering from a long illness.

I found Raymond in the kitchen, frantically rolling out a circle of biscuit dough on a marble slab. Mother's dogs, an aging Pomeranian and a younger Pekingese, came yapping at my ankles, which set the parakeet to screeching. The kitchen reeked of marijuana. A cigarette, a regular cigarette, dangled from Raymond's lips, with an ash about an inch long. When he saw me, he said, "Locusts."

"Raymond," I said. "Have you been smoking dope?"

He looked at me and said, "You don't mind, do you, Marty? One of these college kids who works for me quite a bit, he brought me a joint. As a present. I told the kids absolutely they could not be smoking grass while they were on the job. But I snuck a couple of puffs. I needed something to get me through."

"I don't care, Raymond," I said. "But why are you doing more cooking? Let them go home and eat."

"I should," he said. "I really should."

"Here, give me that rolling pin," I said. "It's just the thing I need for the Mullis sisters."

Raymond thought this was the funniest thing he'd ever heard. He threw back his head and cackled — "Just sneak up behind 'em and knock 'em both out cold," he said between bursts of laughter — and the ash of his cigarette fell down over his chin and onto the dough. "Oh, fuck it," he said, throwing the cigarette into the sink. "You're right, Marty. I'm not lifting another goddamned finger for that bunch. If it wasn't for Helen, I'd . . . you know, I've just been standing here asking myself what I'd really like to do today, and you know what it is? I'd like to go to the movies, that's what I'd like to do. I'd like to go see Burt Reynolds in *Gator,* that's what I'd like to do."

"So go," I said. "We can take care of Mother."

"Well, I guess you really could, couldn't you."

"Of course we could," I said. "If we could only find her."

This struck Raymond as terribly funny too. His eyes wet with laughter, he said, "Has she disappeared?"

"Apparently," I said.

"She was with Felicia last I saw her," he said. "They were standing in the foyer. And something about them made me think they were about to start up the stairs. Marty, are you all right? You look very pale."

I told him I was okay, I was just tired, and that he should go to the movies. I said the party could take care of itself. He'd done enough, the party could wind down unassisted.

Upstairs, I'd just reached the door to Mother's room when I saw Felicia Snow backing out of it, quietly pulling it to. She saw me and put her finger to her lips. Felicia had lost some weight and had had her face lifted again. She was dressed in the abundant black robes of a priestess in *Aïda.* "Asleep," she whispered to me, taking my arm and escorting me away from Mother's door.

"Asleep?" I said.

She nodded. "It's the best thing, Marty."

Just then the door to the guest room opened and Jane appeared, followed by Madeline, who was wearing what I recognized as one of Jane's dresses. "*Tell* me about it," Madeline was saying. It was very disconcerting to see Madeline in Jane's dress, and when they saw me, I must have had an inquisitive, if not accusatory, look on my face, for Jane quickly explained, "Madeline spilled her wine."

Then they each said a polite "Hi" to Felicia and started down the stairs ahead of us, bosom buddies, leaving me wondering, "Tell me about *what?*" Three steps away, Jane turned and looked at me. "Are you all right?" she said quietly, and I nodded.

Max Dolotov stood at the foot of the stairs, and when Jane passed, usurper of his room, all Dolotov did was raise his eyebrows. This exploit seemed to leave him dizzy; he took hold of the newel post.

"Max," Felicia said, placing both feet on each stair before going on to the next. "I want to go home. I had one drink and it went straight to my head."

"Where else would you have it go?" Dolotov said, smiling. He didn't sound as drunk as he looked. "Martin," he added, nodding at me.

I thought his smile turned sly, almost demonic, when he said my name, and for a second he seemed very far away. "Well," I recalled him saying to my father years ago, condescendingly, "I suppose if you like his chamber music . . ."

From the foyer I could see, through the French windows of the library, Madeline and Jane, who had gone out by the pool and were now sitting side by side, dangling their feet in the water. What could they be talking about? I felt I had to put an end to this. It couldn't go on, and yet it was decidedly out of my control. All I could think to do was to walk up to them and say, "Stop talking or I'm going to separate you."

"Please accept my condolences," Dolotov said.

I thanked him for coming and asked whether I might have a word with him.

"Oh, please, you two," said Felicia, already starting for the bar in the sunroom. "I'm not *used* to drinking in the afternoon."

I took Dolotov into the small paneled room behind the stairs that used to be Father's study. I asked him to sit down. I asked him to tell me what he could about Perry.

He looked surprised, then annoyed. He obviously didn't like my tone, and he was immediately defensive. "I don't know what you mean," he said.

"My brother just killed himself," I said. "I'm trying to find out why."

"I'm sure I don't have any idea," he said. "How could anyone? It's not a sane act."

Exasperated, he went to a serving cart of liquor bottles and glasses over by the only window in the room. "I was fond of your brother," he said, pouring Scotch into a tumbler.

"Really?" I said.

"What's that supposed to mean?"

"I know you almost came to blows last spring," I said. "It didn't sound to me as if you treated him like somebody you were fond of."

"Oh, you've been talking to that young woman," Dolotov said.

"Well, didn't you? Didn't you almost come to blows?"

"I wouldn't say that," he said. "He was quite full of himself lately. I attempted to take him down a notch. That's all."

"You seem to have succeeded," I said.

This gave him pause. "Oh, come on, Martin," he said, suddenly the professor. "If you're looking for somebody to blame for this, you'd do well to look closer to home. Your brother didn't jump out of a window because he was angry at *me*."

"Well then, why did he?"

"I already told you, I haven't any idea. Because he was crazy, I suppose." He knocked back the Scotch and turned to pour another.

When he faced the room again, I had closed in on him—I could smell his sweet cologne. "You don't sound very sorry," I said.

He turned his head sideways in order to take a gulp of the Scotch. He put down the glass on the cart. "Thank you for the drink," he said and attempted to step around me.

I blocked him. "You don't sound sorry," I repeated.

"I'm *sorry,*" he said, raising his voice, losing just a bit of his cool. "What do you want me to do, shed tears? Of course it's a great tragedy." He reached for the glass again and finished what was in it. "It's not my fault he went off the deep end. If you want to know the truth, I think he knew he wouldn't ever amount to much. He was so pumped up by your father. By you too, probably. There's nothing worse than the influence of amateurs on a musician of real promise. Your brother wouldn't ever really get anywhere because he always relied on his so-called genius. He didn't think he had to work. God, what an imperious little trumpeter he'd become."

"That's not true," I said, and I felt a tremor in the soles of my feet. "You were jealous," I said. "That's obvious."

Dolotov began laughing now, clearly drunk. His face bright red, his eyes brimming with tears, he began to cough, choking on his laughter. When he regained his composure, he waved his hand at me in dismissal. As he turned away from me, back toward the liquor cart cluttered with bottles, he muttered, "What a bunch of losers. What a disappointing . . . lonely life for your poor mother."

His bringing Mother into it threw me completely off balance. Finally I had arrived at the moment I'd got out of bed for that morning: a fleeting vision—a room of people, Perry's mourners, laughing—then my hands, flat before me. I knew my hands were about to shame me, and I welcomed it. I planted my right hand on Dolotov's shoulder and wheeled him around, then shoved him hard in the chest. There was a sound like gas escaping from a valve and I was stunned—as if I were seeing him for the first time—by what an old man he'd become, in his seventies now. Dolotov retreated backward, grazing the liquor bottles, hit the wall next to the window, and slid down to the floor, his legs splayed like a rag doll's, his trousers hiked up, exposing the white hairless skin of his shins. I heard him say, almost delicately, "Oh my heavens," and then the drop leaf on the liquor cart suddenly collapsed, sending all the glasses and bottles crashing to the floor. I had seen something like this ten years before, in the form of a premonition, as I walked up the lawn toward the house that last Thanksgiving with Father. I recognized it immediately, and my shame took a back seat to a simple yet primary insight: with Perry's death, I had been left on my own. Who else really knew me, who else could confirm for me the truth about myself? Dolotov's eyes were closed. He seemed to be struggling for breath, his hand to his chest. Consumed by loneliness, I reached for his other hand, to help him back to his feet, and I saw, out the window, Jane and Madeline, two women in similar black dresses strolling barefoot down the slope of our lawn, talking their way toward a faraway line of plume-shaped cypresses.

The party at Mother's languished but refused to pass on entirely. The house became a scary place and, on account of the air conditioning, cold as a tomb. Raymond left with his staff of students. No one was in control. Madeline and Jane had not returned from their walk. Stragglers—waiting, I imagined, for some clear climax to the afternoon—milled about the rooms. An obese couple, two men, were having a drunken spat in the library, something about a George II highboy proving how little the one cared for the other's feelings. Out by the pool, a woman in a black suit and heels lay on her back on the diving board, her head at the diving end. A young man who looked like a federal agent or a bodyguard, big and built, wearing black sunglasses, pleaded with her from the rear anchor. And Mother, drugged, slept upstairs.

I recall the odd sensation of climbing the stairs, gaining altitude in eight-inch increments, and somehow feeling that my blood was not coming with me. The heavy drapes were drawn in Mother's room. She lay on her side facing the middle of the bed, at peace under a pale blue satin comforter. She didn't stir as I crawled onto the bed with her and stretched out on my back. The comforter was like touching water. I gently kicked off my shoes and let them fall to the carpet, no more audible than Mother's hushed breathing. I put my hands behind my head and closed my eyes, a man almost thirty and in bed with his mother for the first time since . . . when? Infancy? I had no memory of sleeping with my mother as a child, of cuddling in her bed. I had no memory of Father in bed with her. Wasn't bed the place where she was always alone? Wasn't it her four-poster temple of solitude? I opened my mouth to speak: I wanted to tell her about the shame I felt at having shoved that old man in Father's study (how sadly he had accepted my hand to help him off the floor and then left the room without a word). I wanted to tell her especially about the bottles crashing to the floor—such a familiar sound, breaking glass, a taproot of our shared past—and I wanted to tell her about how I felt I'd never really found my way in life and how completely set adrift I was now, with Perry gone and Madeline gone and Father long gone, how I didn't know what to *do*. But all I put words to was this, a question: "Mother, don't you feel this way too?"

Then I was silent for a while and began to see the faces of young children on the backs of my eyelids, as if *they* were looking *in* . . . children, some black, some white and blond, looking in, then running away across a pasture toward a scalloped line of evergreens . . . I hear the rapid gunfire of their scores of feet on stairs, feel their breath on my face (the sugary scent of grapeade), their forearms on my shoulders . . . they pull at my ears, giggling, their high liquid voices coming out of clear bottles.

Vividly I can see my father, weary from hours of practice, but sober and sturdy and intelligent, standing in the doorway to the library, holding Perry's hand. In a rare moment of irony (irony was Mother's forte, and Perry's) he tells Mother that there's a cigarette smoldering in the rug close to her foot, and adds, "Please try not to burn down the house, Helen. It still has sentimental value to me."

She did eventually burn part of it down the summer following his death, and for financial reasons the burned part was never rebuilt. The fire began in the music room downstairs, where Mother, before staggering up to her room and "falling asleep," left a burning cigarette poised on the edge of an oblong ashtray, a souvenir from Uganda, carved from an elephant's tusk. Altogether five rooms were lost, including my bedroom.

So the night of Perry's funeral, when I woke from a sleep like paralysis, like coma, in the room Mother had given me, it was in Perry's bed, Perry's childhood bed in his childhood room. I lay under a single sheet, and I had only the dimmest memory of how I got there. Had it been Raymond's hand under my elbow in the hall? Finding myself there, in this room from the past, I felt that sleep had transported me over many years. My eyes had been painted shut with a lacquer that illness produces, and they were painful to open. And there was something else, a kind of dull heat behind them, and a radiating ache in my knees and shoulders and ankles. I could hear water pipes somewhere in the house—someone was turning water on and off—a distant, muffled sound like a woman's sighing. This was no dream: a big bright gold razor-sharp sliver of a moon hung in one of the black windows, with Venus set symmetrically like a jewel underneath. I had the distinct sensation that I was not alone. I smelled a faint aroma of roses, and then I saw her in the dark. She glided silently across the rug toward the bed, her glasses off, her hair down. She was wearing a floor-length gown that exposed her shoulders. She pulled covers up from the floor where I'd kicked them off, climbed into the armchair close to the bed, drawing her legs under her, and wrapped herself in a blanket. I sensed her shuddering a little. She was chilled from her journey down the hall. "This is probably weird, coming in here like this," she whispered, her confession surprisingly vulnerable. "But I haven't been able to sleep. I was worried about you. You seemed so out of it."

"I'm sick," I said, and it seemed, by ceasing to try so hard, that I'd turned the key in a difficult lock. Half awake, I could grasp the obvious: all day I'd been getting sick.

"I thought so," said Jane.

"I haven't been taking care of myself."

"I know," she said. "You really haven't."

"I'm glad I'm sick," I said. "I thought I was losing my mind."

"We found you in bed with your mother."

"I remember."

"Weird."

"I know."

"Can I get you anything? How do you feel?"

"Water," I said. "I think I must have some kind of flu."

She went into the bathroom and turned on the light, which spilled into the room in a modest, pleasant way, as if from behind a curtain. She ran the water in the sink for a long time. Funny how a small thing like that can take on meaning. I thought it no less than marvelous of her that she let the water run until it was cool and free of any old-pipe debris. When she returned to the room, she passed me the glass and put her hand to my forehead. "My God, Marty," she said. "You're burning."

"I know," I said. "All over."

Without a word, she quickly left the room, presumably returning to her own room down the hall. She was back at my bedside after a minute, saying, "Here, take these," and she dropped two tablets into my palm. She returned to the bathroom and I heard water again, and some clanking noises. This time she came back with a white porcelain bowl, part of a bowl and pitcher set, and placed it on the table next to my bed. Slowly she dipped a washcloth into the water and wrung it out, a narrow twisting cloud raining into the bowl. I was beginning to enjoy my fever. If sleep had transported me over years, my fever had borne Jane over centuries: at her station by the bowl, her head bowed slightly and light falling over her features in a striking, pointed way, she was a thin version of a Vermeer woman. For a moment she laid the cool cloth over my forehead, then began dabbing it over my face. She dipped the cloth and wrung it again, then brought it down to my neck. I closed my eyes and told her how good it felt. She said, "I liked what you did today, the way you confronted that doctor in the cemetery."

"I was an ass," I said.

"But I liked the impulse behind it," she said. "You know what I mean?"

"If you liked that, you would've loved the scene later in Father's study," I said.

"I heard. I like the impulse behind that, too."

"How did you hear?" I asked.

"Felicia Snow called over here and talked to Raymond. Isn't Raymond wonderful?"

"Yes," I said.

"Felicia was upset, but Raymond thought it was the funniest thing he'd ever heard. And I guess he had Felicia laughing too by the time she hung up. Did you actually knock him to the floor?"

"I shoved him against a wall," I said, "and he slid to the floor, yes. It was pretty sordid."

"God, you're so hot," Jane said, and pulled the sheet down to my navel, which startled me. "I think I'm naked under there," I said.

"Do you feel cold?" she asked.

"No," I said, "I'm boiling."

"Well, I'm not afraid," she said. Then, "By the way, your wife says goodbye."

"Sounds like the title to something," I said.

"To a sad story."

"What were you two talking about all afternoon?"

"You, some. And her new love. And Perry."

"What did she tell you about me?"

"Oh, that you had always felt on the outside of the family.

That Perry had something with your parents that you didn't. Some kind of closeness. That you were a little lost, that you'd always been a little lost. Now relax and just pretend I'm a nurse."

"You're a nurse," I whispered softly, as if I were conjuring something with a line of poetry.

She began applying the cool rag to my chest and stomach, softly, so that I only started to tense and then relaxed quickly.

"If I pull this sheet down nothing's going to jump out at me, is it?" she said.

My sad plumbing below felt lacquered with the same stuff that was in my eyes, and very hot, not with any sexual heat but with a kind of sticky, residual warmth of something already melted. "You don't have to worry," I said, and for a moment I opened my eyes and watched a lovely string of muscle working gracefully in her bare upper arm. "I'm not feeling very jumpy."

"You're a good patient," she said.

That was me precisely, a good patient, slave to her suggestion, even to her scrutiny, if that was what she wanted. I closed my eyes again and mused for a moment about her funny, self-willed preparedness, then drifted into the cool blue grotto of her . . . what? Attention, care, good will, custody? It didn't matter. I liked the drifting.

"Eerie," she said quietly. "I know this body," and she lowered the sheet down to my ankles.

"I'm having a wonderful dream," I said, not opening my eyes.

"No," she said. "This is real. This is *your* life."

She was running the wet cloth up and down my legs, first one then the other, then up again to my stomach and chest, my shoulders and neck, my arms, as if she were erasing my body piece by piece, turning my body to water. I couldn't quite imagine fucking—I was too sick for action verbs—though I tried to imagine it, and each time I did, I felt as if I were holding back, dragging my heels. Jane was taking me somewhere else, and in spite of all that, a surge of fevered blood was collecting *down there*—that now slightly remote but once familiar spot—pooling at some lowest point on a plane and starting foolishly, indiscreetly, to stir, to move, to resurrect me when I felt the cold rag press down hard there and heard her blue voice.

"No-no," she said, "you're sick."

Now I shuddered, and she quickly covered me with the sheet, then with a blanket. She said something about the moon in the window.

Dear Mr. Lambert,

Here is your walit. I kept the $34. Also the watch and the shoes and cloths. There was blood on the pants that cleaned up ok. My brother says this is the stuff of a dead man because of the blood and the tag on the watch. I hope that is not so, if that is so I am sorry. He said I could get money for the i.d. on the black market but I felt sorry in case you were dead. Your Amer. x-press card is expired.

I found this in Perry's mailbox on our return from Norfolk, written in pencil on brown paper (a cut-up grocery bag), wrapped around a black leather wallet. As I sat at the desk in Perry's apartment reading this, Molly ambled over, pushed her nose into my hand, then made a couple of turns and lay at my feet. A while earlier I'd left Jane at her apartment, where we'd had a rather public goodbye in the small entryway; just inside the living room was Dorothy's Monday night support group for women sixty and over. I was holding Molly's leash in one hand, Molly tugging at it, anxious to go out, and a plastic dog dish and a five-pound bag of Purina Dog Chow in the other. On my way to 46th Street, I had wondered if Jane felt some of what I felt—a need to stay together—but, like me, had not known quite how to accomplish this. Or maybe she was sorry she'd let me persuade her to come to Norfolk in the first place. Possibly, she was sorry she'd ever met me.

In Norfolk, we'd had the house to ourselves. The day after Perry's funeral, Mother, with Felicia, had flown to Mother's favorite fat farm in Denver, a place Raymond referred to as the Great Escape. Jane and I spent much of our time together in the pool—the water had provided a balm to the aches and fever of the virus I had—and despite my illness, I'd wanted to think of these days romantically. But always, Jane had been distracted. That first night she visited me in my room (the night of the cold washcloth) had left so much glitter in my eyes that I couldn't see things properly, I knew that, but I felt sure that Jane was worried about something. And it had been unsettling—as if my head were turned in two directions—to have Jane worried and in her bathing suit at the same time. The truth is, I was a raw confusion of symptoms, amorous and viral. I lectured myself quite a bit: not *every* one of her gestures, facial expressions, moods, and desires had to do with me. Perhaps even her exceptional sleepiness didn't have to do with me. She would sleep quite late into the morning, often skip breakfast or have a single piece of toast, then sleep after lunch and again before dinner. She would sleep in the shade of an umbrella on the terrace, on the couch in the library, on an inflatable raft in the pool, and solitary in her darkened room. She slept for most of the flight back to New York, and upon arrival at her apartment, she seemed to want more sleep. She yawned as she said goodbye to me in the entryway. Then, at the last moment, Dorothy had come scurrying to the door, full of baby talk, to plant goodbye kisses on Molly's nose.

And now, to greet me, was the news of the ridiculous fate of Perry's belongings. All of it, every single detail starting with Karajian's phone call in San Francisco, suddenly seemed absurd. I decided that a drink would be in order—what else was there for me to do? But of course there was no liquor in Perry's apartment, so I started down to the nightclub below.

It was a little after midnight, Monday (though technically Tuesday). A sign in front of the club read, "No Show Tonight." I pushed open a door of upholstered leather and stepped into a narrow barroom with a very low ceiling, quite dark but breathing a red glow up from the carpet and out from the walls. As soon as I took a stool at the long bar, I saw that whatever this place may have been at other hours, on other nights, now it was mostly a gay bar, despite the presence of a few women. I had the impression that most of the clientele were show people, gypsies from Broadway. On the jukebox Bernadette Peters was singing: ". . . so make the moments fly, autumn, winter . . ." Lined up on stools at the far corner of the bar were a number of loud older men in business suits, but mostly, people were talking quietly in pairs at the bar and at the even darker tables along the opposite wall. I had chosen a stool among four or five empties nearest the entrance. The bartender, a short, stocky man in his early twenties with a military haircut and a tight-fitting shirt of stretch material, served me two double Scotches, each time allowing his eyes to linger on my face—more the curious perusal of a picture in a magazine than anything blatantly cruisey. This did not bother me. Upstairs in my dead brother's apartment, I had just read a note written by an apologetic thief who wanted his victim to have his identification back, in case the victim was dead. I drank my drinks quickly and left.

No sooner had I arrived back at Perry's when the doorbell rang, the kind of piercing alarm that signals the beginning or end of classes in an elementary school, startling me momentarily out of my drunkenness. But the intercom system and the buzzer for opening the front door were broken, so I had to start back down the wheezing stairs. On the bottom landing, I saw Jane in the vestibule, looking nervous.

She was wearing the same trench coat she'd worn that first day in Karajian's office. And she didn't remove it once we were upstairs and inside the apartment, as if she didn't intend to stay. I looked into her eyes, trying to read her, but all I saw was confusion, anxiety. And then she was in my arms, trembling. "Marty," she whispered against my shoulder.

"I'm glad you're here," I said.

"I can't tell what's going on," she said. "I don't know if I'm falling in love with you or chasing after a ghost or intrigued by the perverse—"

"You're falling in love with me," I said. "Next question."

"That simple, huh?" she said.

"That simple," I said and kissed her gently on the lips.

"That's not simple," she said and kissed me back.

I drew her close, pressing her against me.

"You smell like Scotch," she said.

"Sorry," I said, and I released her quickly and turned toward the bathroom. "I'll brush my teeth."

But she caught my hand. "Don't do anything," she said, back in my arms. "I like you the way you are."

"That's just how I feel about you," I said.

"But not here," she whispered after a moment. "I'm not prepared for that."

"Where, then?" I said. "It's one in the morning."

"I don't know," she said. "I just couldn't. It's too creepy. I feel confused enough already."

"Your place?" I said.

"This would blow Mother's mind," she said. "What little there's left to blow."

"A hotel, then," I said.

"That's silly," she said. "To spend money. Are you drunk?"

"On love," I said.

She broke free from me and went to the bed, sat on the edge of it, appeared deep in thought—second thoughts, I feared. She stretched out on the bed and stared up at the ceiling. When next she spoke, it was with a sad note in her voice. "Maybe we could just sleep for a while," she said. "I could use some sleep." She patted the bed with her hand, indicating a place beside her.

I went and lay there, not touching her. "Wouldn't you like to get undressed at least?" I said.

"No," she said. "Not yet."

We lay in silence for a minute or two. "Would you like to take off your coat?" I asked.

"No," she said. "I think I'll keep it on for now."

"You're a very strange woman."

"I think it would help to turn off the light. Do you mind?"

When I turned off the lamp on the bedside table, the room was lit only by the pink glow of the street lights out on 46th Street.

"Can I hold you?" I said after a moment.

"Yes," she said. "But let's sleep."

I took her into my arms and breathed deeply.

Sometime later, I awoke to the soft sound of her voice. I was no longer holding her, but lying next to her on my back. I noticed that we both were still wearing our shoes.

"My grandparents took me there one summer for lunch when I was a young girl and I was visiting them," Jane was saying, and I realized that we must have begun a conversation before I was actually awake. "It's down by the water on this narrow little cobblestone street," she continued. "I remember it as the most beautiful house I'd ever seen, a huge old Gothic thing. I was a teenager, maybe fourteen. During lunch, I had to go to the bathroom. It was upstairs, and I wandered around these dark hallways for the longest time before I finally found it."

I shifted onto my side, so that I could look at her. She lay on her back, and she was undoing the buttons on her coat as she spoke.

"When I was washing my hands, about to leave," she said, "I noticed out the window another open window across a kind of air shaft. It was a room in another wing of the hotel, and there were some gauzy curtains, but they were open and blowing in a breeze, and I saw a man and a woman making love on a sofa inside the room. I had never seen *anything*, not even pictures, and I stood there and watched the whole thing. It seemed odd to me, I'd never thought about it before, but the woman was lying on the sofa and had her blouse open, and the man was kneeling on the floor kissing her breasts."

I moved close to her, again taking her into my arms. "Like this?" I said.

"Yes," she said.

"She was very beautiful, dark, mysterious looking . . . and then she threw back her head, as if she were in pain . . . but pleasure, too . . . it looked to me as if he were gently biting her nipples . . . but then maybe not so gently, because I could actually hear her gasp . . ."

"Like this?" I said.

"Yes, oh . . ."

"How did she gasp?"

"Like this . . ."

"And what else?"

"He covered her mouth with his, like this . . ."

"Yes . . . what else?"

"He pulled her skirt up and removed her panties, drawing them slowly down her legs—"

"Like this?"

"Yes—"

"Could she have been crying?"

"No . . . she smiled in a heated sort of way, raised her head to watch him—"

"And then—"

"Maybe he even kissed her there . . ."

"Like this, yes . . . Did she take him in her hands?"

"Yes—lovingly, this way . . ."

"Oh . . ."

"She said something, something that seemed to excite him as she drew him down toward her—"

"Yes, like this—"

"This way, just like this . . ."

Jane had grown more vulnerable looking as the hour wore on. Indeed, she seemed to be growing younger, more alive somehow, which was precisely how I felt. I was embarrassed by my lovemaking that first time; we only removed, unzipped, and hiked up what was necessary, and I was much too fast. Afterward, we lay again in silence. Perhaps we drifted in and out of sleep. Though we were still in our clothes, Jane had spread a blanket over us. I recall rain spattering the tall windows of Perry's apartment, the droplets igniting in the light from the street lamps. I heard her voice again.

"Hold me," she said.

"What is it?" I asked.

"There's something I have to tell you."

I took her in my arms.

She closed her eyes.

"Go ahead," I said.

She held me tighter.

"I'm pregnant. There. I've said it." She opened her eyes, smiled, surprised when she saw me smiling.

"Is it mine?" I asked.

She kissed me. "Of course not," she said. "Your brother's."

We made love again, this time with our hands and mouths—and with our clothes off—Jane crying out, contracting seven, eight, nine times and pressing my fingers hard against herself so I could feel the bone beneath the clitoris and the quickened pulse of blood.

Lying apart from each other, like long-joined creatures now happily, blessedly severed, we were silent. And then Jane said, "When I was in the eighth grade, my father came to get me at school one afternoon, early. He took me for a ride in his car, down to Battery Park, and we took the ferry over to Staten Island. I'd always loved the ferry ride, which was why he chose it, I suppose. On the ride over, he bought me a hot dog and a Coke. He sat next to me on a bench and kissed me on the cheek. He told me that he was going to Singapore; he was divorcing Mother and going to the other side of the world. I was close to my father and yet I didn't have the slightest idea that anything was wrong. I thought we were the happiest family I knew. I was totally, completely unprepared. I had to drop out of school for a while. I saw a shrink. And somewhere along the way I made a decision, that I would never, ever be caught unprepared like that again."

"You can't possibly prepare for everything," I said.

"What do you think he would have done?" she asked, and somehow I knew she was referring to Perry and the baby.

"I don't know," I said. "I always thought of him as an honorable person. But I'm not sure an honorable person throws himself out a hotel room window. So I don't know."

"Marty. I only knew about it four days before he—"

"You can't do that to yourself," I said. "You can't think about that."

"But how can I help thinking *what if?*"

"He had a lot of things to keep him alive," I said. "There's no reason to think a baby would have made any difference."

"I just needed a little time. To sort out my feelings."

"You can't do this to yourself. You'll make yourself crazy."

After another long silence, she said, "Do you ever think about taking up the cello again?"

"No," I said. "I'm not good enough. I never was."

"Perry said you were good."

"Perry said I was soloist with the Philadelphia Orchestra."

"But you could play *in* an orchestra. You could teach. You don't have to be Casals. What about your own pleasure?"

"I don't know. Somehow it feels like a sad compromise."

"That sounds like *him,*" she said. "All or nothing, black or white, the top or the absolute bottom."

"I guess that's true," I said.

"But it's not realistic," Jane said. "You know, your wife told me she thought you liked being lost."

"She's entitled to her opinion," I said, not at all pleased that our talk had taken this direction, especially to have had Madeline brought in. "Anyway," I said, "I don't feel lost right now, this minute."

I thought I saw something dark, like fear, cross her face. "I was wearing my diaphragm," she said at last. "I was prepared. But diaphragms are only ninety-five percent effective. And I beat the odds. Which seems to be happening more and more lately."

"What do you mean?"

"Just that it isn't working anymore—all my preparedness. I wasn't prepared for Perry to go weird on me. I wasn't prepared to get pregnant. I wasn't prepared for him to kill himself. And now I'm not prepared for you."

I held her for a minute in silence, then rolled onto my back beside her. "At least we don't need birth control," I said.

"True," she said, and after a few minutes I turned on my side and watched her fall asleep—for me, a kind of lovely meditation.

When I closed my own eyes, I thought at once of Perry, of how, despite his drive to succeed, despite his apparent self-possession, he had been, in his own way, lost. And then I thought how surely the whole family was lost. Certainly we were lost to one another—how else could Father's dying untreated have been allowed to happen? And Father was lost to himself as he groped his way toward his absurd early death. How often he would open the door to a room, surprised to find us there—"Oh, I'm sorry, boys, I was looking for the . . ."—a stray in his own home. And Mother, in the wings, lady in waiting. It seemed the orchestra had lost her music—a temporary delay. Soon she'd be back in the grease paint and fishnet stockings and crinoline petticoats. Wasn't the cancan number up? As for Perry and me, we invented our lives the way all children do, moving from one island of logic and wonder to the next, but we needed also to invent their lives. What were we to make of these phantoms who staggered along the halls of our home? What were we to do with them? What had we to do with them? I was early resigned to the melodrama, so long as I felt apart from it, superior to it, detached, but Perry, precocious and amused, exploited it.

"Where is Perry?" I could hear my mother saying, her eyelids fluttering with anxiety. "Where is Perry?" Raymond has left the kitchen door open, and Perry, now a toddler, has wandered out into the breezeway, sits, seemingly beyond harm, on the dark green and maroon flagstones. He appears to be surveying his dominion as he gazes serenely in the direction of the cypress trees at the base of the lawn.

"Where is Perry?" she asks years later, a different, more developed anxiety in her voice. She has entered the library, where Father, entirely ignoring her, listens to a new recording of *La Forza del Destino*. Now a schoolboy, Perry has discovered how easily and thoroughly Mother startles. He positions himself in dark places, behind furniture, in closets, and waits for the kill. "Do I smell garlic?" Mother asks, sniffing the air in the library—a parting shot at Father and his affection for Italian opera. She climbs the stairs to her room. As soon as she sits on her bed, a nightmare hand shoots out from beneath the dust ruffle and tightly grasps her ankle. Her scream can be heard all over the house.

"Where is Perry?" she asks, still years later, into the telephone, long distance from Norfolk to Cambridge. "He's not in his room." "I don't know, Mother," I say. "It's past midnight. Am I my brother's keeper?" "*Yes*," she shouts and hangs up angry.

And long distance, from the glare and chill of her Norfolk swimming pool, on hearing of his death, she says, flat, without inflection, "Perry."

We were lost to each other, most years, in one way or another.

The summer before Perry came up to Cambridge to begin his freshman year — the first summer without Father — the two of us stayed in Norfolk with Mother. All June she drank heavily and consistently, as if she meant to compensate for whatever brief hours of sobriety she had sometimes mustered in the recent past on account of Father's failing health. Felicia Snow and Little Teddy were there almost every day; sometimes Max Dolotov showed up for a weekend. They took up their games in the library, their smoky, boozy, bantering diversions.

But something, of course, had changed. While Father had been living, his distaste for this group and its silly ways had united Mother's friends, enhanced their sense of naughty fun, subject to Father's occasional, patriarchal eye. Even Max Dolotov, finally, had joined the ranks of Mother's sympathetic companions in the lonely life Father had allotted her. But now that Father's absence was absolute, they lost the thread. It was no longer clear that fun was what they were having. When Perry and I were young children, those afternoons in the library had been extreme and unpredictable and volatile — qualities irresistible to young children. Now they were simply aimless and sad. While once a harsh word or a harsh mood was something to be medicated, moderated with whisky (as if any clash were merely the sharp push that started the delightful forward motion of lengthy, drunken patching up), now these occasions carried the threat of actual estrangement. The element of risk made these afternoons too much like real life, and Mother appeared thoroughly exhausted at the end of them. With Father's passing, "house-drunk" had lost its music, its ring of gaiety; now all it conjured was drunk people in a house.

All this surely had something to do with the striking truth that when Father died, almost nothing of his spirit remained in our Colonial mansion. Some hint of him could be had from visiting his "things," in the music room especially. But soon, even that was to be eradicated.

One very hot night in July, that first summer home, Perry and I took Father's Lincoln and went to a dusk-to-dawn movie marathon at a drive-in theater. We saw *King Rat, El Dorado,* and part of *One Million Years B.C.* For about half an hour we lingered with two exaggeratedly giddy girls who kept laughing at us from the cab of their pickup truck parked next to us on the graveled incline. They were country girls who'd had something to drink, and when they climbed into the Lincoln, one of them became kittenish, curling up on the white leather with the tip of her tongue in the corner of her mouth. The other one, a bit younger, vehemently disapproved of her friend's behavior. "Ar*leeeeen,*" she kept saying, making saucer eyes. In the end, Perry told them the Lincoln had belonged to our father, whom we'd buried only seven months ago. The older one, the drunker one, began to cry, and her friend, humiliated, eventually yanked her by the wrist out of the car. When we returned that night, around one A.M., we came home to a chaos of shouting voices, flashing red lights, and blaring shortwave radio static: Father's family home in flames, burning out of control on its low hill.

Raymond, whose room was on the ground floor behind the kitchen pantry, had been watching television, and had smelled smoke when he went into the kitchen for a glass of milk. Upstairs, he found Mother "asleep" in her clothes, sideways across her bed. He managed to rouse her enough to get her down the stairs and out of the house. Later she admitted having no memory of going to bed, and still later it was determined that the fire had been caused by a cigarette left burning in the music room.

The confusion and anger I felt that autumn, my final year of college, comprised not only Father's recent death and the fire that Mother set in the music room, but also the fact that these tragedies fell against the slowly descending backdrop of the financial ruin Father had left behind: the letting go of advisors, massive losses in the stock market in what appeared to be random investments, a line of disgruntled creditors and bank officers. He had died intestate. Perry and I had our trusts, $250,000 each. Mother had everything else, but the only asset of any major significance was the Newport property, which she sold for the purposes of investing and developing an income. When all was said and done, we saw that Father's family fortune had been reduced by something just over $18 million over the last eight years. In the simplest terms, we were no longer a wealthy family. Mother would be able to continue to live comfortably, but certainly not lavishly. And it didn't come as a complete surprise when we learned that, like everything else, the fire insurance on the house had long ago been allowed to lapse. Some adjustments were made to the house—basically the clearing away of the burned wing—and eventually, Mother put in a pool where that wing had been. Mother drank her way through the early aftermath of the fire, comforted by Felicia and Little Teddy, and drank her way through the decisions that had to be made about finances and reconstruction. And then, while the house was being worked on, she went alone to Hot Springs, Arkansas, and entered a treatment program for alcoholism. She joined AA.

I recall wishing that autumn that the whole house had burned to the ground with Mother in it. I had entered my season of rage. For one thing, I could find nobody to blame for Father's death—nobody, at least, who wouldn't point the finger back at me. And Father's having squandered the family money threw me into a personal dilemma. I wanted not to care, it wasn't politically correct to care, and yet I did care, deeply. I was feeling the influence of the times—the civil rights struggle and the effort against the Vietnam War—and my playing the cello (indeed the whole notion of "classical" music), our empty privileged lives, our Colonial house built by Negro slaves, and the foibles of our drunken mother all got heaped into that convenient catchword "irrelevant." I felt the need to be punished. I wanted all of my family to be punished. I interpreted the burning of our house as a sort of divine retribution, but to my thinking the judgment hadn't been severe enough. I wanted Mother to burn to death. I wanted to be orphaned by justice, to be granted a role I thought I could play very well.

But things didn't work out that way. All the fire really did was to erase more thoroughly Father's life with us—a double whammy, loss grafted on loss. Father's forty-year-old Steinway and his entire music collection burned. His old room upstairs was lost, along with the tape of his recital. Except for a few personal items in the paneled study behind the front stairs—a monogrammed silver letter opener, his reading glasses in their cracked leather case, his old automatic pistol, his wooden Russian Cossack doll—almost all traces of Father, even the oil portrait of him as a curly-headed boy stroking the fur of a Saint Bernard, perished in the fire.

I did not understand the effect of Father's absence on Perry and me, not nearly as well as I understood its effect on Mother and her group of friends. For a long while, Perry seemed bewildered, certainly aloof, more so than usual. There was no joy in him, no joy in our going away together to school, no joy in my company. When I returned to Harvard for my senior year — with Perry in tow, coming up for his freshman year — I was suffering a persistent loneliness. I saw the end of my college career approaching, and I had failed in those years to establish a single friendship that would continue past the commencement ceremony. That last year at Harvard, from a great distance, I watched Perry thrive inside his isolation. He concentrated on his studies in a time when concentrating on one's studies wasn't the thing to do. He was known to give money to various left-wing political campaigns, but he didn't participate in any student demonstration. He didn't experiment with any drug. And yet he grew his hair down to his shoulders. His identity appeared to be intact, even though it wasn't clear to me whether he was supposed to be a long-haired musician or simply a longhair.

What did finally come clear to me, near the end of an endless, brutal winter, was this: with my talent and education I was headed for an instructor's position at some college or university, teaching music theory or ear training, and if I was to spend the rest of my life in a classroom, clapping out a complicated rhythm for my students to repeat back to me like a bunch of stoned chimpanzees, I might as well be in Bellevue. So three months before graduation, I donated my heavy winter clothes — including the heavy cashmere overcoat — to Perry, dropped out of school, and left for California. Technically, I was a draft dodger; I stalled with one thing and another, and eventually stopped communicating with my draft board. Then the lottery came along and Perry and I, with our shared birthday, were in the last third. I had judged California correctly: in those days, it was an easy place in which to get lost. I bummed around for a while, then settled in San Francisco, where I eventually established my business. Young, industrious, intolerant George Michaels soon joined the small company and took charge as efficiently, though not nearly so benignly, as Raymond had taken charge of our house in Norfolk all those years ago. And before long, Madeline came to work for me, on the run from an unhappy love affair. We immediately recognized the fugitive in each other and soon married. After Perry graduated from college, he went to France for a couple of years—"to work"—and we grew more distant than we already were.

I have said that with Father's passing, so passed his spirit. Ironically, sadly, it was the impact of his death, not of his life, that endured. His death had fallen on us like a moon falling into the sea whose tides it used to govern—displacing us, setting us loose, sending us thousands of miles apart. And, more or less, we stayed that way. It took ten years, and Perry's suicide, for me to begin my journey back.

Now, lying next to my dead brother's lover, in my dead brother's apartment, I recalled my visit to him while he was in Europe. After meeting up in Nice, we boarded a boat to Naples, cruising around the boot heel to Brindisi and on to Corfu. There we lived on a beach for a week, camping in a hut we made from bamboo. For meals we bought yogurt, bread, potatoes, tomatoes, and onions from a monastery up in the hills. The air smelled of wild oregano. We drank from a spring under a canopy of myrtles. We showered under a waterfall. Shepherds brought their flocks down the hillside to bathe them in the pounding surf. Elderly Greeks came down and buried themselves in the hot sand—a remedy for rheumatism. At night an apricot moon rose from the Ionian Sea. The water glowed with iridescent plankton.

One day an Englishman, also camping on the beach, a quiet man who had come there with his two young children—and who reminded us very much of Father—was stung in the ankle by a scorpion, a wound that, surprisingly, bled profusely. Civilization was around the other side of a high headland (identical twin to one at the other end of our secluded beach); the monastery was much too far for us to get to over land with the Englishman, and who knew what medical help the monks could provide in any case? We had no boat, so Perry and I swam the poor man around the promontory to the other side. It turned out to be much farther, through deep water, than we'd imagined, and the three of us almost drowned.

We deposited the Englishman in a bus that would take him to a clinic in Kerkyra, and on our return we attempted to cross the headland by foot, which was surprisingly rough going— near its high point, impossible: on the side of our descent, there were sheer rock walls, some as tall as three or four yards.

Seeing this, Perry walked to the edge of the cliff we were standing on, quickly worked his way down to a ledge about twenty feet above the water, and leapt into the sea. He surfaced, slinging water from his hair, and called to me.

"But is it deep enough?" I yell, already scrambling down to the lower ledge.

"Of course," he calls back. "Didn't you just see me do it?"

I have turned all goose flesh. "Show me how deep," I yell.

Impatient, Perry stands up straight and flattens his hand at the water's surface, which strikes him just below the shoulders.

"Are you sure?" I yell.

He pulls an exasperated face.

After a long minute, I jump.

When my feet hit the ocean floor, one knee is driven up hard into my chin. Crouching in the water, only pretending to stand straight, Perry deceived me: the water is actually much shallower than he led me to believe. I'm not seriously injured, but I've bitten my tongue badly and my jaw feels as if it's on fire. I start swinging at Perry, calling him all sorts of names, and crying, "Why? Why?"

He grasps me by the wrists, shouting, "You wouldn't have jumped otherwise, you dummy."

Then I recalled a time long ago. I couldn't have been more than twelve, and though the memory was not precise in all its details, it seemed a vivid and seemingly singular instance of something that had been a repeated occurrence. I am in the powder room at home, hiding out because some of Mother and Father's friends are visiting, and Perry has been playing the piano for them in the music room; they will soon ask me to perform as well, and I don't want to. I will stay in the powder room for an hour or longer, pretending to be sick if necessary, in order to avoid performing. I do not have stage fright. It does not make me nervous to perform. It humiliates me. For one thing, what a disappointment I am after the very young, very amazing Perry at the keyboard, so small that he has to slide back and forth across the bench in order to reach high and low notes. But also, I am the only person I know who plays the cello. Mine is the only cello I have actually seen—what an unwieldy thing to carry across a room, to sit behind, to hold between your knees. And how coarse and bare its sound, how unlike the familiar, the normal, piano.

And more sleepily I recalled a visit to the doctor in San Francisco when Madeline was pregnant for the second time, an early visit. We had a progressive obstetrician, a Chinese woman who, once she had the cold steel speculum inside Madeline, pulled a gooseneck lamp up between Madeline's legs and insisted I come have a look at the cervix.

What I see is a knob of pink flesh with a precise, central opening about the diameter of a pencil. *That,* I am told, is what our child is going to come through.

And then the penultimate visit, the ordinarily routine one, the one (as it turned out) before the D & C, the one where I watch our doctor quizzically struggle with the electronic gadget to find our baby's heartbeat, where I watch panic spread over Madeline's face like black ink in water.

An odd thing. I prayed that night, lying naked next to Jane in Perry's bed. I found myself praying for my brother's soul, whatever that meant, and for the life of Jane's baby, of Perry's baby. I prayed the short, stubby petition of a foul weather friend.

I had thought my dreams—the nightmares, the haunted, haunting dreams—were over, but after I fell asleep, something combustive happened to the fire in Perry's fireplace across the room. It flared up huge and hot and menacing, and Jane and I were fucking furiously again—the massive bed a white violent sea of milk, our acute sexual greed transforming us into animals, all hair and teeth and long arched backbones—so hard I knew I must be hurting her, now from behind, like wolves, like jackals dripping sweat, but I didn't care . . . beyond care, with my bare feet planted on the charred floor, I reach under her belly and grab her in front of her pelvic joints, wedging my hands into the shallow folds there, yank her up hard against each biting thrust so the slapping of our wet flesh cracks the air like a whip . . . frankincense pierces the sweet-acrid scent of our sex, a lurid purple light spills into the room through a stained-glass oculus window over the bed, her moans and grunts pitch deeper, I can see the muscles of her back rippling, straining like a man's as her body grows firmer and harder in response to the fury of my mounting orgasm, and then she turns her shorn head slowly and looks at me over her shoulder: it is Perry, Perry's injured face, tears brimming his eyes, and he speaks my name beseechingly . . . the smell of shit cuts the frankincense and stings my nostrils, I look down at the monstrous thing between my legs and try to stop, try to wake up, to stop, to wake, but I can't, or won't, and holding my eye like a trapped swamp rat, he opens his mouth, lets out an ugly, hoarse groan of pain and pleasure and hatred, his teeth wet and shining in the firelight, and some separate force sucks me into him, some separate disease that is not me and not him . . .

I heard someone outside the apartment, and I leapt sweating and naked from the bed and jerked open the door. But there was no one there, nothing but the ugly green and empty hallway.

In the morning, Jane slipped out of the apartment before I awakened. She left a note—rather businesslike, I thought— simply explaining that she had a rehearsal.

In Jane's place on the bed, Molly was curled up, sleeping.

The nightmare had left me shaky and full of shame. It didn't help simply to acknowledge a subconscious that had a sick sense of humor. I had slept poorly when I slept at all, and though my subsequent dreams had lacked any narrative quality, I was aware of more unsettling images of falling, of climbing stairs, and more Strauss. I also soon saw that somehow, away from New York, in Norfolk, in love with Jane, I'd lost the track of my spiritual decline, the downward spiraling that I thought had climaxed in my shoving Dolotov against the wall in Father's study. But now I had found the track again, or it had found me, and having found me, it would disgrace me and cause me to behave disgracefully to others.

It was after noon by the time I was up, dressed, and out of the apartment. I walked Molly, then, after a bite to eat, picked up Perry's roll of film at the drugstore where I'd left it before going to Norfolk: sixteen exposures out of twenty-four (the remainder of the roll unused), and all of children in a park (Central Park, I thought, Sheep Meadow), girls and boys, six or eight years of age, some black, some Puerto Rican, some white and blond, some wearing baseball caps, mugging at the camera, mugging at each other.

Who were these children, and what were they doing in Perry's camera? Back at 46th Street, I tried telephoning Jane. I got Dorothy, who told me that Jane was still at school.

"Oh, yes," she said when I described the photographs. "He was doing some kind of work with children. Marty, have you seen Jane? She's acting very strangely. She was out all night last night and just stopped in for a minute this—"

"What do you mean, 'some kind of work with children'?"

"I don't know exactly," she said. "You'll have to ask Jane. Some kind of volunteer work, you know. Disadvantaged children. Maybe the YMCA or something. When Jane comes home I'll tell her to call you. That's if she comes home. I don't know what's going on with her."

Jane telephoned two hours later. "It wasn't the Y," she said. "I don't know where Mother got that idea. It was an orphanage or special home for children. In Brooklyn, I think."

"Don't tell me," I said. "You don't know the name."

Silence. "You know very well how he was," she said after a moment. "And he'd only recently started doing it. It's not my fault he was so close-mouthed."

"Do you know anybody who *would* know?" I asked.

"No, Marty, I don't," she said.

"What's wrong?" I said.

"I've had quite a day," she said. "I'm exhausted. I got yelled at for being late to rehearsal. He's still angry with me for missing rehearsals while we were in Norfolk. Then I come home and you're annoyed because I can't provide adequate information for your inquest. Mother is coming at me. My hormones are doing the cha-cha and all I want to do is sleep."

"I can't help it," I said. "I just keep being amazed that you didn't know more. That you don't know more."

"What about you?" she said. "How much did you know?"

"That's different," I said. "We were three thousand miles apart."

"Proximity isn't everything, you know. You can telephone people all over the world these days. Even to out of the way places like New York."

"Is this what happens when two people finally get around to making love?" I said. "They start getting sarcastic with each other?"

"It's just that every time you ask me some question about

him that I don't know the answer to, I feel accused. And I know that's not all in my head."

"Okay," I said. "I'm sorry. You're right. It's not all in your head. Do you want to have dinner tonight?"

"I can't," she said, softening a bit. "I'm eating with my mother. We have a date. I'm going to try to clue her in."

This disappointing exchange, with its disappointing result, didn't lift me out of my funk, and afterward, in a funk, I studied the photographs some more. I'd known immediately that these were the children I'd seen on the back of my eyelids the day of Perry's funeral, when I lay dreaming next to my sedated mother. In one of the pictures, two boys in shorts and no shirts, one in a Yankees baseball cap, one wearing thick eyeglasses, sat side by side on the grass, bare legs and feet splayed out in front. They were photographed from above, from an adult's vantage, and as they looked up into the lens, squinting in the sun, hands folded in their laps, they appeared to be inwardly straining against this willed moment of repose, as if it were only the force of something powerful, like love or gratitude, that could have resigned them to this voluntary capture.

Oddly, sleep became the overriding issue in our lives, both mine and Jane's. She craved it, I feared it. Eventually, I craved it, too, from lack of it. I resumed my drinking, in spades — to enable me to sleep, I told myself — and when I did sleep, my dreams were troubling and exhausting. My dreams were obsessive, and in addition to being obsessed with Jane, I was obsessed with my dreams.

I took long walks at all hours of the day and night, sometimes with Molly, sometimes without. The front page of the

Times was featuring the first photographs back from the *Viking 2* expedition, of the boulder-strewn Utopian Plain of Mars. I thought people on the streets—alien "New Yorkians," I decided they might be called—grew increasingly threatening, scrutinizing me with disparaging eyes. Derelicts, on the other hand, seemed to view me with extraordinary sympathy. One night, on Eighth Avenue at about 2 A.M., a black hooker in red leather hot pants said, "Going out, Marty?" It took a moment to sink in—I'd had many drinks—and when I stopped and asked her how she knew my name, she said, "Is your name Baby? That's what I called you. Is that your name? Baby?" Another time, in broad daylight, an old crone, dressed in the all-black garb of a Mediterranean peasant and seated on a milk crate in front of a West Side fruit stand, looked pointedly into my eyes and said something to me in Italian. I didn't know whether she had cursed me or blessed me, but it felt as if she had looked at my soul and found it in need. I resisted my irrational impulse to stop children on the street and ask them whether they had known my brother.

Yet another time, on one of these walks, I turned a corner onto Fifth Avenue and almost collided with Felicia Snow, in New York on a shopping spree. She expressed her deep sorrow about Perry. She had just spent ten days with Mother at the spa in Colorado . . . how sad my poor Mother was . . . first Rudy and now Perry . . . and what a terrible way to lose a child . . . how many more of our children would we have to lose to drugs?

"What do you mean, drugs?" I said.

"Well, that's what Helen told me," Felicia said. "It *was* drugs, wasn't it?"

"Perry jumped out of a hotel room window," I said.

"Well, I know," she said, distressed by my bluntness. "But I mean drugs was the cause, Marty."

"That's absurd," I said, and Felicia, confused and embarrassed, glanced at her watch and made some excuse to escape me.

I seemed to have found a target for the poison spear of my anger. I went to the nearest telephone booth, appropriately enough inside the door of a liquor store on a side street. I dialed Mother's Norfolk number. Though she'd only recently returned from the spa—presumably a place where she would have got herself into shape—she sounded to me as if she were still on drugs herself. I was able to reduce her to tears in a matter of seconds.

"What am I supposed to tell people, Marty?" she said.

"The truth might be refreshing," I said.

"And what is the truth, Marty?" she said. "You seem to know so much."

"It's not a lie," I said. "It's not something you just make up to satisfy some notion of saving face. I know that much."

"Brilliant," she said. "Thanks a lot."

"You're welcome," I said and hung up on her, a misdeed I had always considered unpardonable. (I recalled that I had hung up on Madeline, too, when she told me about her new love in California.)

I purchased a bottle of Scotch, and when I returned to Perry's apartment a while later, the phone was ringing as I entered the door.

"Don't you ever, ever call me that way again," Mother said. "I don't need that from you. And don't you ever hang up on me again."

And I hung up on her again.

Then, Perry's telephone restored to its usual, perpetual state of silence, I proceeded to get very drunk. I tried calling Ken Karajian to get the name of the construction worker who'd seen Perry's fall, but I was told that the lieutenant was no longer with the department. It would do no good to call his home, because he was out of town until the beginning of the week. He would be checking in with the station then, if I'd like to leave a message. I looked in the yellow pages under Orphanages, which referred me to the general, endless listing under Human Services. It was impossible to tell an orphanage from an abortion clinic. I continued to drink as I sorted through Perry's mail—nothing of any interest, also usual. I pored over the papers on his desk, rifled through his desk drawers, and then I found something I had somehow missed before: a newsletter from Church of the Child Jesus, Atlantic Avenue, Brooklyn. I got the number from directory assistance and phoned the church, but all I got was a recording telling me the time of the next service, which was the following Sunday.

I don't know what hour it was when I eventually fell asleep, but I was awakened shortly afterward by the ringing of the telephone: Mother, clearly drunk and sobbing.

"I'm in the middle of a big slobbery slip," she said, slurring her words. Then, after a pause and more sobs, "Don't you see, Marty? . . . You're all I have left. I don't even have my sobriety now. Just you . . . you and these two dogs."

As gently as I could, I told her to call me tomorrow, when she was sober.

By Sunday, when I took the train out to Brooklyn, I was so strung out from too much Scotch and too little sleep that I was having mild hallucinations: small things, like mistaking a black Seeing Eye dog in the subway for a giant vulture preening its huge umbrellalike wings. I had hoped that Jane would come with me to the church, but she had planned to spend the day with her mother. Dorothy, it seemed, was in need of some soothing; she hadn't taken gracefully the news of her daughter's pregnancy. Besides, Jane was very sleepy. In addition to coping with Dorothy, Jane, of course, was going through the stress and discomfort of early pregnancy, and also, the father of her child had recently killed himself. But I didn't think about any of this; it seemed to me that she was deliberately avoiding me.

I walked from the subway station, about eight or ten blocks, through a bombed-out section of Atlantic Avenue—abandoned buildings, junk stores, transient hotels with open windows and food stacked on the sills, bodegas on corners, sidewalks littered with trash and broken glass, boarded-up doorways, the stench of urine. Though we'd been having cool, pleasant weather the last few days, this morning the air felt stilled with the promise of severe heat. It was not quite eight-thirty, and already I was sweating around my shirt collar.

Eventually, I reached an enormous red-brick building that looked like a National Guard armory, except for the huge mullioned wheel window in its central gable and the small, unobtrusive Celtic cross at its peak — no crockets, towers, or pinnacles. A tall flight of concrete stairs led up to wooden double doors, flung open, exposing the metal straps of medieval-looking hinges. In the surprisingly cool narthex with its flagged floor, I was handed a bulletin by a beautiful black woman wearing a black dress and a small hat with a net veil. I took a pew near the back of the nave. The congregation was about half white and half black, and I noticed that every-one, like the woman in the narthex, was sharply dressed. (I, on the other hand, was shabby and unshaven.) There were quite a few children present, all wondrously quiet and still.

Once the service had begun, even I could tell this was no orthodox Catholic service. Though there was a processional with incense (kindling a distressing vision of my horrible nightmare), those in it were dressed in simple green robes, no miters, copes, or crosiers. The choir was up front rather than in back, on the right side of the chancel, and the processional hymn was "Go Down, Moses," complete with hand clapping. This was not the music I had expected. I had assumed from the beginning, when I first heard that Perry had gone to the church because of the music, that there was some remarkable choir doing Palestrina and Monteverdi.

The sermon was delivered by a black woman — not a conventional sermon given by a conventional preacher. Very eloquent and composed, she talked about the need for rejoicing, the duty we had to rejoice, and said that all week she'd been searching for events to rejoice about. Though she admitted there was not much in the world to set our hearts to rejoicing, happily, she had found two examples. "The first is a Christmas card I bought several years ago," she said. "It shows the Holy Family in a typical Christmas portrait, with Mary looking up to heaven with a big smile. Joseph is looking down at the crib with a startled look on his face. Underneath, the caption reads, 'It's a girl!' "

This provoked a great amount of laughter, both from the congregation and from the speaker herself. She went on: "The second item I found is a little more serious. I'm sure most of you have been following the story in the papers which began last Wednesday, when the management of Manhattan's Park Regency Hotel issued an order to their chambermaids telling them they would no longer be able to use mops to clean the floors of that hotel. They would be issued rags instead. Meaning, of course, that they would have to clean the floors on their hands and knees.

"These workers, mostly immigrants, all women of color, all women in their forties and fifties, protested the order, but the management refused to make any concessions, even after one woman cut her hand on a razor blade. In an interview one of the workers said the new order was cruel and downgrading. The head of hotel management said he didn't see it as a hardship. A maid is a maid, he said, and that was just what they had to do.

"By Thursday, the papers were reporting a return to mops at the Park Regency. In just one day the flood of national attention had been so overwhelming that the management, represented this time by a woman, rescinded the no-mop order.

"What may not have come through in the newspaper accounts was that behind that decision were several hundred representatives of women's rights groups, and all of them were prepared to descend on the hotel on Friday for a protest rally right out in front.

"Now, in one sense this victory may seem small. It didn't require a long-term struggle, nor did it cost much, but if you think about where we were twenty or twenty-five years ago, and how little awareness there was about women's rights—my mother did day work in the 1950s, and there were no protests against the conditions of women's labor—you have to see this event as cause for rejoicing.

"In this event we see all kinds of women in solidarity with oppressed women. To those of us who have grieved over the sufferings of people, or who have marched in protest marches, or who have gone to jail, this is surely a hopeful sign of change. And surely such a change is cause for rejoicing.

"If we want change, we will have to work for it. The Bible describes God as a gardener tending justice like a plant to be cared for and watched over until it blooms. Justice is alive in my life because I see it practiced by the people around me, some of them right here in this room. I rejoice for the people who have given me an example of justice—people who work with the disabled, or with troubled young people, who feed the hungry, take care of the sick, turn out for peace marches, are committed to teaching, who have worked in institutions dedicated to social justice.

"I think a commitment to social justice brings us into the deepest kind of contact with other people. I look at those women claiming their right to mops as necessary equipment for dignified labor and I see the American writer Harriet Jacobs, a woman deeply ashamed of her life as a slave, of having borne two children outside of marriage but who wrote her story because she wanted free women in the North to fight against the enslavement of their sisters. I look at those women with their mops, refusing to be downgraded, and I see Frances Harper and Pauline Hopkins, writing at the turn of the century to transform the lives of black people menaced by lynchings, by racial discrimination, by poverty.

"The dictionary defines joy as 'the emotion evoked by well-being, success, or good fortune, or by the prospect of possessing what one desires.' Thus, our ability to rejoice is related to what we desire.

"But can we learn to rejoice over the coming of justice, over the large and small transformations in our own lives that signal such a triumph? Can we learn to rejoice over the healing of the brokenhearted, the liberation of the captives, over women and men putting on the mantle of justice? Can we learn to rejoice over such things? Can we learn to proclaim our joy when the lowly have been raised up, when the hungry have been given every good thing?

"I think the ability to rejoice is a spiritual gift. It is given to us as we are able to share in the destinies of the poor, the broken-hearted, the lowly. And it is a gift we must continually ask of God."

I could feel a kind of passion swelling in the congregation during this oratory. The "Amen"s gradually grew louder and more widespread, and at the last sentence, the people in the pews erupted into applause. A vigor had been gained that even the solemnness of the Eucharist couldn't check. The portions of the liturgy in plainsong were so ardently sung as to seem almost untamed, on the brink. I sat quietly in my pew while the congregation proceeded to the communion rail, and the blight of isolation that had begun in me—when? surely long before Perry's death—remained untouched and untutored. I felt mocked by this buoyant fellowship as I stood mute during the jubilant singing of "I've Got a New Name over in Glory and It's Mine, Mine, Mine"—an outcast as I stood mute with my hands in my pockets during the endless repetition of the refrain.

At coffee hour, which was held downstairs in an enormous basement room, I was approached by a man who proclaimed, his eyes filled with tears, that I must be Perry Lambert's brother. He introduced himself as Hank, my brother's "trainer," the disciple who'd presided over Perry's studies for joining the church, a young black man with a large Afro and wire-rimmed glasses, a seminarian who had been assigned to this parish for his field work. He was extremely sad about Perry. "I can't get over it," he said to me, shaking his head. "I just don't understand. He was at the threshold."

I asked him whether Perry had spoken to him of any worries.

"He was one of the most positive fellows I'd ever met," Hank said. "I can't figure out how I could've got it so wrong. I thought he was happy to be alive. He was enthusiastic about his studies—I mean his spiritual studies. He was getting involved in things, started working with the kids at Mainstay, taking—"

"Mainstay," I said. "Is that an orphanage?"

"Not exactly," he said. "It's for abused kids. The court's taken them out of the abusive home and they're waiting for trials to be over or waiting for placement in foster homes. Perry used to take them to the Yankee games or to the park, stuff like that."

"Where can I find it?" I asked.

"Here in Brooklyn," he said. "Just a little ways from here, in Boerum Hill. You ought to talk to Faye Barrymore, she runs it. She started it, in fact."

The name was familiar to me, but I couldn't think why.

Hank said, "The woman who preached today in church. I thought you must already know her. She was rushing off right after Mass to catch a plane. On her way down to Virginia — something to do with your brother."

Sunday night, Jane came over to the apartment after dinner, around nine-thirty. A heat wave was enveloping New York, and though after dark the temperature dropped a bit, the walls in Perry's place seemed to have closed in, compressing the stale air. The ponderous black Baldwin crowded the room like never before. Molly stayed in the bathroom, belly-down on the tiles, her tongue hanging out the side of her mouth.

When she arrived, Jane looked at me, noting my slightly yellow sheen, and said she was worried about my health. I took this as half truth: she was really worried about catching something from me. I managed to coerce her into staying over and sleeping with me, overruling her protests about making love in Perry's apartment, about her still not feeling at ease there. But when it came time for lovemaking, she was entirely at ease — and *I* couldn't. This, backed by the force of its cruel nomenclature ("impotent," nasty word), took on the full weight of symbol: it summarized my life. Jane was kind and reassuring, which didn't help because she was too kind and too reassuring, as if she were administering charity to the terminally ill. Most unsettling, she said, "Oh, I don't care," and it was clear that she really didn't.

It wasn't long before she wanted only to sleep—her regular classes were to begin the next morning—but I insisted on telling her about my day: the church, the woman who gave the sermon, the home for children. She listened politely, showing only mild, sleepy interest, and when I mentioned the name Mainstay, she said sleepily, "Oh, yeah, that's right."

"You mean you knew the name all along?" I said.

"Well, now you mention it," she said, "I think he did tell me once."

As outside on the street, even at this hour, children played in fire hydrant fountains, screaming at each other in a patois of Spanish and English, the silence inside grew oppressive, and I began one of those sorry, painfully comic dialogues that goes something like:

Do you want to go home?

No, do you want me to?

Only if you want to.

I want to only if you want me to.

I don't, unless you want to.

Well, why did you bring it up if you didn't want me to?

I thought you wanted to.

Jane ended up staying—from inertia, I thought, more than anything else. She kicked off the bed sheet and lay naked, simple and unashamed, the slightest bulge of pregnancy just below her navel. Her last words were, "Perspiration, the body's air conditioning," before she fell into a sound sleep, leaving me wondering at the ease with which she could drift off and envying her that apparent refuge.

The next morning she climbed out of bed carefully and got dressed while I pretended to sleep. Through one half-open eye I watched her go out the door, the click of the latch bolt in the striker plate a sudden memory. I didn't know what was wrong. Vaguely, I felt she wasn't on my side. But I didn't know what that meant. My side of what?

After she left, I slept without dreaming, and when I woke sometime later, I woke with a sharp longing—completely, unambiguously in love, consumed with a feeling of deep, eternal love for Jane Owlcaster.

Karajian's was the first of a chain of phone calls. "How'd it go?" he asked, too cheerfully, I thought.

I had fallen back to sleep, the phone had waked me, and I couldn't think what he meant exactly. My night of failed lovemaking with Jane? My night of failed sleep?

"The funeral," he added after a moment.

"Oh," I said. "A good time was had by all."

"Sorry," he said. "I only ask because, you know, I feel responsible, hooking you into the Spinellis like I did."

"Everything went smoothly," I said, shamed by my sarcasm.

"You know, I told you they do good work. The son—the brother-in-law—he's a jerk, I mean as a person. But I wouldn't've recommended them if I didn't think they did good work. By the way—"

"The reason I called you," I interrupted, "was to get the name of the man, that construction worker, who saw Perry fall."

"What do you want that for?"

Stupidly, I hadn't anticipated this question. It occurred to me that somehow I blamed this anonymous witness, and I suddenly felt a complete fool. "I just thought I'd have a talk with him," I said finally.

"What for?" said Karajian.

"What difference does it make?"

"I have to tell you," he said, "it's not something I would generally do. I mean, I wouldn't necessarily withhold it from you, but I would recommend you go back over to the station and read the report first. Then if you still have questions and feel like you really need to talk to the guy, you could discuss it with the captain. There's the man's privacy to consider. I don't really understand what you're looking for, to tell you the truth."

"Forget it," I said.

I must have sounded defeated, for Karajian said, "How's it going?"

"I don't know what you mean."

"You know, the brother stuff."

"The brother stuff," I said. "The brother stuff is not going very well."

"That's what I figured," he said. "I was going to call you this morning even before I saw your message. I thought you might still be over there at your brother's place. How long were you down in . . . where was it? Carolina?"

"Virginia," I said. "About ten days."

"I figured. I've got something here you'll be interested in. A Lucy Barr. That name mean anything to you?"

"No," I said. "Should it?"

"A woman named Lucy Barr phoned the station while you were away in Virginia. A shrink. Said she was worried about your brother. He'd missed two or three appointments. She'd been calling his place night and day and never any answer. She wanted somebody to check it out. Anyway, the uniform at the desk ran your brother through the computer and—well, you know. I got her number here if you want it. You want it, don't you?"

Then Jane called around noon: "No, I didn't know. Of course, I didn't know. Don't you think I would have told you?"

"I guess so," I said.

"You guess so."

"Okay, I know so."

"He was seeing somebody a long time ago, but the guy turned out to be crazy. I didn't know Perry had started up with anybody new. Have you called her yet?"

"Not yet," I said. "I'm about to. I was just going to call when the phone rang."

"I'm late for class anyway," Jane said. "I wondered if you could meet me over here at the school this afternoon."

"What for?"

"A surprise. Can you come up to the fourth floor around four-thirty?"

I said okay and hung up. Then I telephoned Lucy Barr. I explained that I was Perry Lambert's brother and very much wanted to make an appointment. Soon. In a friendly voice she told me she was glad I called and that she could see me that evening at six-thirty. She said she looked forward to our meeting.

As soon as I hung up, the phone rang again: Welles Barclay, Father's old lawyer, telephoning to say that he had expected to see me in Norfolk that morning. He had set up an appointment with Mother days ago for the reading of the new will. She had assured him she would let me know. Now neither one of us had shown up.

What new will?

Didn't I know?

About two months before his death, Perry had drawn up

a new will with a New York attorney. The attorney had contacted Mother as soon as he learned—too late for the funeral—about Perry's death; she had put the New York lawyer in touch with Barclay. Arrangements were made, at Mother's insistence, for the will to be read in Norfolk. It had been read that morning, and well, frankly, it had been very embarrassing with no family members present. Where was I? Where was Mother?

In the new will, Barclay explained, Perry had altered all his bequests. He had left nothing to Mother and all his personal belongings to me, excepting the piano. The piano, the trust, and all other pecuniary assets went to—

"Don't tell me," I said to Barclay. "Mainstay."

"A pretty colored woman showed up at the office this morning," said Barclay.

I asked him what we could do.

Certainly, he said, we could contest the new will. Perry's suicide, the new will drawn up so close to it, and Perry's having gone to a new advisor instead of to Barclay himself could all be key factors. Perry was seeing a psychiatrist? That could help too, depending on what the psychiatrist had to say.

A while later, just as I'd begun getting dressed to leave the apartment, the phone rang yet again. "Darling," Mother said, happy and clearly sober. "We're calling from Tahoe. Isn't that grand?"

"Who's we?" I said.

"Raymond's with me," she said, then laughed nervously.

"Raymond?"

"Yes, dear. I needed to get away, as you can imagine, and Raymond, well, he insisted on coming along. Hang on, Marty, dear. He's right here and wants to say hello."

Before I could protest, she was gone from the line, and next I heard Raymond.

"This must be a surprise, Marty," he said. "Us out here."

"What are you two up to?" I asked him. Mother had never taken Raymond with her on any of her trips; appearances alone would have prevented that.

He lowered his voice. "It hasn't been smooth sailing, Marty. I'll explain more another time, but things are better now."

"Raymond," I said, "I just had a call from Welles Barclay. Did you know anything about Perry's having a new will?"

"No," he said. Then, away from the phone: "Helen, do you know anything about Perry's new will? Welles Barclay called Marty this morning."

I could hear a small shriek in the background. Then Raymond said, "I think she knows something about it, Marty. Here, I'll put her back on."

"How could I possibly tell you anything when you were so angry?" Mother said when she got back on the line.

"Why don't you just admit that you forgot?" I said.

"Okay, Martin, if that will make you happy, I forgot. I've had a lot on my mind. What happened?"

"Perry's left everything to some kind of home up here in New York."

"Home?" she said.

"A home for children," I said.

"Oh," she said. "Well, it's exactly like him, isn't it?"

"Welles thinks we have a case against the will, considering Perry's suicide."

"Well, I don't know anything about that . . . I guess we would," Mother said. "I'm sorry I forgot, Marty. It was the slip that did it."

"How are you feeling?" I said.

"I'm happy, darling," she said. "We stopped over in Reno last night, and —"

"Reno?"

"Reno, Nevada, darling, and on the plane this morning to Tahoe the stewardess asked me if I wanted a drink and I just smiled and said ice water. All I wanted was ice water. And that's all I've had. I'm happy. I've decided I'm even going to finally start my book."

"Book?" I said. "What book?"

"Why, 'Everything Interesting,' of course. The story of my life."

"I don't get it, Mother," I said. "How can a shopping bag full of newspaper clippings be the story of your life?"

"Well, I selected them, didn't I?" she said. "I clipped them all out. You just wait. You'll see."

Before Raymond got back on to say goodbye, I could hear them giggling away from the phone. "Like I said, I'll explain more another time," Raymond said. "God, Marty, I wish you could see the view out this window. It's exactly, I mean exactly, like a postcard."

I felt vaguely uneasy after this call. I sat crosslegged on Perry's bed and looked at Molly, who, stationed under the piano, had been surveilling my every movement. She needed to go out, and she was waiting for me to make even the slightest gesture of exit. Sighing heavily, I resolved to finish getting dressed, and I did this—the simple task of putting on clothes—with such a ridiculous sense of resignation that it made me stop for a moment to take stock. I looked around the room: a half-empty bottle of Scotch stood on the floor next to the bed, an empty water glass beside it; my dirty clothes were in a heap in a corner; from where I sat I could see two empty dog food cans on the kitchen floor; a sour bath towel lay across the threshold to the bathroom; the air in the room was stale and warm, and yet I hadn't bothered to open a window. My eyes burned, my throat was dry, and I suddenly felt short of breath. I reached for the bottle, poured a shot into the glass and drank. I looked around me again and made the plainly accurate connection: the apartment had undergone a transformation with my brief tenancy. What had been the studio of a musician was now the sad, gray, and slightly smelly room of a drunk.

I quickly walked Molly, then went for a bus uptown. I knew I should try to get some food into my stomach, but the thought of it made me queasy. I ducked into a place called Charlie's and downed a double Scotch on the rocks, then proceeded to Broadway to wait for the bus. As I stood on Broadway, in the sweltering afternoon heat and amid the scrimmage of tourists and those who feed on tourists, it occurred to me (in a vague, loopy sort of way) that we were all debilitated by the same mysterious pollution, that the demon who'd possessed Perry now possessed me; possessed the bald man behind me who, standing before a phosphorescent pink door, barked, "Girls inside, girls inside!"; possessed the dirty-looking white kid, no older than twelve, who strutted down the sidewalk with a snarl on his face, slapping the end of a lead pipe in the palm of one hand. Our eyes met as the kid neared me, and he gave me such a malevolent look that I actually felt my spine tingle. When he stopped to linger among those waiting at the bus stop only a few feet behind me, I was suddenly, fleetingly certain that this angry ragamuffin child was no less than my executioner. When the bus came, it was not air conditioned. I took a seat at the very back, atop the hot clattering engine, where the exhaust fumes collected. In one of the long seats for three that faced the aisle I noticed a young woman so cowed by the terrible condition of her skin that she kept her head lowered, sneaking horrible, destitute glances at a handsome young boy across from her. Then I noticed that my boy, the one with the lead pipe, had taken the seat next to the rear doors, and that he had turned sideways in the seat and was now staring directly at me. I was sure I saw vengeance in his eyes—even his snarled lips mouthed some venomous, spiteful oaths—and when a man came and stood with his back to me, a cellophane-wrapped package of uncooked shrimp protruding from the back pocket of his jeans, I practically leapt for the doors and off the bus. It was not so far to walk.

A sign inside the glass doors of the school's immense lobby informed me that anyone entering the building was required to show his ID. I assumed this meant student, or in some other way official, ID. Jane had given me no instructions in regard to getting past the uniformed security guard who slouched in a chair behind a desk near the elevators, watching a miniature television. I decided to walk confidently past him, hoping to be taken for faculty. But at the back of my head I heard a Caribbean accent, a magisterial voice something like a heavy electric tool: "What is your business here, please," it said.

I turned, still feigning confidence, and answered, "I'm meeting someone on the fourth floor."

"What is the name of this person you are meeting, please?"

"Jane Owlcaster."

He looked at me for a moment, then shook his head. "I do not know her," he said at last. He continued looking at me, as if he meant to hypnotize me and then get at the real truth. I shrugged my shoulders.

After another moment, he smiled and said, "I do not know everyone. You look okay."

Though I suppose I must have been happy to have been allowed to enter the building, as I rode an elevator to the fourth floor it seemed insulting to have been so quickly judged harmless by the security guard. I stepped off the elevator into a dimly lit, gold-carpeted hallway with glass-slotted doors on either side: practice rooms. I could see Jane far away down the hall, sitting on the floor outside one of the doors. She appeared to be studying some music propped against her knees. Something about the sight of her, engrossed and so far down the dark hall, sent a wave of fright through me. Between us was a young and extremely skinny Chinese girl with a bowl haircut, carrying a violin case and walking in my direction. She touched my arm as we met and said in a very small voice, "I've seen you before."

"I've never seen you," I said.

"Perhaps I made a mistake," she said. "I've never seen you either. I've seen someone who looks like you. I hope you aren't looking for a practice room."

"No," I said.

"Are you a pianist?" she asked.

"No," I said.

"Do you have a dollar?" she asked.

I reached into my pocket, took out a dollar, and gave it to her. She trapped the violin case between arm and rib cage, and turned the dollar over and over in her hands, as if she were checking to see if it was counterfeit. She wore black slacks that stopped above the ankles like pedal pushers, tiny black flats, and a boy's white dress shirt with tails hanging out, buttoned at the neck. She looked up at me, smiled enormously, tucked the bill into her shirt pocket, and moved on.

"I didn't expect to find little beggars up here," I said when I reached Jane.

She stood and kissed me on the cheek. "Her mother's an opium addict," she said. "At least that's the rumor."

Jane opened the door to the room and asked me to come inside. A Steinway grand piano, taking up most of the small room, glared under fluorescent lights; velvet curtains covered the walls. "Cheery," I said as I sat on the piano bench.

"Did you see the shrink?" she asked.

"Not until six-thirty," I said.

"Marty," Jane said. "I say this as someone who cares about you. You look like hell."

"Thanks," I said.

"Are you getting sick again?"

"No."

"Well, what's going on?"

"I'm haunted, didn't you know?"

"Haunted?"

"Never mind. I've had a crazy day. It turns out Perry made a new will leaving everything to that home in Brooklyn. And Mother has suddenly flown out to Tahoe with Raymond and they called a while ago acting very giddy and stupid. She was supposed to tell me about the new will, but it slipped her mind."

Jane was silent for a moment, and when I looked up at her it seemed there were tears in her eyes. She nodded as she said, "That would be just like him"—a version of the same thing Mother had said, but far more appreciative. Jane wore a simple white sun dress, her hair pulled back in a ponytail. It occurred to me that we could cover the narrow glass pane in the door with something and ravage each other under the Steinway, but suddenly I didn't know who the hell she was.

She must have seen bewilderment on my face, for she quickly added, "I mean, as far as the will goes, does it really make any difference?"

"I had thought," I said measuredly, "that *you* might do with some of that money."

"I don't want it." She shook her head. "That was a part of my decision to have this baby. That I could manage alone."

"Well, we're going to sue to reverse the will, anyway," I said. "That's family money. Father gave that money to Perry. It belongs to the family. Mother could use it."

"For what?"

"Never mind," I said.

"Marty, think about it. Perry obviously wanted to do something good. It seems wrong not to honor his wishes."

The little room seemed to shudder slightly as its velvet-draped walls inched in a bit. The long fluorescent tubes buzzed over my head. Now I could see clearly that, from the beginning, I'd had a sense that Jane Owlcaster had betrayed my brother in some way—it lay just beneath the surface of my infatuation for her. Hadn't I had enough nightmares to warn me away from her? I wasn't haunted at all. Perry had only been trying to protect me.

"You haven't been on our side from the beginning," I said to her quietly, surprising even myself.

She looked incredulous. "What on earth are you talking about?"

"I've felt all along that you betrayed him in some way," I said. "And that's why you're so afraid of my finding out the truth about why he killed himself. It's why you've been so unhelpful."

Now tears brimmed her eyelids—tears, I thought, at my having found her out. But she said, "Marty, have you had any sleep at all?" She reached out to touch my forehead, but I pulled away.

"First of all," she said very calmly, "Perry was not Jesus of Nazareth. We need to establish that. And second of all, all I have said here is that I think his wishes concerning his own money should be honored. I think you're much more strung out than either of us realized. I think it might be a good idea for you to see a doctor."

Her unexpected concern for me, as well as her logic, disarmed me for the moment. I saw immediately that she was right. The echo of my own words inside my head did sound like the drivel of a lunatic. I wrapped my arms around her waist and held on. I said I was sorry. I said that she was right, I hadn't had much sleep. That I couldn't eat—the sight of food made me sick. I said I thought I was coming apart. I said I needed her with me. That I didn't want to be alone. That I felt afraid to be alone.

She stroked my hair. She did not say anything about being with me—I wasn't even sure what I meant by that—but said I just needed to rest, to get some sleep. Maybe I should ask Perry's shrink for some pills. When I said I thought that was a good idea, we held each other for a minute longer.

"Now, do you want to see your surprise?" she asked, pulling away.

She walked behind the piano and lifted an instrument case up from the floor. She opened the case and removed a cello, pointed its red scroll at me like some kind of deformed knob of flesh in a nightmare. "I checked it out for you," she said. "I've got some music here, too. Stuff I can fake my way through at the piano if you're up to it."

I smiled, but I did not reach for the cello.

"Maybe this isn't the best time," she said.

I looked at her and nodded. "Is this supposed to be a test?" I said.

"What are you talking about? I've never heard you play."

"I don't like this," I said.

"Don't like what?" she said, her eyes wide. "What have I done wrong?"

"If you had wanted to hear me play, you could've asked," I said. "You didn't need to trap me like this." I stood up and went for the door.

"Trap you? Marty, I don't understand what it is you think I've done."

"I can't trust you, that's all."

"It's just a cello, Marty. A musical instrument. I don't know what you mean."

"You're playing dumb," I said. "You don't want me to find out why Perry killed himself. You haven't wanted me to from the beginning."

"Marty, Perry killed himself because he wanted to die. It's that simple. It wasn't a conspiracy."

She sat down on the piano bench, lowered her head, and began really to cry. I thought, rightly, that it was her first frank moment of bereavement, and maybe this would have moved me—fanned my last smoldering coal of humanness—maybe, called on to console, I could have come to my senses, but she began speaking again, through tears. "Don't you see, Marty?" she said. "All this searching and anguish is what you're doing instead of grieving." She paused, gathering strength for what she was about to say next. "It's just like you and me falling into bed together. It's crazy. We don't really love each other. How could we? We're just trying to grieve. Or trying not to."

This was the last piece of the puzzle, and now I could see

the exact, unambiguous picture of why she'd called me up to this torture chamber. I wondered when exactly she had meant to spring it on me—just after our jolly duet, perhaps?

Someone knocked at the door, and I yanked it open to a robust-looking man with a red beard, who looked past me at Jane and said, "You know, Owlcaster, if you're not rehearsing in here, I could use this room."

"Fuck off, Spooner," Jane said.

I pushed rudely past the young man and started down the hall toward the elevators. Jane called to me from outside the practice room door. When I turned I saw her and the red-bearded man standing in a trapezoid of fluorescent light, both of them so white they might soon evaporate, their flat faces fogged with anticipation, as if they expected something from me, some word, some pardon, so I said what came into my head: "If you had told him you were pregnant, he wouldn't *be* dead."

The last thing I heard before the elevator doors shut was the distant, still slightly hostile but softened voice of Spooner saying, "Are you pregnant, Owlcaster? I didn't know you were pregnant."

Lucy Barr, a woman of about fifty, freckled and almost radiant in the dim lamplight of her darkened study, smoked little brown cigarettes and crossed her legs in that slanted, entwined way that only very thin women can accomplish, one knee over the other, one foot hooked behind the other ankle. I sat in a green leather recliner right next to an air conditioner, its drone in my ear heightening a sensation that I had come to Lucy Barr's study with none of my vital systems intact. They'd been shutting down one by one all day long, all over town—short-circuiting, hissing, and sputtering out. (This impression might have had something to do with the two additional Scotches I'd had in a bar on Sixth Avenue just before announcing myself majestically to Lucy Barr's doorman on Central Park South. I'd been asked to wait—which I did indignantly, next to a planter of dusty plastic delphiniums in the orange-carpeted lobby—and eventually a signal was sent down to the doorman indicating that I'd been granted permission to proceed.) At her door, Lucy Barr remarked on my resemblance to Perry, a response that had become tiresome.

Inside, she first explained to me her policy of confidentiality. Implicit in her contract with Perry was an understanding that he had to stay alive—he had in effect breached his end of the deal by killing himself—and now it was a matter of her own discretion what she chose to reveal to a close family member. Then she quickly added a kind of disclaimer: she had just begun with Perry, had seen him only three times. She actually knew very little about him. There was nothing in what he'd told her that she felt she needed to exercise discretion over. He had been experiencing some depression but had never mentioned suicide. As far as she could tell, he'd been suffering what most clinicians would call a philosophical crisis—he felt his life and work were meaningless—and he struggled with coming to terms with certain resentments about his past.

Prematurely, I mentioned the new will—a tactical error that caused me to lose and never to regain her confidence.

"I can't help you there," she said unpleasantly. "Your brother was of sane mind as far as I'm concerned."

"Then why did he kill himself?" I asked.

"A lot of people kill themselves," she said.

"He was going to be a father," I said. "He has an heir he didn't know about."

"The question of the will isn't any concern of mine," she said, shaking her head. "I didn't know that was why you wanted to see me."

"It's not the main reason," I said. "I thought you might tell me why my brother killed himself."

She lit a fresh cigarette, thoughtfully. "I'm afraid I didn't know him well enough to help you," she began and quickly ran down a list of what she called Perry's "issues." He'd come to think the composition of art music was esoteric; he thought there were about twelve people in the world who had any genuine interest or appreciation—and he thought that was about the size audience it deserved. And of course he felt terrible about Father's death, about his having been allowed to die at such an early age. Perry saw a pattern in the previous generation, in our grandfather's having been allowed to fly that airplane in Colorado while drunk. And he was very angry with Mother, because of her having threatened to take us boys away from Father unless Father agreed to give up his intended recital career. Oh yes, and Perry was worried about *me,* worried that I had a serious drinking problem. "But I'm certain you must already know all this," she concluded.

Lucy Barr wanted to be rid of me, that was clear. It occurred to me that she was in need of some comforting—after all, a client of hers had killed himself and she hadn't even known he was suicidal—and I'd turned out to be nothing more than a voyeur with a calculator in my pocket, seeking the dark secret that would win me my brother's estate. "I'm very sorry about your brother," she said conclusively, rounding her desk, ready to show me to the door.

Rejected, I informed her that there would probably be something for her to fill out, a deposition or something, when we went to court.

"That would be a waste of everyone's time, Mr. Lambert," she said. "Perry was perfectly sane, perfectly capable of making his wishes clear."

We were at the door. "That's probably a matter of opinion."

"Yes," she said. "That's exactly what I would be called on to give, wouldn't it? A professional opinion."

I left her office without the sort of answer I wanted, and certainly without her good will. Still, without knowing it, Lucy Barr had surprised and disturbed me. I had not known that our grandfather had been drunk when he crashed the Piper Cub into the side of that Colorado mountain, killing himself and our young grandmother. And I had not known that Mother had threatened Father with taking Perry and me away from him.

As I walked toward Columbus Circle, the sky began to release a heavy pelting rain, and I stalled under the nearby canopy of another apartment building on Central Park South. The young doorman—he might have been a drum major in his black uniform with lavish gold trim and a double row of brass buttons—came and stood next to me. He yanked at his collar, then jammed his hands into his pockets, gazing out at the rain. "Thank Christ, huh?" he said. "Some fucking relief at last."

I didn't mean to, but I must have turned on him the face of a condemned man. Though Lucy Barr had held me at bay, finally, her accidental news had been sobering, and with sobriety came a good deal of shame: the unearthly image of Jane Owlcaster rose before me, waxen and bleached in that garish trapezoid of light, miles away down a hallway, holding the neck of a cello. Wasn't my behavior of the last few hours only the culmination of a lifetime of misguided stupidity? Wasn't I doomed to bungle things?

"Days are getting shorter, too," said the young doorman carefully, raising his eyebrows, quietly turning and sneaking back toward his glass doors, back toward safety.

As I climbed the creaking stairs in Perry's building, I thought of Father, late, near the end, standing with his back to the library windows, rapt, listening to the bleak voices that must have chronicled his life. At such moments he might have been hearing music, but none played. He'd always been ready to admit that he was shattered by the sudden death of his parents. He was ready to admit that he blamed his father for the death of his mother—and he blamed this tragedy for the failures in his own life. But he had always blamed his father's age, his father's poor judgment, never his drinking. Was he blind to this truth, or did he know it, deep down, and only deny it? I saw now that of course he must have known it—otherwise, how could Perry have known it?—and that it was one of the truths that generally got voiced inside the dark well of his stupors, of his sad reveries. That one, and the truth about himself and Mother, about their little arrangement. If I'd ever thought about it, I would have realized that Mother's simply threatening to leave Father wouldn't have been any threat at all. She would *have* to have threatened to take us away from him. It didn't matter whether or not she could have actually done it (after all, she was a drunk, too). All that mattered was that she'd come up with something Father wouldn't dare to risk. And why did Perry know these things while I didn't? Simple: I had never asked.

Once inside the apartment, I telephoned Jane. It was shortly after eight o'clock. The rain had stopped, leaving New York in a steam bath. I wanted to tell Jane that Lucy Barr had been a bust, and I wanted to say how sorry I was for everything, that she had been right all along, about everything, that probably she was right even about us.

When Dorothy answered the phone, she faltered, stammered: "No . . . Jane . . . isn't here right now . . . uh, she . . . can I take a message?"

I could envision Jane clearly, standing a few feet away from Dorothy, coaching her with hand signals.

"Dorothy," I said. "I really need to talk to her. Will you please tell her I really need to talk to her? It's very important."

"Hold on," she said. After a moment, she returned to the line and said, "I just needed to get a pencil."

"Some actress you'd make," I said to her. "Please tell her I don't blame her for not wanting to talk to me, but I'd really like to talk. Tell her I think she's right about everything. I'm at Perry's. Please."

Poor neglected Molly came over to the bed and wedged her nose under my hand. I pushed her away, went to the kitchen, where I poured a drink, and then returned to the bed, bringing the telephone on its long cord and the bottle of Scotch with me. I placed the phone on the floor next to the bed and stared at it as I drank. I don't know how much I drank, but I did it earnestly, with so grim a sense of purpose that it felt like a punishment.

Sometime later in the night, I was startled by the ringing of the telephone right near my left ear. In an alcoholic sleep, I must have continued to struggle with the problem of Jane Owlcaster, for when I reached for the phone, it was as if no time had passed since I'd tried reaching her, and I was certain that this was she, calling back. "Thank you," I said into the receiver. "I'm sorry. I'm going crazy—"

I heard brief laughter and a woman's voice saying, "Excuse me?"

It was Faye Barrymore, the woman I had heard preach . . . when? Could it have been only the day before? She was calling to invite me to Mainstay and wanted to give me the address in Brooklyn. She had heard through the grapevine (which could only mean that Welles Barclay had told the New York lawyer about my intentions) that Perry's family was not pleased with the new will. "But before you do anything," she told me, "you should at least come down and see the place. Your brother was devoted to us, Mr. Lambert."

A sharp pain, a stab of heat, passed through my head. "Frankly, I don't think we should even be talking," I said. "This is a legal matter as far as I'm concerned."

"I realize that, Mr. Lambert. I realize that it is a legal matter. But it is also a human matter. And I think you should see Mainstay. Don't you want to at least see the place your brother was so deeply devoted to?"

"I appreciate your concern," I said. "But this isn't a very good time—"

"Someone told me you looked like him," she said quickly.

"I really must go," I said.

"Well, I hope you'll come and see us," she said. "Just take the IRT, get off at Hoyt Street, and walk south six blocks."

"I really have to hang up now," I said.

"We're in the building with the big windows," she said. "And the vine on front."

*

Jane did not return my call. Who could blame her? I had another drink and collapsed onto the bed. From my position so near the floor and on my back, the large room seemed imposing, forbidding as its lines and curves rushed at me. I thought of Perry's teacher, Max Dolotov—the irony in his having called Perry an imperious little trumpeter when Perry himself saw his life as meaningless, saw his successes as failures, his promise as weakness. And how ironic that Max Dolotov should have been so close to the truth when he advised me that if I was looking for someone to blame for Perry's death, I should look closer to home. I thought of my own dull perceptions of the two of us, my having always cast us in opposing roles, Perry playing "found" to my "lost." And that night, when I fell into a deep, long-needed sleep, penitent and self-loathing, I had what was to be my last nightmare on the subject of my brother.

We are piloting a small airplane, the dome of its cockpit impossibly huge and paned with the muntins of our library windows at home. We are in high spirits, and in an entirely dreamlike way I know that we are en route to see Father—I have the sure sense of Father's waiting for us somewhere. Outside, I can see only the white gleam of the engine cowling and the pencil-roughed hoop of the propeller blades against the white clouds that envelop us. Perry, too, is milky white, as if drained of all blood, and I think it's only the blinding glare of the clouds. But the whiteness enters the incisive whir of the engine and a white heat begins to pulse the metal floor beneath my feet. Perry says something funny, something that tricks me and makes me laugh as he points a finger at my chest and says "Gotcha," but suddenly his face changes and I look out the French windows just in time to see the wall of rock, the hideous surface of an asteroid with no bottom and no top and no sides, loom up and rush toward us . . .

Trembling, not fully awake, I telephoned Welles Barclay at his home in Norfolk. When finally he answered, I said in a voice I couldn't quite identify as my own, "We've got to get that fucking money, Barclay. What I didn't tell you is that Perry was going to be a father. He's going to have an heir."

"Marty Lambert," said Barclay. "Do you know what time it is?"

"No," I said.

"Well, call me in the morning, for Christ's sake," he said and hung up.

I threw the receiver at the telephone and sat on the piano bench, dazed. Then I went on what could only be called a rampage. I tore books and records down from the shelves. I pulled clothes from the dresser drawers and the closet, searching the pockets. I rifled through Perry's desk, flinging papers as I went. I even dumped the silverware from the counter drawers in the kitchen. I did not formulate an idea of what I was looking for. I had no notion of how much noise I was making—some peculiar sounds of rage, not words, erupted from me. God only knows how this fit would have climaxed had I not suddenly seen Molly cowering in a corner of the kitchen: Perry's black retriever, frightened for her life, pressing one side of her face against a wall, glancing at me, looking away and whimpering, scraping her feet against the floor and slipping, trying to force herself through the wall.

I moved toward her carefully, knelt on the kitchen floor, and coaxed her to me. Doubtful, she dropped her head and lumbered slowly toward my hand. Seated crosslegged on the cool linoleum, I pulled her awkwardly into my lap, helping her to fold her legs, holding her, comforting her. I told her I was sorry — sorry for having frightened her, sorry for having neglected her these last few days, very sorry for everything. I rocked her and told her I had been mistaken about so many things. I told her I missed my brother — You miss him too, I said to her — and that I missed my father, and that I was having some kind of trouble that seemed bigger than me, and that neither of them was around to help me. I continued rocking her and told her that of course it wasn't Perry's *money* I wanted back.

The following night, I asked the taxi driver to let me off at the gate to our long driveway, just as I had done ten years earlier at Thanksgiving, but this time I walked up the sloping lawn toward the house with my new best friend, Molly, at my side. My brother's retriever ran ahead, leaping and bounding, herding me up the gentle hill, very happy to have been released from the cargo bay of the plane and from her fancy kennel (which the airline let me leave in a store-room at the terminal). It was a windy night, though warm — warmer even than New York — and now and then a half-moon found a clear spot among the rapid clouds. Floodlights on two corners of the house burned bright, and lights inside as well, both upstairs and down. On either side of the house, the pecan trees erupted into motion, sagged and swayed, their lower branches so heavily laden that they nearly swept the ground. Horses stood dozing in the pasture beyond the dark cypresses, emerging and fading in the intermittent moonlight, and farther away, beyond the farthest line of trees, heat lightning flashed two, three, four times. There was the hushed, momentary sound of wind in a bordering field, and for an instant I thought I heard music coming from the house—the long brassy slur of a sax, a brush on a cymbal—and then it was gone . . . gone, and a swell of nostalgia broke over me, so abrupt it took my breath away.

I have said that my childhood began with Perry, which is to say that my life began with him, and in some way, ever afterward, he was my focus and my legitimate link to my family. I have also said that on my first day in New York, as I visited the police station, full-blown sorrow over his death, still brewing at sea, had not yet reached shore. The time of its eventual arrival remains distinct for me. It was precisely as I sat on the floor of Perry's apartment, rocking and consoling his dog—finally stripped of any hope about the survival of my marriage, finally stripped of any illusions about sidestepping grief by taking up a new passion (possessing Jane Owlcaster, overturning Perry's will), finally resigned to the truth that the reason for my brother's suicide was not, as Jane had put it, a single answer. I did not cry. Sorrow's arrival was not marked by tears but by clarity: the next morning I knew I wanted to go home. And that night, as I walked up the long drive to our house, that general truth took on detail. I had needed this heavy air with its occasional coastal scents, this slope of crabgrass and dandelions and dogwoods, these massive trees and surrounding pastures, these vistas and all they summoned. It could no longer be true that my life began with Perry, for what did that mean now that he was gone?

I had not drunk on the airplane to Virginia, though I'd felt a strong compulsion to. I sat in the john the whole time cocktails were being served, choosing the awful disinfectant and exhaust fumes over the risk of relieving my symptoms with the thing that had caused them. Another aspect of my new clarity: the agitation, insomnia, loss of appetite, nausea, even the vivid dreaming and the powerful sensation of short-circuiting, were surely all symptoms of the seesaw of drunkenness and alcoholic withdrawal I'd been riding daily. In the john, I had a bad case of the shakes, but the roar and rumble of the jet engines saturated me, resonated with my poor jittery cells, which felt like a kind of sympathy. I thought I might be running a fever. Periodically there was a knock at the door, but I figured I had paid my fare and if I preferred to travel in the toilet I had every right.

It did not escape me that I was hiding out just as I had done as a child in the powder room at home, and I had a clear, suddenly explicit recollection of being sick as a young child, running a high fever, delirious in the middle of the night. My nurse, Marion, in tears, is having a heated exchange with Mother in the hallway outside my bedroom door. A single lamp burns next to my bed—a cowboy roping a steer—a towel or scarf thrown over its shade to darken the room. Mother appears, her face pasty, eyes bleary, Marion behind her. They both wear long dressing gowns, and from my vantage point it looks as if Marion's head grows out of Mother's right shoulder. Oddly, this has a kind of logic to me. I am much more concerned about my ankles feeling so swollen they might burst, and about the long flat piece of timber I can see floating outside my bedroom window.

Mother says something solacing, not quite convincingly, and I ask her, "Do I have to ride on that board in the sky?" It seems to me that the large piece of lumber hovers outside because it means to take me away.

"No, no, darling," Mother says. Then over her shoulder, to Marion, bitterly, "He's hallucinating, for Christ's sake. Get on the goddamn phone. I'll stay with him, okay?"

As soon as Marion leaves the room, Mother rests her head on my stomach, her suddenly copious hair reeking of perfume, and in another moment she's sound asleep. A raucous wind kicks up outside, Mother begins to snore, and I am crying, completely convinced that our house is going to collapse — I can hear it creaking deep within, plaster cracking, beams splintering, the shrill sucking sound of nails torn from wood . . .

As I turned onto the lawn and continued up the slope toward the house, Molly advancing and retreating on the grass, I recalled how this febrile sense of our house falling down lingered with me long after the illness (rheumatic fever) had passed, how sometimes at night, throughout my childhood, I would awaken doused with terror of our house collapsing.

Mother and Raymond had not yet returned from Tahoe. Possibly I *had* heard music out on the lawn: a radio played in the kitchen, though the program, as I entered the house, was a talk show. I spent the first few minutes wandering around the rooms, touching things — the bronze deer on the mantel in the library, the red spines of the *Encyclopaedia Britannica,* the pink strawberry-shaped soaps in a basket in Mother's bathroom, a glass box in Perry's room that itself held, among other objects, a set of onyx studs, a silver puzzle ring, a miniature pine cone, a small tin harmonica, several sea shells and sea-smoothed rocks — as if these items were amulets and I meant to conjure good fortune for myself. What I actually felt was the need to connect.

I happened to be walking down the front stairs, thinking

about connections—and the sense I had, in my craving drink, of not being properly wired—when all the lights in the house went off. It took me a minute to understand that the lights, along with the radio in the kitchen, were on a timing device, and I thought how implausible this abrupt blackout would look to any enterprising burglar who might be watching the place. Molly, having identified the bottom of the stairs as some sort of midpoint in the house, had fallen asleep there, and I almost tripped over her in the dark.

For the next several days, glorious and dramatic weather moved in: stark blue skies and hot sun, cumulus clouds stacked high and sailing with monumental laziness, then violent, passing electrical storms each afternoon. I bought what groceries we needed at the nearby market, simple things like dog chow and corn flakes (a bowl of cereal around midday was all I could stomach). I turned off the air conditioning in the house, opened the windows, and let in the warm weather (the cold air gave me the chills). I let my beard grow (the very thought of drawing a razor across my face gave me nausea). Mornings, Molly and I took long walks into the countryside and sometimes napped in a grove of oaks (I was alternately restless and sleepy). We drank from a spring in the side of a rock wall in the woods (my thirst was immense). At home I became an ardent nudist (fabric against my skin seemed to sting). I lay naked by the pool and let the sun purge me, let it sweat out any poisons, then washed them away in the pool. Any time, day or night, that I felt myself lusting for a whisky fix, I went outside, stripped, and threw myself into the pool— a ritual that felt, with its inherent qualities of surrender and immersion, almost religious. If I meant to atone and purify, I had taken a primitive tack. I had become a worshiper of sun and water. When I slept, I often dreamt of drinking, of being drunk. Once, I had a very elaborate Shakespearean dream full of suicide, fratricide, patricide, and conspiracy in which all the characters had the brand names of Scotch: MacGregor, Sir Dewar, King Henry IV, Glenlivet and his doppelgänger Glenfiddich. I suppose, too, that in wandering naked among the rooms of my childhood, I meant to make myself more vulnerable to their influence.

Molly displayed all the esprit de corps of someone in love and on holiday. Romping in the fields and leaping after dragonflies were her favorite pastimes, but she was also attentive to me, the Joshua who'd brought her to this promised land. She most often followed me on my naked excursions around the house. She even kept me company by the pool. At first, she would leap into the water each time I did, despite the chlorine's making her sneeze. With time, she merely walked to the tiled rim and barked. By the third or fourth day, from her prone position in the shade, she would only raise her head and direct an apathetic gaze at the naked fool splashing in the water, and eventually she didn't even do that, but simply let her brown torpid eyes do all the work. In the evenings, she took up her post at the bottom of the stairs, or if there was a thunderstorm, lay at my feet in the library.

I had found, in a deep drawer of Perry's bedroom desk, the spiral notebooks he used to write in when we were teenagers. Mostly they contained fanciful stories with caricatures of people we knew: Felicia and Teddy, operating a housekeeping scam in Newport, pilfering valuables from rich people's homes; Max Dolotov, running off to a trained-seal act in a circus; now and then a straightforward entry, usually about Father's health; some comical drawings—one of me playing the cello with my feet. But most eccentrically, page after page of definitions copied out of Webster's. Some of these seemed to reflect a kind of vocabulary building, and others a fascination with semantics ("obdurate—hardened in feelings, resistant to persuasion or softening influences"; "gyroscope—a wheel or disk mounted to spin rapidly about an axis and also free to rotate about one or both of two axes perpendicular to each other"; "ditty box—a box used for the same purpose as a ditty bag"; "music—punishment for a misdeed"). At night I read these, sitting in the wing-back chair in the library, the chair where, years ago, Father had chosen to sit and drink into the wee hours. Outside in the trees, the penetrating whir of cicadas rose and fell and eventually went unnoticed. My reading transported me: more than once I looked up from the page surprised to find myself in the library; I hadn't gone to the various settings of Perry's narratives, but had imagined myself just across the hall, in the now extinct music room.

One of these nights, I looked up from the page aware that I was ravenously hungry for elementary foods, meat and eggs and bread. And another night, I found that I no longer had the shakes. Something inside me had ceased to tremble.

Still, when it was time for sleep, I felt a certain dread—that loneliness and insomnia awaited me at the top of the stairs. But I slept in Perry's bedroom, and each night, in the minutes before drifting off, I was flushed and filled, lulled and kept unlonely, by memory. The piecemeal history that emerged reassured me; for the first time, I began to see myself as a primary player in this history—or at least that was how my memory began to work. I recalled again, for example, my first day of grade school, and walking home in the afternoon along a dirt road—Lambert Road, named for us, the family who owned the biggest house. I could see the Colonial mansion on its hill in the distance, the four columns supporting a portico, the porte-cochère outside the library's French doors. The weather is still very warm; the leaves have not begun to turn. Dewberries grow along the wire fences on either side of the road, cloaked in dust. A truck barrels out from around the curve ahead, leaving me in a dense cloud that makes me cough and wipe my eyes. My first-grade teacher—a heavily made-up elderly woman with dyed red hair, a clown in a nightmare—yelled at me today during reading period. We sat in a semicircle before the green chalkboard and took turns reading out of a soft-cover primer. I was first to read, did well, then closed my primer and looked out the window. (Two enormous crows were fighting for position atop a telephone pole.) The story was about an imprudent boy who painted the floor of his playhouse, but stupidly began at the door and painted himself into a corner—which, either in its details or in its moral, seemed overly familiar to me. My closing the primer angered the teacher, who shouted from across the semicircle, "How do you expect to learn anything sitting there with your *book* closed?" She was extremely thin, and somehow her voice matched the sharpness of her bones. *Book,* the way she'd fired it, sounded almost exactly like a gunshot, and I noticed that some of the other children in the group cowered. I did not cower. There was nothing especially new to me about this sort of ballistic explosion from an adult. I knew that at another time, the teacher would be quiet and gentle, affectionate, even gushing: what I had come to expect.

The great, new thing is this change in my life, school—an occupation that takes me outside the big house on the hill with its deceptively still and solid-looking exterior. Even before I mount the front steps, I can hear the sound of Father's piano. His playing means that he has been sad. These days, he only plays when he has been sad. He wanders despondently into the music room and stares into the huge oil portrait of himself as a boy, the painting with the Saint Bernard. Sometimes he inspects one of the carved, scary-looking African masks on the grass-cloth walls of the music room, and laughs or shakes his head, amused. But after laughing, he is immediately sad again. He takes a bottle of whisky out of a bamboo cabinet and refills his glass, then finds his seat at the piano. Most often, he fetches me to sit on the rattan couch and listen to him play, or if not me, then Marion, our nurse (never Mother). And as he begins to play, something wonderful happens: he changes. Often he appears angry during the process of this change, but by the time he stops playing, he is normal, himself, calm and kind and sleepy.

Today he plays Beethoven. I will soon turn six, and I know Ludwig van Beethoven, both the music and the man, the deaf composer, though when I was a bit younger I occasionally confused him with the inventor of the light bulb, Thomas Edison, who lost his hearing as a boy when he was pulled by the ears onto the back of a moving train. This did not happen to Beethoven—it happened only to Thomas Edison—but I still have to remind myself of that now and then. I have a child's artistic impulse to marry the two events, the composition and the moving train. And I am very fond of imagining deafness. At night, when I think I hear our house disintegrating, I try to intercept this terror by pressing pillows against my ears and willing myself deaf. How odd that in this musical family one of my earliest longings is for deafness: the silencing not only of the nocturnal creakings of the Colonial mansion but of the regular jagged peal of breaking glass, of the grownups' zingers and spiny laughter, and of Father's terrible, smashed wrong notes.

Inside the music room, Marion sits on the couch and holds my baby brother in her lap. Perry is nearly two and strikingly handsome with his perfect features and perfect white teeth, though right now, the way Mother has drunkenly cut his platinum hair, bowl-like but uneven with very short bangs, makes him look slightly idiotic. I have been mindful of Perry's care, a mindfulness that Marion encourages. In the beginning, when he was an infant, I envied the kind of fussing my parents did over him. Rightly, I saw that something was different with Perry; they were devoted to him in a way they'd never been with me. But when I studied my parents' faces and saw that they appeared happy, my envy waned and came to be replaced by hope: I wanted Perry to be good, to succeed where I had failed. I put great store in his success at changing our mother and father. And it seemed to work for a short while. Now I have my doubts. Our parents went overseas for quite a long time—a surprising, inexplicable thing to do—and soon after their return they seemed to take the baby for granted. Now they are unhappy again.

When I enter the music room, Perry sees me and lurches forward, out of Marion's arms. His feet hit the floor and he begins running toward me, squealing my name. It is the day I have recalled before, the day my family all converged on him as if we meant to tear him apart, as if we each meant to possess a piece of him. Perry's foot comes down in a puddle of liquid on the floor—spilled whisky, no doubt—and he flies forward, his chin connecting with the wood. There's the overturned whisky glass, the starburst of glass splinters, Mother's perfume and hysteria, and soon I've wrenched Perry away from the others, I've got him under the arms and I am running with him out of the room, out the front door, down the lawn toward the line of cypresses at its base. I'm pressing him tightly against my chest, his legs swinging back and forth, his hard shoes kicking into my knees. When at last we are under the trees, I sit with my back to the house, holding Perry in my lap. Very soon he stops crying and climbs down. We both kneel under the low branches of the trees, and I breathe in the piny scent of the leaves as I examine Perry's face. His nose and chin are red and splotchy, but there's no blood. "Are you okay?" I ask him, and he nods, sniffling. With his hand he brushes aside some of the dry brown leaves, like brittle lace on the ground, to reveal the insects underneath — pill bugs, earwigs, and smaller, black things with twitching antennae. He likes to touch the pill bugs and make them coil into their neat, gray-armored globes.

I turn and see Father out on the lawn, his hand sheltering his eyes, scanning the expansive stretch of grass for where we might have gone. Finally he spies us and begins walking slowly down the slope, his white shirt rippling in a breeze. When he reaches us he sits close by, Indian style, not quite under the cypress branches, and doesn't say a word. He looks at me and smiles. But suddenly tears mount in his eyes, and he stands quickly, walks between the trees and into the adjacent field. Perry and I both stand, too, and move out from under the cypresses. We watch Father go into the field, down toward a distant grove of oaks. Perry points a finger at Father and asks "Where?" just as Father stops, folds his hands behind his back, and looks straight up at the sky. Perry and I look up, but there's nothing there, not even a wisp of cloud, only a boundless dome of pale blue air. I have a moment of dizziness, in which the world seems to turn bottom side up — I am staring *down* into the blue well of the sky — and a rush of anxiety lodges in my chest, like a hummingbird trapped in my rib cage. I've had this feeling before, this breathless motor of apprehension . . .

Another time, earlier, perhaps a Saturday morning—hard to tell, since each day is more or less the same. Mother and Father have not yet returned from their long trip abroad. I sit on a high stool at the long oak refectory table in the kitchen. Upstairs, Perry, an infant, wails. He hates diaper changes, being lifted or moved too fast, having his face washed, people leaving rooms, and loud noises. Understandable complaints, but often he cries for no apparent reason. Marion—once my nurse, now his—has explained that he cries to let us know he's hungry, or sleepy, or not feeling well, or missing Mother and Father, or just about anything else that makes him feel unhappy. She has been teaching me how to do things for the baby—how to feed him, bathe him, rock him to sleep. She and Raymond both say that I'm a good helper. Once, when Perry began screaming so loud that we all thought he was having some kind of attack, I was the one who discovered that a diaper pin had come loose and was sticking him in the hip.

But now, this morning, I have awakened from a night of bad dreams, and Perry's crying bores me. I feel tired of everything in this house, especially tired of the daily struggle of *what to do*. Upstairs, Marion asked me to entertain my baby brother, and I told her, in my most petulant tone, "That's *your* job." She referred to the passage from the Bible about "my brother's keeper." The first night after Mother and Father left for overseas—swept away in a whirlwind of gaiety and forgotten details and leaving me amazed in the entry hall— Raymond produced a book of Bible stories filled with terrifying illustrations of bearded men and snakes and strange,

Egyptian-looking architecture; now he reads from it each night at my bedside. Cain and Abel is the story in which the word "slew" means "killed" and does not mean "a lot," as in "a slew of people" or "a slew of toys." It's ridiculous for Marion to conjure Cain and Abel, since even in my most passionate fits of jealousy, it has never occurred to me to kill my brother.

At the table, I watch Raymond polish a huge silver epergne, at which he appears to be angry. He concentrates very hard as he works; he's even forgotten the cigarette that burns away in a nearby ashtray. He has just advised me that I must remember to cooperate with him and Marion, and I have told him that he is not my father and Marion is not my mother, that I don't have to do what either of them tells me, and that if he were my father I would run away from home.

"And just how would you do that?" he asks, keeping his eyes on his work.

"I would ride one of the horses," I say, meaning the horses that graze in the pastures around our house.

"And where would you sleep?"

"On the ground."

"And what would you eat?"

"Leaves."

"Well," he says, "it sounds as if you have things pretty well worked out. Maybe it's not a bad idea after all. Maybe you *should* run away."

Silent for quite some time, I think about what he has said. Because Raymond appeared in our house so close to the time that Perry was born, I have mistakenly thought that Raymond was acquired, like Perry, at the hospital, that he was part of a package; though he's often kind to me, Raymond seems, in my struggle to know what's definite and mine, just another part of Perry. I hold my breath for a moment, then begin to breathe shallowly as I lower my eyes and keep my head very straight so I can see, through the blurred crosshatch of my lashes, only what is directly in front of me; it is what I do to calm the fretful pulse of apprehension I so often feel inside my chest. After a moment or two the pulse is absolutely quiet, and I begin to feel so numb and light I think I might float to the ceiling. I can still hear Perry's wailing, but it seems far away, like something heard over Father's old console radio in the library.

Without another word, I carefully climb down from the stool and go into Father's study behind the front stairs. On the broad mahogany desk I see a picture postcard: biblical-looking men, robed and turbaned, on camels, enormous palm trees, three pyramids in the distance, turquoise sky; on the amber-colored stamp, an engraving of the aqueduct near Akko. I have memorized the words written on the card addressed to me and Perry. It reads, "We ate lunch near here . . . missing our darlings . . ." I open the right-hand drawer of Father's desk and take out the heavy black automatic pistol that I've been told never, ever to touch. I carry it back into the kitchen and stand at the opposite end of the refectory table from Raymond. I aim the gun at the spot where the stone from young David's slingshot hit and killed Goliath. Raymond looks up just as I pull the trigger. Complete silence follows the dull click—there is no clip in the gun. Raymond comes toward me. I believe he will slap me, though he has never done that. I follow him through the rear sight on the pistol and pull the trigger twice more before he takes it out of my hands. He kneels beside me, puts his arms around me. I stiffen at first, but then I feel tears sting my eyes.

"I'm sorry," Raymond says.

When I say nothing, he says, "Do you know? I've heard it's been so cold they're skating on Wilmer's Pond for the first time in half a century. We could go ice skating."

I already know that it's winter, an unusually bitter one, but I feel oddly surprised by this knowledge, this reminder.

"Now let's put this nasty old thing away," says Raymond. "Somewhere we'll never have to even see it again."

We did go skating that day. We bought ice skates and Raymond took me to Wilmer's Pond. More than twenty-five years later, as I lay half asleep in my brother's childhood bed, I recalled vividly the wobbly feeling in my ankles, the colorful sock caps on the heads of the skaters, the smell of woodsmoke from the fires along the shore of the pond, my amazement at Raymond's gliding away across the ice with his hands behind his back and my bitter, inexorable pang of remorse. Even many years afterward—after the day I aimed the gun at Raymond's third eye—I could not determine for sure whether or not I'd thought the pistol loaded. I thought I hadn't known anything about the specific processes attending bullets and guns, and I thought "loaded" had been a word, like "drunk," that I'd heard hurled between my parents when they meant to hurt each other. Father would tell Mother that she was too loaded to do whatever it was they had planned to do in the evening; Mother would say she was not loaded, but Father would cancel their plans anyway. And when she protested, he would say, "Helen, for crying out loud, you're *drunk*."

For years I heard them say this to each other. Father finds Mother in the library playing solitaire at the game table, cursing the cards under her breath, cigarette hanging from her lips, its ash about to drop. "You're *drunk*," he says to her from the doorway, disgusted. "You're *drunk*," Mother says to Father in the music room as he lies on the couch staring at the ceiling, the record on the phonograph having finished some time ago, now rasping again and again in its last groove. In the entryway, gripping her braceleted wrists—is she about to hit him?—he says to her (a harsh whisper, for there are guests in the library), "You're *drunk*." Long before I knew what the word meant, I identified it as the meanest thing they said to each other. And when I finally knew that it was what you got from drinking whisky, it seemed a very strange thing to accuse each other of, since they were always drinking whisky.

Or used to be. Father quit drinking whisky for several months while he was rehearsing for his recital, and on that rainy afternoon when he and Perry and I lay on our backs in the music room, staring at the wooden ribs under the Steinway, I thought about this. I was eleven now, to Perry's seven. (We enter the house together after school, Mother sees us in the entry hall, calls to us in her overly loud, afternoon voice, "Well, if it isn't seven come eleven!") It's pouring outside this afternoon, and Father, beside me, is sound asleep with his hands folded over his heart. It's been a long time now since Mother said to him, "You're drunk," though she seems even angrier with him these days than when he used to drink. They have had one of their cryptic showdowns this afternoon, and Father has brought Perry and me with him into the music room, where he'd been practicing. The three of us have crawled under the piano—to rest and talk, I suppose—but now that Father has fallen asleep, I'm not sure what we're doing here. I sit up and start to slide quietly away.

Perry sits up too and whispers, "Where are you going?"

"He's asleep," I whisper back, as if this is the obvious answer to where I'm going.

Perry shrugs his shoulders and lies back down, folding his

hands exactly like Father's. (I think of the Russian wooden doll in Father's study, the hollow Cossack whose body comes apart at the waist to reveal a slightly smaller, identical soldier inside.)

I return to the library, where Mother, Felicia, and Little Teddy are playing cards. They sit at the inlaid game table Mother brought back one trip from Italy, a beautiful thing now scarred with cigarette burns. Its top flips over — a chessboard on one side, backgammon on the other — or comes completely off to reveal a roulette wheel underneath. There's a terrible odor in the room, like the smell of burnt hair.

"I think he actually intends to go through with it," I hear Mother saying as I enter the room.

"I don't think it's such a bad idea," says Teddy, and Mother rolls her eyes.

"You wouldn't understand, darling," says Felicia, patting the back of Teddy's hand.

"Marty," Mother says, seeing me. "The prodigal returns. Come here, darling."

I go to her and she wraps her arms around me, squeezing me tight. "I'm glad you're back," she says. "Teddy has something to say to you."

I look at Teddy, whose eyes grow very wide as he inhales on his cigarette. "This is ridiculous," he says softly to no one in particular. He rises and moves to the bar.

"Me too, me too," cries Felicia, holding up her empty glass.

"Down, girl," says Teddy from the bar.

"We're all waiting," Mother sings, still cradling me with one arm.

"Oh, for heaven's sake. Martin, I'm sorry I called you a stick-in-the-mud before," says Teddy quickly, all in one breath.

I look at Mother, then down at my feet, where I notice a large black burn in the carpet.

"Well, what do you say?" she asks me.

I think for a minute, then say, "I don't know," which is the truth.

Felicia says, "You say, Go sit on it, Teddy."

"Felicia!" Mother cries, but they both immediately erupt into peals of laughter. Mother, releasing me, begins taking cigarettes out of a pack on the table and throwing them at Felicia, who bats them away, squealing.

As I turn to leave the room, I hear Teddy say, "Oh, very funny, Felicia." Then, "Honestly, Helen, sometimes I honestly can't tell when you're serious and when you're not."

"Neither can I, Teddy, neither can I," says Mother, still laughing.

I go to the front door and look out one of the sidelights at the endlessly gray, pelting rain. It's time I should be practicing my cello, but since Father, the enforcer of practice, is asleep, I decide to put it off until he awakens. I see our mailman, Mr. Minor, coming slowly up our drive in his old beat-up green Ford. Most of the houses have mailboxes down on the road, but Mr. Minor has always brought our mail to the door. I step outside under the portico, and when he sees me, he pulls the Ford up alongside. He rolls down the window, saying, "Hello, Marty. How are you getting along on this wet day?"

"Fine," I say.

We're half shouting at each other because of the noisy rain.

"And Master Perry?" he asks.

"Fine."

"And your folks?"

"Fine."

I notice that he's wearing his short-sleeved shirt, and I'm wondering whether or not I'll see the dread elbow when he hands me our mail.

"Well, that's just fine," he says, smiling, and then I do see it, the horrible patch of seed warts on his right elbow, caked and cracked like the dried-up alluvial plains I've seen in the pictures of my geography book.

When I return to the entry hall, I hear Mother in the library, giggling. "Maybe just a little one, okay?" she's saying.

"Oh, come on, Helen," Felicia says, "more than a little one."

Naturally, I think the subject of this exchange is a drink. But just as I'm about to pass the library door, I hear Teddy say, "It's that wretched nurse who's responsible."

"Oh, she is not," says Mother. "I'll concede that he's a *little* stick-in-the-mud, okay? Maybe he's seen some things he shouldn't've. He's an awful lot like his father. Now please shut up about it."

. . . I stand in the powder room under the stairs, the door closed and locked. Safe, but I can't stay in here forever. I'm expected outside, meaning "in the world," anywhere outside this room. It isn't musical performance I dread; I have not yet begun to play the cello. This is dim, early, before Perry, before music. I look down into the toilet, and inside my chest there's a motor going—I can't get a deep enough breath . . .

. . . behind a door, the triangle behind an open door, the world comes through the inch-wide crack between the edge of the door and the jamb—comforting to have it narrowed this way, contained, spun into a rope, but I still hear the voices, and I can't breathe deeply enough, and something hums and pulses inside my chest, a gyroscope on the string of my breath . . .

For thirteen days the telephone never rang. Except for the cashier at the local market, to whom I announced one afternoon, pointing to a bag of tangerines she'd just thrown onto a scale, "Those aren't mine," I spoke not a word to another human. The gardener stopped by one morning very early to do the lawns, but I only waved to him from a great distance. I became brown out by the pool, my hair and beard sun-bleached. Occasionally, I talked to Molly about some of the things going on inside my head. (Dozing intermittently in a chaise, I turn to her and clear my throat. We each open one eye. "If he'd only stayed alive," I say to her, "we might've eventually discussed some of this stuff." Or, dreamily, "Was I really that frightened and unhappy before he came along?" Or, emerging from a reverie, "Oh, I get it—punishment for a misdeed, as in 'face the music.' ")

On the fourteenth day, around noon, the phone rang (Mother had installed a ghastly bell under the eaves of the terrace, a shrill alarm designed by a hysteric). In my dream at poolside, Molly approached me as the dog-queen of paradise, adorned in an enormous necklace of magnolia petals, and when the bell rang, I thought it signaled the end of the world.

George Michaels had inadvertently tracked me down. He'd been telephoning Mother to ask if she knew where to find me, and he hadn't expected me to answer the phone. Caught off guard, he couldn't quite correct his tone of repugnance. Our conversation was minimal. He said, Where the hell are you? I said he should know the answer to that question, considering that he'd just dialed my home in Norfolk. He reminded me of some important contract meetings we had scheduled for the first of October and asked me how I expected to run a business if—

I interrupted him. I told him I did not intend to return to California and that he should get his investors lined up as soon as possible; I was granting his long-suffering wish to buy the company. He asked whether I meant it, because if I really did, he had had his partners lined up for some time. He figured "something in the neighborhood of two hundred *K*." I said that would do—which surprised him, I could tell. I said he should get in touch with Ben, our mutual lawyer, to draw up the papers. At the end, his voice took on a penitent cast. Perhaps he even recalled that I had gone back East to bury my only brother. He asked me how I was doing. He called me Boss. I didn't answer his question, but said I wished him well and that I'd always been grateful, even though I may not always have shown it, for the careful way he'd run the company. He stammered for a moment, then said, "Oh, by the bye. Some woman named Faye Barrymore's been phoning out here from New York. Left several messages. You want the number?"

I told him no, then he stammered some more until I helped him get off the telephone.

As soon as I hung up, I went into the butler's pantry where the liquor had always been stored and opened the cupboards. Except for a single deep-cut crystal decanter, pushed way to the back of a shelf, containing about three fingers of what looked decidedly like Scotch, the cupboards were bare of liquor. I pulled the decanter forward. Around its neck, a little silver ID bracelet: Hooch, it said. I took down the decanter, carried it to the kitchen counter, found a short glass and poured it half full. I don't know how long I stood there naked, staring into the glass of amber liquid, not quite daring to pick it up, but eventually I caught sight of Molly through the windows above the kitchen sink, gamboling on the lawn and rolling in the grass. I thought of her in my dream, how silly and innocent she'd looked, and I was moved by the fact of her entering my dreams in so giddy a way. I thought such an instinctively whimsical image must surely betoken, however ephemerally, a will to live. It could be that this mannered reasoning was a trick of the mind or a gift from God, or both. But it worked. I emptied the glass and the decanter into the sink and returned to the pool, where I threw myself in the cool water.

A short while later, the telephone rang again. This time Molly followed me into the house and stood at my feet, as if she'd been anticipating a call. The woman at the other end—her voice vaguely familiar to me—asked to speak to Mrs. Lambert. When I told her that Mrs. Lambert was out of town, she said, in a surprised tone, "Is this Mr. Lambert?"

"Yes. Martin Lambert."

"Oh, Mr. Lambert, how provident. This is Faye Barrymore calling from Brooklyn. I've been trying to reach you. To see when you might like to come out to Brooklyn. To see Mainstay."

I told her I didn't have any idea when I would be returning to New York.

Molly worked her nose into the palm of my free hand, and I began stroking the top of her head.

"Oh," Faye Barrymore said, disappointed. "Well, I do hope you'll make a special effort, Mr. Lambert. I don't think you can get an idea of how important Mainstay was to Perry without . . ."

Outside, I heard what sounded like an invasion of sea gulls, a birdlike yapping, and then Molly was charging for the pool, pushing open the screen door, and out. I told Faye Barrymore that someone or something was outside and that I needed to hang up. Quickly she told me again the directions to Mainstay, gave me the Boerum Hill address, and the next thing I knew I was squinting, trying to focus on an odd tableau across the pool: Molly, frozen, growling fiercely, had Little Teddy pinned against the Roman brick wall next to the terrace gate. Teddy was wearing a Hawaiian pineapple-print cabaña outfit and holding a bird cage, with a panicky parakeet inside, high up over his head. Next to his pale, thin, extremely hairy legs, Mother's two miniature dogs yapped excitedly.

I called out to Molly, but she wouldn't relent until I'd gone over and grabbed her by the scruff of the neck. I squatted beside her, saying, "It's all right, girl, it's all right," and Teddy slowly lowered the cage, wide-eyed, still visibly frightened. "Teddy, it's Martin," I said. "I'm Martin and this is Molly."

He stared for another moment and then said, "Good heavens! Marty, you look like some horrifying thing out of . . . I don't know what. The Bible, I guess."

I laughed, surprised by how glad I felt to see Teddy.

"You better put something on," he said. "Felicia's right behind me. And hang on to that black beast, will you?"

I was just slipping a robe on when Felicia Snow appeared in a bright pink muumuu, jingling her many gold bracelets. Unlike Teddy, she recognized me immediately and greeted me warmly.

"Would you look at him," said Teddy. "He's like something out of the Old Testament. He's like Robinson Caruso."

"That's *Crusoe,* darling," said Felicia. "Caruso was a tenor. And neither one of them were out of the Bible."

"Whatever," said Teddy. "He almost scared the daylights out of me."

"Don't tell me," said Felicia to Teddy. "You need a drink."
Then she asked me what on earth I was doing home.

"Actually, I came down to see Mother," I answered.

"They're coming back today," Felicia said. "We're making a little party for them. She's going to be surprised to see you here."

"That's if she recognizes him," said Teddy.

"Oh, don't be silly," said Felicia. "Of course she'll recognize him. Oh, Marty, you do know about Helen and Raymond?"

"What do you mean?" I said.

She paused for a moment, trying to read my face. She glanced quickly at Teddy. "Well," she said at last. "Helen and Raymond have gone and got married."

"Now what do you think of that?" said Teddy.

"Married?" I said.

"That's precisely what I said," said Teddy.

"Well, I think they're deliriously happy," said Felicia.

"Or just delirious," said Teddy, and Felicia stared a dagger through him.

"What brought this on?" I asked.

"Well, I think Helen needed something . . . well, something new," Felicia answered. "She's become so very serious since—you know. She needs something new now. A new life, and she sounded very happy to me on the phone yesterday."

"Ha," said Teddy.

Rolling her eyes, Felicia said, "Teddy thinks Raymond is after Helen's money or something. Teddy doesn't understand about things like love and history."

"Oh, bull," said Teddy. "I understand plenty. Don't get me wrong, Marty. I've always liked Raymond. I can't say that I ever thought him the marrying type, but I always liked him."

"You don't know anything, does he, Marty?" said Felicia.

"Your brain doesn't even start working until after five. I'm just glad Helen has something . . . well, something *new*."

With one hand, Felicia shielded her eyes from the glare of the pool and looked hard at me. I suddenly thought how, in her own boozy, bumbling way, Felicia had always been a good friend to my mother—certainly not a good influence, but at least a steady presence, maybe a buffer against loneliness. I smiled at her. All I could think to say was, "Well, if they're happy . . ."

"They're blissfully happy," said Felicia. "Marty, I wonder if maybe you ought to pretend you didn't already know about this. Helen'll kill me for telling you. I'm sure she wanted to tell you herself."

Then Felicia told me I looked like an absolute berry, and told Teddy to help her fetch the things from the car. "Marty," she said, "wait till you see the glorious *saviche* and French bread we've brought from Anthony's."

As they moved through the gate, Teddy whispered something, to which Felicia said aloud, exasperated, "Yes, I brought the bloody marys."

When I turned back to the pool, I saw that Teddy had put the bird cage, a wire bell jar, on the diving board. And the two little dogs, Pomeranian and Pekingese, were quietly sniffing the ankles of the black giantess, Molly, who stood polite and regal and patient in the shade of an umbrella.

Mother and Raymond were scheduled to arrive in Norfolk at around four in the afternoon, but when we telephoned the airport to confirm the time, we learned that a fuel leak had been discovered in the plane that was to carry them from San Francisco to Chicago. The flight had been canceled, and the passengers were being farmed out to various other flights. All we could do was wait at the house, checking with the airline from time to time and hoping to hear from Mother or Raymond. When they finally did call, around five, I answered the telephone, which was a shock to Mother. "Oh, Marty, what are *you* doing there?"

"I came down for a rest," I said.

She quickly explained about the plane and said they would keep us posted. Then there was a pause on the line; I heard her say something away from the phone. Then she said, "Marty, darling, brace yourself, because I have to tell you something. Are you braced?"

"Yes," I said.

"Well, this is nutty." She began laughing now, squeezing the rest out in fits and starts. "But Raymond . . . our own dear Raymond . . . asked me to marry him . . . the poor dear thing."

"I know," I said.

"Felicia told you," she said.

"It was an accident," I said. "She assumed I already knew."

"I wanted to tell you myself, dear. I wanted you to know how very sweet Raymond's been. Said all he'd ever really wanted to do in his life was take care of me. And I thought, well, why not, really?"

"But Mother," I said, "I always thought Raymond was, you know, not really straight . . ."

She lowered her voice. "Oh, who knows? He's straighter than you'd think. Mainly he wants to make a commitment, and I think it's very sweet. I mean, he deserves it, Marty, don't you think? I don't have that much anymore, God knows— I'm not exactly Happy Rockefeller—but he's entitled, don't you think? He's always been just like family anyway."

she would join them soon, but at five-thirty she had still not appeared. By then, I'd had my fill of Teddy and Felicia, while Raymond—who hadn't planned for them to stay to dinner and wanted them to leave too—was looking more and more flustered. Felicia and Teddy still treated Raymond like a servant. Sprawled on the sofa with her stocking feet in Teddy's lap—he was administering a foot rub—she asked Raymond to make her a drink. When Raymond said that he didn't think she needed another, both she and Teddy were amazed at such insubordination. Felicia handled the moment with aplomb. "Raymond," she said, "I give you my solemn oath that I'll go to one of Helen's AA meetings if you'll get over to that goddamned bar and make me a double martini, two olives."

Teddy thought this was the funniest thing he'd ever heard.

Raymond, ignoring them both, led me out of the library and into the entry hall. "Somebody's going to have to drive them home," he said.

"What's with Mother?" I asked.

He shrugged his shoulders and turned toward the stairs. This time I followed him up. Mother was coming down the hall as we reached the top landing. "Helen," Raymond said warmly, almost as if he were surprised to see her, and offered his hand.

"Sorry, darling," she said. "This was the best I could do."

She had changed into black silk pajamas and a matching robe with huge eruptions of blue-dyed ostrich feathers on the shoulders, something a female impersonator might have worn in a Bourbon Street revue. "Marty," she said to me, smiling. "I'm so glad you're here."

"Are you all right?" I asked.

"Whatever do you mean?" she said.

"Well, if you're content to—"

"Oh, Martin, please don't be that way. Why don't we face it, darling. I'm an old drunk. What other prospects do I have? And he does take good care of me. You've always been fond of Raymond. I think you even love him in your way. Isn't that true? And I know you know he loves you. Now will you just say hello and be very nice?"

Before I could protest, she was gone from the line, and next I heard Raymond.

"You don't have to approve, Marty," he said. "I don't expect you to approve. I know you'll have to get used to it. I know it must be a shock. Oh, she's been so sad, Marty . . . if you could only see her . . . well, I don't expect you to get used to it over-night."

"It doesn't matter what I think, Raymond," I said after a moment. "I'm happy if you and Mother are happy. It's just a big surprise."

"I feel proud, if you want to know the truth," he said. "I'm very proud, Marty. Take some time to get used to the idea. I know it must seem like some kind of crazy whim to you. We don't expect you to love the idea overnight."

"Raymond," I said, "how long have you been thinking about this?"

"Marrying your mother?" he said. Then, proudly, "Oh, Marty, I've been thinking about it for at least ten years."

The "party" Felicia had planned was nothing more than a light supper, the guest list comprising only herself and Teddy—and then spontaneous me. So we ate the *seviche,* and Teddy and Felicia drank an indeterminate number of bloody marys. Early in the evening, Felicia and Teddy competed with each other for my attention. "Stop interrupting, Felicia," Teddy would say. "I'm *trying* to talk to *Marty*." But as they grew drunker, their sense of rejection at my not joining in grew deeper — which eventually united them, and they began to talk about me as if I weren't in the room.

"Well, what can you do?" said Felicia to Teddy. "Martin was a serious child and he grew up to be a serious man."

"Really incredibly rike Ludy," said Teddy.

"Oh, yes," said Felicia. "Incwedibwy wike Wudy."

Gales of laughter.

At dusk I took all three dogs for a walk and stayed away until past dark, hoping Teddy and Felicia would leave. The dogs and I walked a mile or so down the road, away from town, to the marsh beyond the pastures, a place where, as an adolescent, I had collected insects. I let the dogs run free, and found a large stone to sit on that afforded me a view of the sunset over the marsh. I thought about the news: as far as I could tell, Mother and Raymond had married in order to cheer each other up, which may have been as good a reason as any. And I felt surprised by my own easy acceptance of the news. It seemed more evidence of my new clear-headedness. Still, I was plagued a bit by the past — by the other news, about Mother's scheme to take me and Perry away from Father — and I meant to confront her with this. I meant to make her sort out some of this history with me.

But right now I felt oddly at peace. Despite Teddy and Felicia, I had stayed in good spirits. And I was glad that Mother would be home soon — I felt ready for her. I composed in my mind a poem about Molly among the sedges / While the little dogs kept to the edges. I became entranced by the effects of the dying light on an enormous flock of red-winged blackbirds. They seemed to grow agitated as the light waned, flying out of the rushes and lighting in nearby trees, returning quickly to the marsh, only to repeat the pattern time and again, as if they were debating where to spend the night.

On our way back home, under the black arms of the live oaks on either side of the road, fireflies put on quite a show.

At the house, I happily saw that my plan had worked: Teddy and Felicia had jumped ship, leaving me the food, dirty dishes, and ashtrays to clean up. In the kitchen I found a note from Felicia, which began, "Marty where *are* you?" It seemed Teddy had a splitting headache . . . Mother had telephoned again from California . . . still didn't know when they'd get a flight out, might even go back to the Huntington . . . delighted that I was home.

I went to bed early, and for once fell asleep quickly and slept like a stone. Sometime during the night, I was awakened by the sound of adult voices—Mother and Father, coming home very late as usual. They didn't seem to be quarreling. Mother spoke to the dogs in baby talk. Doors opened and closed. Toilets flushed. I went back to sleep hoping tomorrow would be a good day, hoping they wouldn't be too sick, and that Father would maybe take us downtown to the docks and a movie.

Their mountain of luggage was in the entry hall in the morning. I did my best to keep the dogs quiet. I showered, then clipped and shaved off my beard, exposing the considerably lighter skin beneath. When I went out to the pool, I wore swim trunks. Raymond was first to appear, around noon, in a long white bathrobe and carrying a tray—a pitcher of iced tea and some glasses. He was very cheerful and tanned. He told me with great amusement that last night had been his and Mother's first night in the house as husband and wife, and that they hadn't given any forethought to sleeping arrange-ments. "I followed Helen into her room," he said, taking the chaise next to mine and crossing his legs. He pulled a kitchen match from a pocket of the robe, struck it on the terrace bricks, and lit a Kool. "I wish you could have seen the look she gave me. It was like the look you'd give an intruder. She's been very nice, Marty, very happy. We've been very close. And then she looks at me like, What are *you* doing here?" Raymond thought for a moment, apparently recalling Mother's face, and cackled. "Everything in good time," he said.

"Where did you sleep?" I asked him.

"In my old room, of course," he said. "I actually didn't mind. It's just that we have to make changes. It wouldn't be right just to go on as usual."

I pointed out to Raymond that even Father had never shared Mother's room and bed — not overnight anyway.

"I know," he said. "But that was different. Helen and I are good friends. It'll just take some getting used to. For all of us. She wants to make changes too. She wants me to become the man of the house. She said so. I can't very well do that and live in the servants' quarters, can I? I wish you could have seen her face. She pushed me out of the room."

And from the screen door to the kitchen we suddenly heard Mother's voice: "I did not *push* you."

She strode onto the terrace as if it were a stage, her best face forward, hair and make-up just so, pink silk dressing gown billowing behind her. Mother was still a beautiful woman, striking, but this entrance was too artificial even for her. It meant that she was nervous. After we embraced, she looked at me and said, "Marty, you have a two-toned face. You look wonderful, but your face is two distinct colors, tan and bright red."

She was not thoroughly glad to see me. I explained about the beard, and she began enumerating several tanning lotions and après-sun creams she had upstairs in her bathroom. Why had I not used any? And oh my God, what were the babies doing out there on the lawn with that immense black creature?

"That's Perry's dog," I said.

"Perry's?"

"Yes."

"I didn't know Perry had a dog."

"Molly."

"Well, she's—she's lovely. She won't hurt them, will she?"

"No," I said. "She's very gentle. They seem to be great friends already."

"Well, good." But something had happened. She turned quickly for the house, crying, "God, that sun is *hot,* you two!" At the screen door, she said, "Raymond, I think something's wrong with the air conditioning."

"I've turned it off," I said.

"Oh," she said. "Why?"

"We don't really need it," I said. "It's been cool at night and I wanted real air."

"Oh," she said again. "Well, I think maybe I like it too. It's interesting."

After she was inside, Raymond quietly said, "She's not quite okay yet. She seems chipper. And she never looked better. But that's how she acts every time his name comes up. That's not completely okay, if you ask me. I mean, his name has got to come up sometime."

"I don't think she's very happy about my being here," I said.

"Well, Marty, you know she loves you very much," said Raymond. "But I think right now, at this particular time, you might remind her too much of him. It makes sense, if you think about it. As far as I'm concerned, you're very welcome here. For as long as you like. The longer the better, as far as I'm concerned."

"Okay, Raymond," I said. "I don't plan to stay much longer."

"Well, it's your home, Marty," said Raymond. "It's not my place to say what's awkward and what isn't. I know you must be in shock."

"Not really," I said.

"I'm not a complete fool, Marty," he said. "I know what people will think."

"I don't know what you mean."

"About me," he said. "About the sex issue. I mean, of course, everyone assumes my marrying Helen is about money, but it's the sex issue that's behind the money issue. Some people will be very cruel about it. But everything isn't what meets the eye, Marty. Let me assure you."

"That's not any of my business, Raymond," I said. "Believe me, it's not what's on my mind."

"I know what I am," said Raymond. "I have a certain way about me. I'm not macho. I've done a lot of what people consider women's work. And I've never been much interested in women, not in that way. But hell, I don't give a hoot what any of these other old toadies and drunks around here think about me. I just wanted you to know the truth. What I'm trying to say is that I love your mother very much."

I think he would have embraced me then had it not been

for the clumsy chairs we were in. As it was, he gave me a couple of rather manly pats on the shoulder. I told him I had been remembering the time I tried to shoot him with Father's pistol. Could he really have been as calm and kind as I remembered?

"Oh, Lord, I'll never forget that," he said. "But you don't think I'd let a loaded pistol lay around *this* house, do you? I knew the thing wasn't loaded. Besides, I thought I understood what you were going through. Helen and Rudy were off gallivanting around the world, Marion had a new baby to take care of, and what kind of a sorry excuse for a father did I make? But I knew the gun wasn't loaded, Marty. We went ice skating that day, I think. Coldest winter on the books, as I recall. Marty, why did you really come back down here? Why are you actually here?"

"It seemed the best place for me to start sorting out the past," I said.

"I was afraid it might be something like that," he said.

"What's the matter?"

"Helen's not okay yet, like I said. Not at all okay about the past. And I was hoping you might talk to her."

"I will," I said.

"But I don't want you to," he said. "Not if you're going to dredge up unpleasant memories for her. That's the one thing she doesn't need any help with. If you have to, couldn't you just talk to her about the good times? Make her feel a little bit better, like things are going to be okay?"

"I don't know if I can do that, Raymond."

"Well, try. Will you?"

"Raymond," I said. "My grandfather crashed his plane into the side of a mountain and killed himself and my grandmother because he was drunk. My father drank himself to death at a point in life when most men are coming into their own. I just lost my only brother—I don't know exactly why, but I see it as some kind of link in this chain. And now that Perry's dead, I've finally started to believe something he'd been telling me these last few years, that I have a drinking problem of my own. Madeline's divorcing me because she's in love with another man. Yesterday I consented to sell my business because I no longer have the heart for it. Somebody I thought I was in love with in New York isn't speaking to me and I don't blame her. I'm going to turn thirty next week and I don't know anything about anything. When you ask me to try to cheer Mother up, I don't really know if I want to."

Just then we heard Mother in the kitchen, gaily crooning "I Left My Heart in San Francisco," which made the idea of her need for cheering up seem ridiculous. But Raymond lowered his voice and said quickly, "Just be careful, Marty. She's afraid that if she starts to feel guilty about things, there may be no bottom to it."

"What's she got to feel guilty about?" I said. "Just because she stayed stinko the whole time her children were growing up, just because she disappointed Father every possible chance she got, just because she threatened to take us away from him unless he gave up his dream of a career—"

"Jesus, Marty," said Raymond, looking stunned. "Don't you love her at all?"

After a moment, I said, "What kind of a question is that?"

Mother complained of jet lag and spent the early afternoon in her room. Around three-thirty, Raymond brought a cardboard box of liquor bottles from the cellar and set up a bar in the library. Felicia and Teddy arrived around four, already drunk. Raymond carried down messages from Mother, saying

"You're so late coming down," I said.

"I am?" she said. "Raymond, am I late?"

"Marty means that Teddy and Felicia have been here—"

"I don't think I realized that we were on a schedule," Mother said.

"It doesn't matter," I said.

Then, as the three of us were midway down the stairs, we heard Felicia's gritty voice. ". . . such an old lady," she was saying. "What was that wonderful thing Max called him?"

Teddy, between spurts of laughter: "An hermaphrodite . . . scullery maid!"

Felicia, uproarious: "That's it! Hermaphrodite scullery maid. Oh, God, that is so *perfect!*"

We had all three stopped on the stairs, and Raymond, without a word, turned and started back up. Mother put her hand on my arm. "Marty, darling," she said, "do you think you could possibly get rid of them?"

I left Mother on the stairs. At the library door, I saw Felicia standing, laughing, bracing herself at the table where Raymond had set up the bar. Teddy was doubled up on the sofa. They stopped abruptly when they saw me. "I'll drive you home," I said.

"Home?" said Felicia, tears streaking her cheeks. "But we haven't even seen Helen yet."

When I returned to the foyer, a single blue ostrich feather was floating slowly down from the upper balustrade.

Teddy and Felicia sulked the whole way back to her house, only a fifteen-minute drive. I brought along Molly, who sat regally up front with me in Felicia's pastel green Cadillac. Then Molly and I walked home together, through the woods and across the fields. A wind was kicking up, and the sky had turned a beautiful lavender, gold near the horizon. I thought I smelled apples in the air. Altogether, we were gone about ninety minutes, to Felicia's and back. On our return, I found Mother in the pool. She wore a white bathing cap and was doing some sort of aquatic exercise involving a large blue rubber ball held under water between her thighs; she appeared to be sitting in the water, and paddled herself from one end of the pool to the other. When I had placed myself in her line of vision, she said, "Oh, Marty, thank you so much, darling. I'm afraid I would have strangled those two had I allowed myself near them."

She stared straight ahead, dead-eyed—apparently what she was doing required intense concentration—but then she toppled over and went under.

When she surfaced, laughing and spurting water, I said, "Are you okay?"

"You keep asking me that, Martin," she said. "I'm fine. This is out of this world for the thighs and buttocks, even the tummy."

She made several attempts to get back on the ball, but continued to slip off. She seemed extraordinarily amused by this. Just then, I noticed a bottle of whisky and a glass on the table at the opposite end of the pool. "Have you been drinking?" I asked her.

She stopped splashing and for the first time looked at me. "Now don't be angry, Marty," she said. "I didn't mean to."

"Where's Raymond?"

"The poor thing," she said, now moving toward the edge of the pool, her arms extended at shoulder level, as if she were walking a high wire. She was unnecessarily thin; she looked to me as if she'd lost weight. "He said he was going for a drive," she said. "But I'm sure he'll end up at the movies. That's what he's always done, you know, when he was upset."

She slipped and went under again.

"Will you please get out of the pool before you drown," I said.

She was moving in the general direction of the ladder now. "You're very angry, aren't you," she said.

"Those people are lowlifes, Mother," I said. "They've never been anything but lowlifes. And I don't see why you sent them home if all you were going to do was get drunk yourself."

"Well, those lowlifes have meant a great deal to me over the years, Marty," she said, her voice going flat. "You can't know. I'm sorry Raymond got his feelings hurt. He doesn't deserve to be hurt. It was horrible of Max to say such a thing—whatever it meant—and horrible of Felicia to repeat it. But you have to understand that Max Dolotov has been in love with me for many years."

"You're kidding me," I said.

"I'm afraid he's taking the news of my marrying Raymond very hard."

"Don't tell me you *slept* with Dolotov?" I said, surprising both of us.

Mother pulled herself up onto the first rung of the pool ladder. "That's none of your business, Marty," she said, "who I've slept with and who I haven't. But I'll tell you that I did not sleep with anyone while your father was alive."

I moved to the ladder and gave her a hand getting out of the pool. She reached for her robe, which was thrown over the table on the terrace. She removed the rubber cap and let her hair fall down around her shoulders, found her cigarettes and lit one. Without the slightest visible shame, she poured whisky into her glass, lifted it to her lips, and knocked it back in one shot, just like the old days. Then she came toward me. I watched her face: it was the hardened Las Vegas girl she put forward now and again, and I found myself steeling against the moment. But when she was quite near, she looked at me deeply, as if she were trying to ascertain something about me, and her own face changed — it went almost fragile — and then, all at once, I knew what she was seeing: Perry.

At last she said, "Oh, Martin, I've done everything wrong."

"What do you mean?" I said.

"Come over here and sit with me," she said. "Drink with me if you want to. I don't think I've ever told you the story of my life."

I declined her offer of a drink, and when we were seated in the chairs by the terrace table, she said, "First of all, I don't know what I've got myself into. You know how dear Raymond is to me, but now I see that he imagined that I was in love with him."

"I guess you should tell him," I said.

"But I have told him," she said. "He couldn't care less. His devotion is simply too loud for him to *hear* anything else. He's really very sweet."

Then she said, "But, Marty." In the half-light of dusk I could see her eyes sharpening with tears. "I don't know what to do about Perry," she whispered.

"What do you mean?" I said.

"I don't know what to *do* with him," she whispered.

I leaned forward and whispered back, "I still don't know what you mean."

She took a deep breath and put out the cigarette. She poured another drink. "When I met your father," she said, "it was like an answer to a prayer. No, I take that back. It wasn't *like* an answer, it was *exactly* an answer to a prayer. I was twenty-six years old, which was about twice as old back then as it is now, and I hadn't made it out of the chorus yet. You haven't any idea what that life is like, Marty. Everyone in Las Vegas is dying of some terminal illness. They're all being eaten up by something—ambition or greed or booze or grief or all the above. Just when you think you might be getting close to somebody, it turns out they were just hoping you might introduce them to somebody important. Or just when you thought somebody was about to do you a good turn it turns out they just wanted to see if it was true what whatch-amacallit said about you in bed.

"I was getting nowhere because I'd never learned to play the game as well as I needed to. I could sing and dance all right, but that wasn't good enough. I was getting nowhere. I had abandoned all hope, as the saying goes. In another couple of years I would be an old maid. Nothing was happening with my singing. I knew it wouldn't be long before I was going to be replaced by a younger girl with younger tits-and-ass—you should excuse the expression. I'd stopped praying for a break in my career. I just didn't have the heart for it anymore. I'd started praying to meet a rich man, you see. So when your father showed up and started ordering *bottles*, not drinks, to our table . . . and then started showing up at my room with little thousand-dollar earrings and such . . . well, it was a definite sign from above, nothing less. I never for a moment questioned it.

"You won't believe this, Marty, but I didn't have a drinking problem until I moved into this house. It was a way of life, you see, when I got here, and it was great fun. There didn't seem to be any real price to pay. Nobody went downstairs before one in the afternoon and there were servants to nurse you through your hangover. But then you came along, Marty dear. You were an answer to a prayer too, believe it or not. Not a very virtuous prayer maybe, certainly not an unselfish prayer, I now see, but an honest prayer at least. I prayed that a baby would make me seem like less of a mistake to your father. And it did help off and on.

"You see, for a number of years your father went back and forth about me. Like a typical drunk . . . he went from one extreme to the other. One moment I was the old lasting passion of his life. The next I was some tramp who'd brought him a few minutes of good luck at a craps table when he was on some crazy binge. But as it turned out, I wasn't a very good mother. Not for very long anyway. I was drinking too much by then. That's the simple truth. And by then Rudy's parents had died in that stupid plane crash and he was no help. Honestly, I think everyone thought we were having a good time, with our travels and our parties. But really, we enjoyed each other for about three hours out of the day. From cocktails until shortly after dinner, when we were both completely falling-down."

She stopped and lit another cigarette. When she spoke next, there was a catch in her voice. "Then, when you were three, I got pregnant again."

That was all she said for about a minute—she was fighting back tears. She poured another and drank it quickly. "Well, it was a disaster," she said at last. "It felt criminal for me to bring another child into that marriage. I was already guilty for not caring for you more than I was able to—"

She stopped again, to pour yet another. She let the mouth of the bottle slip off the glass and spilled whisky through the wire mesh of the table.

This is what Raymond saw when he suddenly appeared at the kitchen door and turned on the pool lights. When he reached us, he was glaring at me. I looked up at him and said, "It's not what you think, Raymond."

He took the bottle out of Mother's hand, saying, "Helen, Helen, what on earth are you doing?"

"Nothing, Raymond darling," she said. "You weren't supposed to come back so soon. I guess you're angry with me now, too."

Raymond looked at me again. "How could you, Marty?" he said and began lifting Mother under the arms.

"Wait a minute," I said to Raymond. "She's trying to tell me something. Leave her alone, will you?"

"Yes, Raymond," Mother said, pulling herself against the back of her chair. "Leave me be. I'm trying to tell Perry about Marty, I mean Marty about Perry . . . when I was pregnant."

"Oh," Raymond said. "Can't you let that silly thing go, Helen?"

She sat up straight and said, "It is not silly."

In the light from the pool, they were both blue-white, like ghosts. They looked at each other. Mother's robe had fallen open, exposing her legs. Finally, she said to Raymond, "You tell him."

Raymond sighed, then pulled a chair up so that he was between Mother and me, facing us. He restored Mother's robe over her legs, saying, "Helen, aren't you cold?"

"No," she said, "I am not cold."

Raymond sighed again, then said to me, "Your mother has drawn some harebrained connection between the abortion and Perry's killing himself."

"He doesn't *know* about the abortion, Raymond," Mother said. "That's what I'm trying to tell him."

"What abortion?" I asked.

Raymond stood up and screwed the cap onto the whisky bottle. He reached for the glass, which had a small amount left in it, but Mother beat him to it.

"It doesn't matter how drunk I get, darling," Mother said to him. "A slip's a slip."

Raymond put the bottle back on the table, then sat back down. "Well, that's the point," he said calmly. "There wasn't any abortion, actually."

"Marty," Mother said, exasperated. "I'd heard about this old black woman, you see, and I had her come out to the house one weekend when Rudy was in Washington. I'd made up my mind to tell Rudy when he got back that I'd had a miscarriage. But what happened was, Rudy came home early. He was supposed to spend the night in Washington, but he didn't. So he caught me in the act . . . well, just before the act, really."

She was silent, staring into the blue glow of the pool. I looked at Raymond. "That's it?" I said.

"That's it," he said, shrugging his shoulders. "She got it into her head that Perry would never have killed himself if she hadn't *almost* had an abortion. It's crazy."

"It is not crazy," Mother said, leaning toward me. "You see, Marty, he must've had some kind of memory or something that his mother wanted him to die. Maybe he wasn't even aware of it. You know, it was just planted way down deep. Don't you see? I tried to make it up to him — what I'd done — by being extra nice to him, but I knew that I would be punished, and . . . well, as you can see, I was right. I thought when Rudy died that that was the end of my punishment.

And then when the house burned I thought that was the end. And then when Perry killed himself, well . . . what I want to know, Marty, is when is it supposed to end?"

She had leaned so far forward that she appeared on the verge of falling out of the chair. Raymond took hold of her again, but she looked over his shoulder, directly at me. "Do *you* know, Marty?" she said. "Do *you* know when it's supposed to end?"

"I don't know much about it, Mother," I said. "But I don't think God works that way."

"You don't think so?" she said.

"No, I don't."

"Well if it isn't God who's punishing me," she said, "then who the—"

She stared suddenly into the pool, as if she were startled by some sea creature swimming there, then sagged onto Raymond's shoulder.

"I think I better get her upstairs," Raymond said. "There's a sack of cold cheeseburgers in the kitchen, Marty, if you want one."

As they were going through the door, I heard Mother say, "Boy, I better get to a meeting tomorrow."

"Definitely," said Raymond.

"Dear Raymond," she said. "Why are you so good to me?"

"Because you're good, Helen," I heard him answer. "Basically you're good."

Later, when I went up the stairs, I heard Raymond's voice through the door to Mother's room, reading a prayer. I stopped and listened: ". . . Helen, for whom our prayers are desired. Look upon her with the eyes of thy mercy; comfort her with a sense of thy goodness; preserve her from the temp-

tations of the enemy; and give her patience under her afflic-
tion. In thy good time, restore her to health, and enable her to
lead the residue of her life in thy fear, and to thy glory . . ."

And late that night, in bed, I recalled the frightened old
black woman in her long feed-sack dress and white baker's
apron. I'd been awakened by my father's shouting, and I'd
wandered out into the upstairs hall. I walked toward my
mother's room, where the shouting was coming from. The
double doors to her room, which swung outward into the hall,
stood open, and I moved behind the near one, where I could
watch what was going on through the crack between the door
and the jamb. In the room, which, unusually, was very
brightly lit, the old woman stood near the side of Mother's
bed, crying, her eyes shut tightly. She wore a handkerchief
tied around her head. Mother, sitting up in the bed, was crying, too. Mother looked very beautiful, but pale. And Marion
stood on the other side of the bed, holding Mother's hand and
also crying. Father, his back to the door, stood at the foot of
the bed, gripping the round wooden railing with both hands,
as if he meant to control himself. He had never shouted this
loud, and I couldn't much make sense of most of what he
said—Father, who had always been kind to black people, was
angry that the old woman was in our home.

The old woman's lips were moving. I think she was saying,
"Please please please please please," and now and again she
clasped her hands to her heart. I closed my eyes for a minute
and studied the afterimage of that long vertical strip of light
with its crying shadows. When I opened them, Marion had
released Mother's hand and had walked to a window. Father
was asking Mother many questions, which she did not answer: Have you lost your mind? Do you know what could
happen to you? Have you any idea what you're actually do-

ing? The canopy on Mother's bed shook as Father shouted. Then, suddenly, his voice stopped. All I could hear for a moment was the old woman's "please please please please." Marion moved back to Mother's side, Mother started to say something, and Father began all over again. But soon he stopped again, turned away from the women, and seemed to look, with his very red eyes, through the crack, directly at me. (I know he couldn't have seen me, for if he had, he wouldn't have said what he was about to say.) I thought I had never seen so much sadness, so much crying, when he, too, began to cry, lowering his head and pressing his fists into his eyes. "Helen," he said, "how could you even think of it. How could you honestly want to kill our child . . ."

And of course I thought he meant me. My big toe stuck out of a hole in the foot of my pajamas. A shaky coldness seemed to begin there and move into my body, making me tremble and eventually settling into my chest. In another moment, the old woman was out in the hallway, carrying a doctor's bag made of brown alligator, which she set down on the floor in order to close Mother's doors. When she saw me, she let out a little gasp. I stood still as a statue. The woman said, "Why, who is this pretty child?" and wiped tears from her cheeks with a corner of her apron. I made no answer. "Why, you must be a little angel done lost his wings and doesn't know where to find them," she said. "I bet I got something for you." She reached into her apron pocket and pulled out a toy harmonica, made of bright shiny tin, and handed it to me. I immediately put it to my lips, but she shushed me, saying, "Hold on, Gabriel. Later, boy." Then she turned and hurried down the stairs, waving her hand high up in the air over her head like a gospel singer, and was out the door.

I have said that the memories that began unfolding for me

in Norfolk did me no harm, that on the contrary, they reassured me and kept me from loneliness. But that last night in my old home, in my brother's childhood bed—after I had rewitnessed my parents' enormous sadness and my own terrible misinterpretation—I thought of the walk back from Felicia's, across the fields in the afternoon. It had been such a fine, warm autumn day, Molly and I found a spot on a rise in the woods where we could lie and watch the sun go down through the pines. And a while later, as we left the woods and the house came into view on its distant hill, I had a certain feeling I wouldn't name, a glimpse of something I let slip quickly away. But here, now, at the end of this remarkable day, it returned, and I was visited not by memory, but by the kind of vision that is the brutal side of grief: the vision of an impossible future.

It is a bright late-summer morning along the ocean. A sea gull wheeling overhead cries, not ruefully, but as a hunter praising the weather and the sheer joy of good health. It is a day we have all looked forward to for some time, a day of celebration, perhaps Father's sixtieth birthday, and we've all gathered one last time before the end of the season, before we return to our separate autumns of responsibility and hard work. Madeline and Father (long sober) are already down by the breakers with the kids, the cousins, our lovely girls and Perry's boys, with their full bellies and brown backs and white hair. Perry is playing backgammon with Mother (long sober) in the shade of the cabaña. Jane looks on, standing behind Perry, her hands resting on his shoulders. I (long sober) have been reading a good book, but the gull's shrill cry has caused me to look up, and I am momentarily blinded by the sun. As my sight returns, and the forms of the people I love reemerge out of the brightness, as the squeals of the children fleeing the cool surf and the laughter attending the backgammon game reach my ears, I am filled with the faith and quiet confidence that belongs to those who were given the heart and willingness to survive, to those given the great fortune to have continued.

There is an item in Mother's hoard of "Everything Interesting" newspaper clippings about a woman who wrote in lipstick on the bathroom mirror of her home, "I can't go on," then closed herself in the garage, which was attached to the house, started the family car, and soon died of asphyxiation. This was in the middle of the night, while her husband and two teen-aged children slept. What she didn't realize was that the central heating furnace, also in the garage, would carry carbon monoxide through the duct system into each room of the house and kill her entire family. The teen-aged daughter had been engaged to be married. Her fiancé, a close friend of the family, called on them repeatedly, both by telephone and in person. After some days, and assisted by the police, he entered the house by force and discovered the horrifying, inexplicable tragedy. Stricken, he told reporters that it had been the happiest family he knew, high on love and happiness as they anticipated the imminent wedding. The family's community was duly shocked and, for a short time, baffled. Eventually, it was revealed that the investigating police had found, in the wallet of the father, Polaroids of his teen-aged daughter, posed in the nude.

Reported in another of Mother's clippings is the story of a man who, horsing around one Christmas Day with the new shotgun he'd received as a gift, pointed it at his stepdaughter amid her protests, pulled the trigger, and blew her brains out through the picture window behind the couch she was sitting on. Her mother had been sitting right next to her. The man, who had thought the gun was not loaded, who had just *sworn* that the gun was not loaded, now quickly loaded it, handed it to his wife and begged her to kill him. When she repeatedly refused, he took the gun back, awkwardly got the barrel into his mouth, and shot himself.

These stories came to me somewhere under the East River, as the IRT train I was on stalled for several minutes in its tunnel to Brooklyn. I was not sure when I might have read them. It didn't matter. What mattered was that they were the kind of scandalous answer I'd started out looking for when I was first called by Detective Karajian to New York. These stories, cast in the clean reduction of journalism, were nutshell suicide stories, immediately comprehensible—anybody could see the reason in them at a glance—the grisly harbored secret, the terrible twist of fate. That was the sort of answer I had wanted, and the sort I was not to have.

But as the lights in the subway train flickered on, off, and on again, and we eventually rattled and clattered into Clark Street station, I felt close to my brother, or closer to him somehow.

I sat in the extreme rear car of the train, and when I got off at Hoyt Street I stood directly in front of the brass revolving doors to the basement of Abraham & Straus. The store had only just opened. I went inside, up a flight of stairs to the street level, and back out through another set of revolving doors. Winter clothes were displayed in the store windows: mannequins in brown and gray tweeds standing with their feet buried in paper leaves of yellow and orange and red. I stopped before one window to watch a young woman, with a storm of black hair of her own, try two or three different wigs on a female mannequin. She was having a great, hilarious time, turning to me with each try, to get my opinion. We agreed, in mime, that none of the wigs looked very good, and as if to settle the matter, she shrugged her shoulders and screwed off the mannequin's head, carrying it away under her arm like a basketball. I turned the corner onto Hoyt and nearly collided with a man wearing a sandwich board so crowded with writing that it might have been the blown-up pages of some sacred Sanskrit text. "My wife left me for another man" was all I managed to read.

At the corner of Atlantic, a head shop, painted all black on the outside and decorated with psychedelic designs—mandalas, yin-yang, a Maltese cross—blasted loud Jimi Hendrix through its open door. And across the avenue I gazed through the dirty windows of an antiques store, an amazing jumble of silver tea services and candelabra, clocks, andirons and mirrors, davenports and cupboards. In a rocker set precisely in the middle of all this, a dusty old woman, white-headed and white-skinned, dipped snuff and meditated—Miss Havisham among the cobwebs.

Farther along Hoyt Street, I came to a block in which all the buildings had been demolished—a field of old painted bricks heaped in low mounds, a kind of burial ground enclosed with a hurricane fence—and soon I entered a very poor area of dilapidated brownstones: Boerum Hill.

Early that morning, I had awakened in Perry's New York apartment with a shadowy memory of my mother's having telephoned in the night: sorry she'd been too sick in the morning to say goodbye, she had read the note I left her, though, about the grandchild, and did she dare believe something so wonderful could be true?

Molly lay next to me on the bed. I shook from cold and at first I couldn't figure out why, but after a moment I understood that the weather had changed. I got out of bed and quickly closed the windows. After coffee, I pulled on a red sweater and took Molly for her walk. The definite surprise of autumn in the air made me sad, as it does many people, but I didn't mind. I liked the simple clarity of the feeling. It had the appeal of a primary color; it promised a range of complementary hues to come.

The evening before, I had met Jane Owlcaster, hurriedly, between a rehearsal and a concert at the school. Though nervous—it was the concert she had been rehearsing the chorus for all of September—she seemed glad to see me. We sat on the low stone wall surrounding the fountain in the plaza outside the school. The yellow-pink glow of dusk rose up from behind all the white granite buildings. I had prepared formal atonement for Jane, but as it turned out, none was necessary. She could see at a glance that I was better—calmer, more human, no longer plagued. She told me that she hoped we could be friends. I said I hoped so too.

"It's important," she said. "After all, you're my baby's only uncle." She was dressed for the concert, in a long black skirt and a white silk blouse. She wore her pearls and smelled of roses. Through the lenses of her glasses I could see a certain light in her eyes, an optimism that hadn't been there before. "I'm going to do this right," she said. "I'm getting myself prepared." She smiled as she said this—a kind of inside joke between us. I told her I thought she would make a wonderful mother.

"I was thinking about that," she said. "I've been worried—you know, that I might smother the kid, drive him crazy with details. But then I thought I might not be too bad. I figure that if your mother won't obsess about you, who will?"

The plaza began to fill with concertgoers; the fountain lights came on. I tried apologizing for that shameful afternoon in the practice room but Jane stopped me, said that actually she had faced up to something that day. "It was like clouds parting," she said. "You were in such bad shape that even I couldn't fix you. I decided you had to fix yourself."

"You were right," I said.

I went on to tell her about selling my company, and briefly about Norfolk, about my mother and Raymond, about that last night there—and somehow, inexplicably, the sound of the plummeting water in the fountain lent plausibility to all that I said.

"So what are you going to do now?" asked Jane at last.

"I think I'll just sit still," I said, relieved at the promptness of my answer.

"Well, if you're interested," said Jane, looking at her watch, "I'm going to be looking for a childbirth coach. *He* would like that, don't you think?"

But before I could reply, she stood and told me she had to fly. Instead of a kiss, she took my hand in hers and pressed it gently to her stomach, and, thoroughly surprised, I went away walking on air.

I slept peacefully that night, and dreamed that I was attending Jane Owlcaster's choral concert, a wondrous affair: two double choirs, the sixteen-part music profuse with imitation, the overlapping sibilance in the lyrics eventually creating nothing less than the sound of the sea; the lyrics spoke of human history and human compassion, of charity, hope, and forgiveness. And then the telephone rang, waking me from the dream. On hearing my mother's voice I recalled how, before leaving Norfolk, challenging her about our past no longer seemed the least bit useful or important. Mother was overjoyed about the baby, oh what a beautiful gift, a grandchild, could it really be true? At the end, she said, "Marty darling, I've been thinking about Perry's will. After all, it was what he wished." I told her I had already come to that same conclusion, and after we hung up, I fell back to sleep so quickly that even her call seemed part of a dream.

On our morning promenade, Molly and I walked to the docks at the end of 46th Street, passing the friendly aroma of soda bread baking at the Landmark Tavern. The *Queen Elizabeth II* and a Russian ship, the *Maxim Gorki,* were berthed. It was still so early in the day that the liners' white paint appeared a lovely light blue. On the Russian ship I could see two men jogging on an upper deck, holding hands as they ran. As I continued watching them and drew closer, I could tell that something was not quite right with one of the men — perhaps he was palsied in some way — and that the other one was helping him run. I felt oddly moved by this, and past the traffic, on the wide, dimpled sidewalk at the docks, I let Molly off the leash — and releasing her, I knew that I would go to Brooklyn that day.

✳

A Catholic hospital occupied the block cater-corner to the field of bricks, and two streets beyond, on a corner lot, rose a stark anomaly: an enormous house set back from the street with an L-shaped yard overgrown with forsythia and untended roses. The house itself was four stories high, with a tower rising to a height of five stories—wildly ornamented, ogee roofs, some window heads round, some flattened, some set in bays, all extremely tall and wide, even the ones in the tower. Covering most of the façade, woodbine, flame red, rippled in the wind, causing the house to appear almost liquid, two-dimensional, as if it were only painted on a scrim, the coming-unglued backdrop in a mysterious diorama. The ornate roof cresting was broken in places so that it looked more like weaponry than decoration, here and there a crumbling bracket or keystone. A jet passed overhead, setting the sky to thundering, and a car sped by on Hoyt, the music of its radio—a strange Rumanian drone, like an ostinato out of Bartók—making a sharp, sudden arc before fading. As I neared the house, I saw a nurse in white cap and uniform standing in a fourth-story window. She waved a friendly hello, then seemed to be pulled away by someone behind her.

At the top of a high stone landing, the front doors stood ajar. There was no bell visible, so I stepped inside into a wide hallway with a huge staircase on one wall and a cork bulletin board along the other. The wind rustled the hundreds of fliers and notices tacked there, a soft whisper that made me think of the sibilant choirs in my dream, and then I heard a woman's voice, seemingly from a room near the end of the hall.

Faye Barrymore stood in a cluttered office behind a desk piled high with papers and books and file folders. She wore a gold-colored turban and an oversized purple sweatshirt. A telephone receiver was nestled between her jaw and shoulder, freeing her hands to open mail with a silver letter opener. "You're not *hearing* me," I heard her say into the phone. "I've got Niagara *Falls* over here in the kitchen. Hang on a minute." She fixed her eyes on me, and her face quickly went from surprise to great happiness. "My goodness," she said, "you *do* look like him." Then she told me she was going to be tied up for another ten minutes or so, and why didn't I have a look around. She shooed me away, kindly, with the hand that held the letter opener.

Across the hall, I peeked into a large dining room with two long refectory tables; on each stood a vase of chrysanthemums in burnt colors—brick, amber, rust. I could hear a gushing sound of water coming from a door at the opposite end of the large room—presumably from the kitchen—and when I looked inside I saw water spurting in a high arc from around the base of a sink faucet. Dodging the spray, I moved to where I could see beneath the sink, but there were no valves. I went back out through the refectory and into the hall, and there found the door leading to the basement. Eventually, I also found the light switch and the water pipe leading to the kitchen, and closed the valve.

Faye Barrymore greeted me at the top of the basement stairs. I explained that I had shut off the water. "That's just what the plumber told me to do," she said and thanked me. She led me back into the refectory, and we sat at the end of one of the long tables. "I don't want to talk about your brother's will today," she said when we were seated. "I just wanted you to see the place."

I told her she didn't need to worry about that anymore. Perry had made his wishes clear, and we intended to honor them.

She closed her eyes and brought both hands to her chin in an attitude of prayer. "You have no idea what this means to us," she said. "Oh, God in heaven, we can get the furnace fixed before the cold weather gets here, we can put on storm windows, we can hire people to help and pay them a decent wage, we can . . . oh, Lord, you don't know what a good girl I've been these past couple of weeks, Mr. Lambert. I just kept praying for God's will, you know, like you're supposed to. But all the time thinking deep in my heart, You just *better* come through on this one, buddy, or we are going to have to rethink our relationship."

"It's the right thing," I said.

"You may rest assured of that, Mr. Lambert. Of that you may rest assured."

She folded her hands on the refectory table. "You know," she said at last, "he often spoke of you and I wished you hadn't been so far away. I was worried about him from the first day he came out here and said he wanted to help us and teach music to the kids. I told him he was going to need a strong heart and he assured me that he had, but I never entirely believed him. You see, Mr. Lambert, being around these kids is not heartbreaking, I don't think. It's just that sometimes things don't work out in the courts the way you'd have them work out and they get sent back into the situation they were trying to escape. And *that's* heartbreaking. I thought your brother was out here trying to prove something to himself. I thought he was penitential. I thought he was in despair. As if he was trying to work off some kind of great sin from the past. I was afraid he was in too vulnerable a condition, if you know what I mean."

She stood and said she would show me around. As we walked into the hall, she said, "I could never think what such a kind gentle young man like Perry could have done so wrong. Do you know what he could have done so wrong?"

I thought about this. In my mind, I saw Perry as a young boy in short pants and knee socks, sitting on the flagstones outside our kitchen door in the afternoon—an unruly party dying inside the house, the phonograph playing at the wrong speed, grown-ups asleep on the couches in the library—Perry, alone, in the flagstone breezeway, gazing out toward the fields—the trees and the horses—one hand shielding his eyes from the glare of the sun. And I heard myself say to Faye Barrymore, "He was just a child, Miss Barrymore. He didn't do anything wrong."

She didn't seem to think this answer the least bit odd. She asked me when I expected to return to California, and I told her I didn't expect to.

"Oh," she said. "What are your plans, then?"

"Actually, I'm looking for a job," I said.

She looked at me suddenly, smiled, and said, "How's *your* heart, Mr. Lambert?"

"Of the two of us," I said, "mine was always the stronger. Not better. But stronger."

Just then the telephone rang inside Faye Barrymore's office. "Go on," she said. "Explore. I'll catch up to you."

I started up the stairs. The floors in the upper hall were covered with worn runners, and the paint on the walls was peeling, but despite these signs of wear, everything had a scrubbed look. I peered into what were once parlors and bedroom suites, now converted to work rooms, some of which appeared to be classrooms, with flat-topped desks in rows, others art rooms, with larger work tables and drawings and paintings hanging on the walls. A sign on one door read, Dark Room.

All the rooms were empty. No people. This was true of the third floor as well, where I found a long hallway and two dormitory rooms. But as I started up the next flight, I heard what sounded like approaching machine-gun fire, and suddenly two dozen children of various ages raced by me on the stairs, flattening me against the wall. Behind them came the nurse, who smiled pleasantly, said "Hello, Mr. Lambert," and continued down. Two or three stairs beyond, she stopped, turned, and pointed her finger toward the ceiling, saying, "Oh . . . you'll find a new arrival up in the tower room," and she disappeared with the children around the lower newel post. Then there was an abrupt silence during which something passed through me, something subtle but definite, like the moment when a school of fish turns in precise unison and there's a flash of brilliance from the mosaic of their scales, like a sustained orchestral chord's changing colors: I felt him so dramatically on the stairs that I had to sit for a moment. Immediately I believed that nothing had prepared me for this, and yet somehow I knew to say goodbye. I said it aloud, then closed my eyes and whispered it.

And after some time passed—I don't know how long—I stood and climbed to the next landing . . .

The instant I saw the spiral stairs to the tower I also heard the frustrated sound of the cello, the labor of the same passage over and over again, the fits and starts, the startings-over. In the high room at the top, the wood floor was painted a pale sky blue, its tall windows draped with white sheers. The door stood partway open, and I could see the young boy with the cello, staring at the rickety music stand before him. On one wall was a long chalkboard with staff lines on which someone had drawn treble and bass clefs and written the words "Every Good Boy Does Fine" and "Good Boys Do Fine Always." The boy with the cello had not yet noticed me at the door; he stared at the music and tried again. He was struggling with the opening passage from the gavotte in Bach's sixth suite, the one that goes

—a passage more devilish than Bach meant it to be, since the instrument he'd written it for had five strings instead of four. For a moment I watched the boy, and when I pushed open the door a bit further and stepped inside, he turned and gave me a mostly neutral look, shaded slightly with impatience.

Later I would learn that his name was Francis Cam (you may have heard of him), thirteen years old, called Frankie. His father, a widowed auto mechanic, had been uneasy about having a cellist for a son—he feared that Frankie wouldn't turn out to be a real man, a strong man who could protect himself. So sometimes, after a few beers in the evenings, he would give Frankie boxing lessons. It had been a neighbor who eventually let it be known that these lessons always ended with Frankie unconscious.

But now I only knew him as someone funneled to me in a dream, and as I stepped closer, I could see that he was a good-looking boy, though there was something asymmetrical about his face, as if it had gone through the misshaping trial of re-peated injury and healing. What I was about to do felt like something I wasn't fluent enough for—like trying to be tactful in a foreign language—but at least I knew I needed to be careful, and I made an effort to return his neutral look.

"You're letting your left hand lock up on the chords," I said to him. "You're crunching them. Do you want me to show you?"

Apparently unthreatened, he stood, now interested, and offered me the cello. I accepted the bow and sat in the scarred wooden chair in the otherwise empty room. I cleared my throat as if I were about to sing. Frankie Cam stood behind me, looking over my shoulder at the music on the stand. "They've got to *ring*," I said, waited a moment, then began.

The first try, I flubbed the passage, but on the second, I got through it perfectly, miraculously up to tempo. Over my shoulder I said, "See?" and when I turned to look at Frankie, Faye Barrymore was standing in the doorway to the room, watching, listening.

"And don't forget to breathe," I said, handing Frankie back the bow, standing, offering him the chair. "You've got to breathe."

On Frankie's young, handsome, permanently ambivalent face I saw a mixture of comprehension and self-doubt. The long sheers billowed into the room, weightless, heavy, like white banners under water, and Frankie moved quickly to close the windows, then returned to my side.